2084

JOHN B. DUTTON

Copyright and Legal Notice

This book is a work of fiction. Names, characters, places, and incidents either are products of the author's imagination or are used fictitiously. Any resemblance to actual persons, living or dead, events, or locales is entirely coincidental.

To the extent that the image or images on the cover of this book depict a person or persons, such person or persons are merely models, and are not intended to portray any character or characters featured in the book.

North American Paperback First Edition License Notes

This edition published by Utopiatainment, a subsidiary of the United Corporations of Canada.

Cover by Kevin Lacombe, Executive Design Officer, UCC

Acknowledgments

Bobbie for your ongoing work, support, and love.

Tara and Yasmine for your valuable input.

Note to reader

A substantial amount of vocabulary used in this novel is from the future.

To aid comprehension, an alphabetized glossary has been included at the back of the book. It includes the difference between "oky" and "kay". Okay?

There are a couple of blank pages between the end of the story and the glossary to make sure that you don't accidentally see how it all turns out.

Preface: The history of the future

There used to be a country called the United States of America. Then came the pandemics. And the heat and the storms. And the quake. The markets collapsed and the people migrated. The USA dried and drowned as the Great Green North blossomed and thrived.

The tech giants relocated to the country once called Canada, merged in the ultimate economy of scale, and rebranded their currencies with a common name. The uDollars issued by the United Corporations flowed seamlessly from employer to chip implant to device to webstore. The banks swiftly withered, becoming storehouses for pointless paper and worthless metal. Governments lost control of the monetary supply and pensions were converted by gutless unions. Soon, the corporate carpetbaggers won elections in both countries, vaulted into office by the political power of lobbyists' bottomless pocketbooks and the public influence of news stories carefully crafted by UC artificial intelligence and shared on UC-owned media.

In the early 2040s the municipal land selloff began, and by the middle of the decade privatization had achieved unstoppable momentum. The UC evolved from a disparate patchwork of corporate campuses and gated communities to a coherent tapestry of branded havens straddling the border from Calgary to Chicago to Toronto to Montreal and down to the sodden remnants of New York City.

A flurry of Freedom from Taxation laws passed in

2047, voted for by the urban majority who now worked for United Corporations companies, lived on United Corporations property, went to United Corporations schools, received healthcare at United Corporations hospitals, and saw no reason to contribute to the wasteful spending of the governments that gave them nothing. Within two years, the tax bases collapsed and the governments' whimpers fell on ears deafened by the UC's media.

2051 was a tipping point: the impoverished northeastern and Great Lakes states seceded to join the provinces that neighbored them in the newly minted United Corporations of Canada, where all citizens became shareholders, the government shrank to a board, and the military was run by the UCC's proprietary AI technology.

A ravaged, mutated United States of Amexica declared itself the keeper of the flame of democracy, but within two months platoons of UCC fencebots had shut out the gun-wielding savages to the south, leaving them to fight among themselves for the few pockets of land that weren't poisoned and parched.

The United Corporations of Canada was recognized in all corporate communications to be the pinnacle of human achievement. A place where security was assured and health was genetically optimized. Where income was guaranteed and uDollars could buy anything. And where being uHappy was the only goal worth striving for, in a life where everything *just worked*.

1.

"Our grandparents worked with computers. We work *for* computers."

"That's a good thing, Santi."

An eyeroll. "Ride off, kid. Of course you'd say that."

"No, I mean it. I've got a squirtload more perspective than you. The CEO's, COO's, CFO's... they were basically CFU's."

"Ha."

A knowing pause. "Santiago Khan. Seriously? Have you really forgotten the zeitgeist of your youth? Managers were power-hungry dudes who groped their interns, and their bosses rose to the top because they were sociopaths or, if they weren't, because they copied their behavior."

An embarrassed clearing of the throat. "We don't say things like sociopath anymore."

"Yah, yah. Bite me a lychee."

Santi reclined his cocoonchair and smiled. His memoryself floating in the convocast projection smiled back. "Kay. Happy Monday, kid. Talk soon."

"See you later!"

Always the same ironic sign-off.

Santi flicked his hand dismissively and the convocast vanished. He looked around his studio. Plentium, the element that keeps on giving, was piled up beside the 3D printer in neat foot-square bricks ten high. Enough for three or four sculptures. He could deliver the week's statue commissions and still have some left over for the masks.

So, what was bothering him? Why the social angst?

After all, he counted himself lucky to be one of the few in the new Canada who didn't work for an AI-run corporation. He was his own boss, and Sculpturize had given him the freedom to do what he loved on his own terms. The commercials that people plugged into for hours to earn their basic YouBucks? Not only was he not forced to watch them, some of the ads were for his own company. So why had he wandered out of the bathroom with an existential frown?

Life was good. But that was the problem – life was too good. That's exactly why his father began his stand-up routines with this deceptively simple joke: *It's a dog-eat-dogfood world.* Everything was convenient, everything was easy.

A rumble in his belly. His wristline flashed a low blood sugar level.

"Room, help me with breakfast," he said.

The room answered. A warm, engaging voice like an accomplished mother of three: "Two slices of AuthentiCo toast with thin slices of uCheese topped with Agralife blueberry jelly. AuthentiCo green tea."

"Do it," he said, and the thought crossed his mind that AuthentiCo was featuring more frequently among his food brand options.

"Emeraldia is awake now," said the room.

He felt a tingling in his dick. The sexologist had been absolutely right: rebranding his wife had made the mere mention of her name trigger the hormonal reaction that had seemed hobbled or hidden. Everyone's uHappy rating was improved by engaging in unselfish love, intimacy, and care. But Santi actually enjoyed the *feeling* of love. Did that make him selfish? Did it matter?

He adjusted his genitals and walked out the door. The light from the wall panels dimmed and extinguished. It was still dark outside. The studio's bust-lined shelves receded into shadow. A trio of life-size Sculpturize models that Santi had printed the day before communed silently in one corner, awaiting that afternoon's approval sessions. The Rodin-styled statue was of a middle-aged woman with both arms raised, fists clenched in triumph. Maybe a fiftieth birthday gift? Or a cancer victory tribute? The Brancusi's ageless curved planes and impenetrable eyes belonged to a younger woman, though it was hard to place her age. She stared, head tilted, at the figure in the middle – a classical Greek statue of a man with folded arms and legs planted firmly apart. The curves of the man's muscles seemed to flow into his leonine afro of the mid-century fashion.

Santi hurried along the hallway toward the bedroom. He was becoming more aroused by the second. Her morning scent. Her unfolding limbs. His stomach rumbled again and he stopped in his tracks. His wristline reflashed its low blood sugar notification. To his left was the kitchen. Should he grab something quickly? A Slabfruit? Could he risk a negative ReasSure outcome if he followed his dick's wishes? But what if Emeraldia also became hungry in the two minutes he spent eating, or had gotten out of bed and dressed? The moment might be lost, the hormones flushed. Fuckit, he'd take a chance. After all, sex would boost his ReasSure wellscore – and surely that would offset any detrimental impact on his bioscore? The dick won the debate, and he continued to the bedroom.

Santi's eyes adjusted to the darkness. The curve of Emeraldia's right hip as she lay on her side formed an enticing sheet-shrouded question mark.

"You told the room you were awake just so I'd come," he said in a slow, low voice.

"Uh-huh," she groaned, stretching and twisting onto her back.

He climbed onto the bed and knelt astride her. She opened her eyes and focused on his crotch. "Good morning!" she said to the extended fabric of his shorts.

He brushed a curl of indigo hair away from her eye and she kissed the palm of his hand. She shifted beneath him and thrust her hips against his pelvis. He pulled down the sheet and yanked it to one side. She was wearing the deep violet silk nightdress the sexologist had recommended. Her labia was just visible below the hem, the triangle above it covered by a trimmed bed of fine curlicues. Her wristline glowed deep lava orange.

Santi kissed her. She grabbed the back of his neck, keeping his head close as she opened her mouth and her legs at the same time. Supporting himself on one elbow, he reached down with his other hand and gently massaged. She moaned and kissed him harder.

"I want you," he said, reaching over to the nightstand. He padded around with his hand, feeling for the lube tube that wasn't there. He opened one squinting eye as he kissed her.

Emeraldia was sick of using the lube. Santi knew from their shared search history that she'd been researching Genedit's uCuff. Had she been seeing another sexologist who'd implanted the idea in her mind? In a general sense, she was all too ready to please him, and although this had been truly awesome during the first few years of their togetherness, he was now concerned that she was allowing generosity to submerge her own authentic desires. And that couldn't be a good thing in the long run. Her uHappy rating was off the charts but what if it all came crumbling down one day? What if she suddenly realized she'd mined every last seam of selflessness, leaving nothing but a pretty husk, drifting aimlessly toward self-term?

She broke away from the kiss. "I want you, too," she panted, "but I've ordered the cuff."

He sagged everywhere.

She smiled optimistically. "It's coming today and I stashed the lube in the drawer."

He flopped onto his back.

"I wanted to surprise you."

"Right," he said. "Have you been seeing someone else?"

"Seeing?"

"Another sexologist?"

She propped herself up on one side. "No! How long have you known me? I would never do that!" Lovingly, she brushed the beads of sweat off his forehead.

"So why change things?"

"It was... my memoryself suggested it."

He looked away from the ceiling and into her eyes.

"Last week – we were chatting," continued Emeraldia. "She had no idea the uCuff even existed – of course – and her first reaction was, like: What are you waiting for?"

"That checks out."

Santi recalled the young woman he'd met in her thirties. The woman named Sophie. The woman buoyed by a fresh outlook on this life that he shouldered so heavily. The woman who loved the tech. No surprise that she was excited by the idea of a targeted gene-editing wearable. She was sure to grasp the chance to rejuvenate.

"It's oky, honey," he said, straining upward to kiss her burgeoning disappointment away.

She smiled. "Oh, don't you worry, it's going to be very oky."

Emeraldia pushed his chest and he fell back onto the bed. She moved her hand down his belly and into his shorts. He was hard again within seconds, and her head followed her hand.

As she fellated him, he ran his fingers through her curls and tried to extinguish the doubt and the angst. Had any life ever been as happy as his? The UCC's main business line was happiness and he was most definitely a major beneficiary.

He twitched and caught his breath. Her lessons were paying off.

She shifted her ass around and he ran his fingers up the back of her thigh. She cupped his balls and slowed her head movements. The sensation felt so good he was sure that his daily uHappy quota would be 70, maybe even 80 percent achieved by noon. But he needed to stop thinking about ratings and concentrate on erotica. The virtual Emeraldia they had designed together in Doctor Markova's office popped into his mind. She was a soft-core veeporn version of Sophie – slightly firmer, slightly shapelier, and slightly younger. But the combined effect was a whole lot sexier, and his breathing became shallow as the real-world Emeraldia increased her speed.

His stomach let out a huge squelch. A cartoon sound effect that betrayed his hunger. Emeraldia gamely continued, suppressing laughter. Santi made an effort to reactivate the mental image of his virtual wife but to no avail. Emeraldia withdrew and now she did laugh.

"Oh, Santi! I'm hungry too! Let's reset and repeat later."

He had lifted his head from the pillow, but now let it flop back down. He hated it when she repurposed advertising taglines in general conversation. Everyone did it, but the artist in him recoiled. Ah, who was he kidding – he did it too, he'd just stopped being aware.

Emeraldia crawled on top of him and playfully tapped him on the cheek. "Don't get mad!"

Santi looked at her and had to smile.

"We'll have a wellness breakfast together and this afternoon maybe a sexy siesta with lube for the last time," she said. "Then we can dump the tube in the garbage and look forward to the new me."

"I've got approvals."

"Kay, tonight then?"

"We'll see. You know what Markova said about being spontaneous. Scheduling sex is a pheromone killer. If our wellscore rating doesn't get that pheromone boost, what's the point?"

She sat upright, hands on hips, ass on his thighs. "What do you mean, what's the point? Why do you think I'm getting the uCuff? Shit, Santi, I've already done all this." She gestured reflexively and with annoyance at her hair and nightgown.

This was getting nonHappy. He was concerned about the negative effect on both their wellscores. But within seconds he became conscious of a wider problem: he must not allow his concern about their nonHappiness to produce additional nonHappiness. This was the classic nonHappy vicious spiral and he couldn't let it ruin the day.

So he did what every UCC shareholder was trained to do in such circumstances – he placed the first three fingers of both hands onto his closed eyelids, breathed in deeply, and pressed lightly while exhaling. Seeing him in the emergency wellness pose, Emeraldia was obliged to do the same.

Santiago focused on the floating, fleeting sparkles and forms created by the pressure of his fingers. Their impermanence and randomness were all that mattered. Not his feelings, not his situation. Only the lights moving in the darkness and the sound of his breathing. Emeraldia synchronized her breathing with his, still sitting astride him. They had to let the forgetting take over. They had to forget until they had forgotten what they needed to forget. And once their minds were empty, they were allowed to repeat the uMantra silently to themselves until one of them murmured it aloud, then the other, then in harmony:

"United we are uHappy."

"United we are uHappy."

"United we are uHappy."

2.

Emeraldia unboxed the uCuff with mounting excitement. Her uPersona glowed on the video projection as she shared the event online. She was contractually obliged to livestream the unboxing for a minimum of five minutes as part of Genedit's terms and conditions of purchase. The AI camera on her desk transformed her face and body into the avatar she had chosen for her uPersona years ago – an aquamarine-skinned cat-faced humanoid creature wearing a flower-print sari who she'd named Katine80. The flat-lay camera pointing down from the ceiling showed her feline fingers as they manipulated the packaging and product inside.

"They really did a kranpow job with the packaging design," she purred. "Sleek, yet tactile. Tech, yet human."

The slim rectangular box was decorated with a stylized double helix and a photo of a smiling blonde mother and pre-teen daughter. Katine80 pulled a discreet tab at one end of the box and slid out the insert containing the cuff.

"So here's our first look at Genedit's uCuff. I love how the first time you see the device it's nestled snugly inside this, um, interior compartment thing."

Emeraldia frowned at her lack of fluency. Viewers of the unboxing livestream could view either camera angle or a split-screen of both at once. Streaming numbers would fall instantly after a stumble like that, and she recalled her training: when you mess up, laugh. So she laughed.

She placed the box on the desk and removed the cuff. It was enclosed in a translucent biodegradable membrane that she pulled off gently. The wrapper disintegrated into a fine dust as she crumpled it in one hand. She blew the dust off her palm with a quick puff.

She turned the cuff over. It was about three inches wide and thin as a wristwatch strap. The synthium it was made from was babyskin soft and slightly darker than Emeraldia's pale skin tone. Its color contrasted pleasingly with Katine80's hands and arms in the livestream.

"It feels so soft," she said, rubbing the cuff lightly between her fingers. "I could totes imagine wearing this comfortably for the time required to complete the procedure." She held out her left wrist and carefully attached the cuff. "I guess it holds firm with some kind of lizadhesive coating." She peeled the overlapping end of the strap away from the other end. "It's super easy to unstick and restick," she said with a giggle as she reattached the cuff. Katine80 fluttered her long-lashed eyelids engagingly.

Emeraldia was happier with how this was going now. She reattached the cuff, then had a pang of panic. The timer on her desksplay showed that the unboxing still had over two minutes to run. Even with the recap and uPersona sign-off, she would struggle to fill the time. She wasn't even sure what would happen if she fell short. Would the cuff fail to work? Would she be charged an additional penalty fee by Genedit? These thoughts flitted through her mind as Katine80 looked up from the cuff on her wrist and blinked blankly at the camera.

"So… yah." She picked up the empty box and turned it over. "I can hardly wait to finish the setup process and… start hacking my genome!" She laughed again, but this time it was nervous and forced. "I've been… looking forward to this for so long, and… I'm super excited to share this unboxing with all my fans… all over the UCC." She put down the box and removed the cuff. "Let's see how it feels on my other wrist!" she exclaimed perkily. "I'm right-handed, so this might not be as easy… Ah, there you go! So, as it turns out, the uCuff is so kranpow that you can attach it to either wrist with ease and… um… enjoy the many benefits of the product."

Emeraldia winced. She was lapsing into formulaic praise. She imagined it wouldn't affect her contractual obligation but knew all too well that her stream count would plummet any second. Maybe she could wrap things up and get away with it?

"It's been soooo exciting to share the unboxing of the Genedit uCuff with you today, and I'd like to thank you all for watching and Genedit for creating this… kranpow device. I'll keep you posted on how things go after I've activated it. Yah, so… again, you guys are all super amazing and I really appreciate you taking the time to view this livestream of the Genedit uCuff unboxing! Hit subscribe for more videos and this is Katine80 saying see you soon!"

Emeraldia pushed a button on the desksplay and the livestream ended. She dropped her head down to the desk and sighed. The sign-off was the part she disliked the most about her Katine80 livestreams. It wasn't like anyone watched them out of choice – all UCC shareholders had a duty to log two hours per day viewing user-generated streaming content. Oh well, it was done. Now she could watch the how-to video.

She removed the cuff from her wrist. Genedit must have notified the device that the unboxing obligation had been carried out because a half-inch-wide halo now glowed a soft pink, in the very center of the cuff, surrounding the words, "Press to begin". She pressed, and a convocast displayed a sober text above the desk: "Genedit uCuff – Instructions for use."

Emeraldia motioned toward the arrow underneath the text. A woman appeared in the video wearing a white lab coat and holding a uCuff. Her instructions were accompanied by close-up shots of the device being used by an unseen female. With soft features matching her voice, the presenter was the embodiment of reassurance.

"Congratulations on choosing the uCuff for your personal gene editing needs. If at any time you need to go over these instructions again, just wave left to rewind. Your unboxing livestream has been reviewed by Genedit and it appears that you didn't see the pharmsert underneath the uCuff container. Please locate the pharmsert now by pulling the marked tab and lifting the uCuff compartment out of the box."

The box on the desk seemed empty. She swiveled it around and noticed a tab marked "Pull" midway along the longest side. Lifting it upward, she raised the part of the box that had housed the cuff. Underneath it was another, much shallower compartment housing the pharmsert. The woman in the lab coat looked like she was waiting patiently, blinking and smiling, in a short video loop.

"Do you have the pharmsert in your hand?" asked the presenter with a warm smile. "If you do, please activate it using the fingerprint scanner located on its upper surface."

Emeraldia turned the pharmsert around. Made of medium-flexible charcoal-colored EcoPlast, it was about an inch wide, two inches long, and maybe a quarter-inch thick. She placed her forefinger on a lightly indented oval at one end, and a thin strip of algae-green light pulsed down its center. The presenter jolted back to life.

"Thank you! Activation has been registered by Genedit Security. Before connecting the pharmsert to the uCuff, please take a moment to familiarize yourself with the uCuff and practice attaching it to your arm. As a right-hander, you should lay the uCuff open on a flat surface with the arrow on the interior surface facing away from you, then place your left wrist onto the uCuff with your veins facing downwards. Try it now!"

Emeraldia did as she was told. In the unboxing livestream, she had clutched the cuff against her torso to attach it, now she used the desk as a support. The woman in the convocast seemed to be watching her efforts attentively, but with a patient, gentle smile. "The adhesive part of the strap is marked turquoise and must overlap the other end of the strap to attach the uCuff firmly. You should feel a slight pressure similar to a smartwatch but not as strong as a blood pressure monitor. Once the activated uCuff is attached properly, a green smiley will appear on the reverse side of the turquoise section. Try it now!" The smiley appeared. "Good job!" said the woman. "You are now ready to connect the pharmsert – your personalized gene editing Crispr formulation."

But Emeraldia wasn't ready. Not in the emotional sense. She picked up the pharmsert and turned it over. She was overcome with a sickly unease. But why? Tech was her thing.

Back when she was Sophie Langlais in suburban Ottawa, Emeraldia had been part of the first wave of tech-paths – kids on the spectrum with an affinity for second-gen AI devices and quantum computing. Her Asperger's had found common ground with artificial intelligence.

Personality disorder became a social asset. Sophie soon found herself branching out from realigning the behavior of her parents' uCleanser to providing 700-YouBuck-an-hour therapy sessions for the elderly and their smarthomes. Put her in a room with a stranger and she would avoid eye contact; activate the room's AI and the conversation would flow.

"Turn your arm and place your hand palm-down, then hold the pharmsert in your other hand with your index finger once again positioned on the scanner," instructed the woman, performing the same actions.

What bothered her about the pharmsert, Emeraldia now realized, was that DNA was a messy affair. This wasn't the kind of predictable code she was used to. The junk code in the human genome almost made her retch. On top of that, the pharmsert worked by physical injection. Which circled back to the original problem: her own body was failing her relationship with Santi. She had grown up at ease with the idea of autohacking, but now the time had come to do it, she was anxious.

"Align your index finger with the finger outlined on the uCuff and press firmly down until you feel a mild suction pulling the pharmsert into place."

Emeraldia couldn't do it. She closed her eyes and breathed deeply. Rationally, she knew from the UCC rating that the procedure was risk-free, but she felt squeamish as she imagined the injection itself. She breathed in again and tried to relax on the exhale.

"Are you having trouble attaching the pharmsert?" asked the presenter. "If you are, just replay the previous instruction by waving back." She folded her arms, waiting with oppressively infinite patience.

Be logical, Emeraldia told herself, you're just upgrading your hardware. No wait, your software. No! Hardware… by modifying the software. Right? Kinda like machine learning. You're retraining your body. It's just a tweak. Just a tweak.

"You made a hot decision by choosing the Genedit uCuff," said the presenter. "If you have any concerns about allowing your future self to enjoy the awesome advantages and possibilities of improving your genome, just remember – the UCC encourages shareholders like you to benefit from an improved and extended existence through genetic modification. Your life is yours to control."

Emeraldia attached the pharmsert to the cuff. The thin strip along its center glowed fuchsia and her wrist prickled around its circumference as the nanoneedles punctured her skin.

"Good job!" said the presenter, unfolding her arms and clasping her hands together. "Now it's time to let your personal Crispr formulation do its magic. Except…" she added, leaning forward as though confiding with Emeraldia, "that it isn't magic – it's the pinnacle of Genedit's proprietary scientific advancement. Your body is changing now – for the better. It's best to leave the uCuff in place for an hour or so, to allow the pharmsert's nanoheal to function optimally. When it's safe to remove the uCuff, the notification strip will turn from pink to green. In the meantime, why not lie down and relax with a Genedit advertising session? After all, you've earned it!"

The video faded away and Emeraldia found herself staring at the space where the woman's smile had been. She was right, it was a good idea to spend the next hour fulfilling her daily ad-watching obligation.

Emeraldia left the office and walked a few feet down the hallway to the bedroom. She took her AdVisor mask from its stand in the corner, strapped it onto her face, and lay on the bed. She activated it with two index fingers to the temples, blinked three times, then stared at the virtual screen in front of her eyes.

Eyeball-tracking sensors followed her gaze as she watched commercial after commercial. Skipping was permitted, with a glance at the arrow at the base of her field of vision, but sixty minutes of completed ads had to be watched per day to achieve a baseline uHappy rating. Having preselected Genedit as her preferred advertiser for the session, the company's commercials played. Some were shorter than thirty seconds, others lasted up to five minutes. She had seen the majority of them many times before, but she knew that the AdVisor AI adjusted the frequency of their repetition for optimal product awareness, and she gladly assimilated all the information and benefits. As a key subsidiary of the UCC, AdVisor Inc.'s finely tuned advertising distribution system was a cornerstone of the corporate paradise in which shareholders like Emeraldia and Santiago dwelled.

She watched and listened attentively. Over the next hour, she considered changing her hair color and texture to a lustrous copper, while a simulation of her face smiled back at her, swishing the projected hairstyle left and right in a sun-bathed meadow. She imagined strengthening her joints so she could take up rock climbing. She toyed with the idea of enlarging her buttocks. Maybe Santi would like a juicier ass… And all the while the Crispr formulation was delivering its genetic payload and altering her cells.

3.

Santiago's Sculpturize approvals had gone well. Only a few tweaks to be done to the grandfather. But he'd been expecting that. The more realistic the sculpture style, the more likely the client would request changes.

He activated his curated vidnews stream. The first item featured harrowing footage of lifeless bodies being dragged aboard a rescue ship rocked by waves in an angry, landless sea. Then an overhead shot of a much smaller capsized boat.

A grave male voice-over reported: "Terrible scenes earlier today, twenty miles off the coast of Nova Scotia, as a vessel carrying refugees from Amexica sank in stormy weather. This video obtained by the UCCBC is from coastdrones that discovered the wreckage while performing a routine sweep of the area." Cut to body bags lying next to each other in a school gymnasium. "Fifteen bodies were recovered but it is not known at the present time exactly how many perished making the perilous crossing from New Jersey."

A golden-skinned spokeswoman in uniform spoke somberly from a press conference podium. Behind her hung the national flag, with vertical red bands flanking a white center and the UCC logo where the maple leaf used to be. "This tragedy should serve not only as a cautionary tale to the inhabitants of Amexica, but also as a reminder to UCC shareholders across Canada how fortunate they are to live in a place that is so coveted by people south of the border."

Santi shook his head as the next item began. They were already onto sports. Tragedy was only effective in small doses. He wondered how people managed a hundred years ago, with a daily, almost hourly, dose of terror, disease, war, and loss. Good thing his grandparents didn't have a uHappy rating to maintain or they would never have received any bonus uDollars. Not that anyone's lifestandard depended on a universal basic income back then. My Sim, he thought, no wonder people killed themselves, took drugs, drank themselves silly, gambled, and gamed – the turn of the millennium was an economic jungle that drove pre-shareholders to despair. It had always made him laugh that the so-called Great Depression referred to a decade-long blip when it should have been the name given to three centuries of democrapitalist pain. He stretched up to the ceiling and cracked his knuckles. Thank Sim for the corporations that took care of them now.

Two tattooed hockey players smashed into each other on the projection. Esports did nothing for his wellscore rating, so he waved the vidnews off. Before his gymtime he needed to feed the horselettes and give them a run in the yardzone. In fact, if he wore his tuneec while chasing them around, he could kick his bioscore up a few notches and have some FilterfreshAir fun. Best not to bother Emeraldia again until the evening. He should order a bottle of wine. Get the playlist right. Take a shower. Then let spontaneity and genetic engineering take their course.

4.

Mira Cool peered in the bathroom mirror and painted on her purple eyebrows. She curved the left one upward at the outer tip, then angled the other one down for optimal dissonance. Her thin, short, magenta mohawk (she called it a mauvehawk) tapered to a point above her forehead like the world's most exaggerated widow's peak. She took a step back and analyzed the overall effect. Her bacteria-infused Elastrium jacket shimmered aqua-blue. The more eye-catching the better when you're planning a daylight raid.

Outside on Queen West, she waited for the taxibot, watching its approach as a blue dot on her garmscreen. A late-November breeze made it feel colder than the 28 centigrade displayed on the trolleystop across the street. The condo block rose up in front of her, the sheer glass façade mirroring the identical building behind her where she lived on the 15th floor. The screen on the bottom of the 50th-floor skywalk bridge between the twin buildings showed an ad for the very event she was on her way to: Mandzukic's Horrortario. Enormous block lettering appeared on the screen against the cloudless afternoon sky: CHAOS, STRIFE, POVERTY, HUNGER, SICKFEEL. The words scrolled across from one building to the other, followed by images of feral children picking through garbage dumps and teeming marketplaces where the meats of unidentifiable creatures hung from wooden stalls.

A buzz on Mira's arm. The blue dot sent out ripples on the garmscreen. As her taxibot pulled over in front of her, a trolleycar glided to a halt at the stop across the street, its entire exterior plastered in advertising for the same event. From one of the trolley windows, a man in his early twenties was staring at her, his mouth covered with a mask on which was printed a lurid cartoon smile with a drooping tongue sticking out from it. The taxibot's door slid open. The man lowered his mask and raised an arm. The garmscreen on his sleeve glowed orange. Mira's garmscreen buzzed and glowed a matching orange. The sinuous uTender logo uncoiled in the center of the screen above a throbbing question mark and a photo of the man. He was shirtless, with arms crossed and sinewy muscles flexed. The photo zoomed in to his angular face framed by a Betty Page haircut. He tilted his head back slightly, flaring the nostrils of his narrow nose. Mira recoiled automatically, not expecting a video. She looked back up at the trolleycar window. The man did the same head tilt. She liked this vibe. Her wellscore would get a boost if she hooked up with him. Maybe even her bioscore if he was as athletic in bed as he seemed in the video. The taxibot's welcome chime sounded. Mira swiped a checkmark on the screen. The man smiled slyly, then repositioned the mask over his mouth and turned away as the trolleycar pulled away. Below the uTender video was the man's username: Jan Magus. She closed the screen and breathed in sharply, refocusing on the task at hand.

Mira entered the taxibot and fastened her seatbelt. The vehicle crept silently away from the curb. Old-fashioned chamber music began to play and the side windows dimmed. She frowned – some joker had hacked her preferences. Probably Rex. Well, that's what siblings were for. Tev. She would go with it for now – artsy music seemed appropriate for an artheft. Mira pressed the button on the drinkstributor screen to her left. A cup dropped down and filled with instalatte. The receipt appeared on her garm-screen. She left the cup where it was and looked out the windshield at the vehicles gliding in their equidistant convoy like assembly line components. Mira didn't want to drink the coffee, she had to make absolutely certain that the authorities would trace her movements after she completed the artheft, and the taxibot refreshment data was an additional piece of evidence.

Thirteen minutes later Mira arrived at the Canadian Art Co Museum and disembarked. She stood on the sidewalk, legs apart, arms akimbo, smirking at the venerable CACoM building's two-century-old brickwork. She needed the security camdrones to get a good look at her before she entered. The spangled heels of her faux-fur cowboy boots sparkled in the afternoon sun. Her indigo skortlet rippled as a pre-storm wind descended on Toronto. In the sky behind the museum, the thunderheads gathered. This was all too perfect.

The doors swung open and she entered the museum, waving her uCharge at the payment sensor. The side walls of the darkened vestibule were lined with twenty spot-lit Sculpturize statues of a bare-chested Mandzukic, each with clasped hands reaching up and bald head thrown back in a horrified expression reflecting the show's theme. As her eyes adjusted to the light, she saw that the statues were only likenesses of the artist from the waist up. Below, each one featured a different pair of legs, some female, some male, some old, some young, producing human chimeras of varying heights. Mira approached one. Mandzuckic's rippled torso was supported by the thin brown legs and bare feet of a child in dirty, ragged shorts. A six-inch-wide band displayed the Horrortario logo where the two bodies joined. To the left of the child-legged statue was another with the legs of an incredibly fat woman teetering on tatty, rancid running shoes. Mira recoiled at the artsmell and in doing so nearly backed into a vendbot that had wheeled up to her in silence. "Snack?" it asked in a perky warble. Before she had time to respond, it flashed up a holovid of curly beige undulating discs falling in slow motion onto a silvery platter. "Try AgraLife's newest yum – our Elvis-flavored veggie chip!" The chips piling up on the platter suddenly morphed into a tiny version of Vegas Elvis swinging a microphone stand around and singing, "Don't you step on my veggie chips," to the tune of Blue Suede Shoes. Mira sighed. The recent Presley revival knew no bounds.

"Nothing right now," she snapped at the vendbot, which promptly shut down the holovid and spun around to harass a group of high school kids who were milling about the vestibule. That would cost her a uClub point or two.

She made her way through the vestibule, past the coat-bot, and through the entry barrier, which swooshed open at the flash of her uCharge. And then she was in. A cavernous, dimly-lit circular hall with visitors clumped around the outer walls, and in the middle a sheer column of light twenty feet wide projected down from the ceiling. Low, dissonant reedy notes enveloped the viewers. She glanced at her garmscreen – only one minute to the start of the show.

The schoolkids entered the hall, shushed by their teachers as the doors closed behind them. A sixty-second countdown appeared on the floor in the middle of the light column. The gentle murmuring of the visitors grew momentarily louder in anticipation, then fell to silence as the countdown advanced. With twenty seconds remaining, a male voice boomed out, "Welcome… to Mandzukic's Horrortario. Please dark your garmscreens and uDevices. You may move freely around the room during the show but be sure to respect the enjoyment – or horror – of your fellow art lovers."

At zero the spotlight abruptly shut off, plunging the hall into darkness. The music continued, rising in pitch and volume. As it reached a deafening crescendo, the first miniscreens began to fall, fluttering and floating in the air-conditioned breeze like gleaming blossom. The music ended with a reverberation that overlapped the whispering of a female child in a foreign accent:

"We are the other world. The orphans of politics and faith. Unable to escape the flow of misery, we grow brittle and timid, scratching and biting as we seek food, water, and air."

At the word "air" the breeze became stronger. There were now maybe a thousand wispy screens drifting down and outward from where the light column had been in the center of the hall. Mira watched the audience's faces illuminated by the faint glow of the miniscreens as the viewers edged forward to see them more clearly. One of the screens wafted into her field of vision. It showed a video stream from some other part of the world: bloodied, injured brown-skinned men, women, and children clambering over the rubble in a bombed-out Middle-Eastern city.

She nodded in recognition. Mandzukic had been the

first artist to repurpose the televacation camdrones for an artwork. His Beats of Burden piece in the same museum a year ago had projected images from cubicle farms onto a giant treadmill installed in front of the UCC's downtown headquarters, accompanied by thumping destrock. Mira had considered performing an artheft on that work, but couldn't figure out how to uncouple the treadmill from its axle. Today there would be no such impediment. And she'd done her homework. The Horrortario itself would provide the cover for the heist.

The drifting, falling miniscreens now filled the central area of the hall. Visitors gaped at the scintillating cloud of video flakes drifting in front of their faces and landing at their feet in a carpet woven from thousands of unique livestreams showing the abject poverty and unimaginable suffering being experienced that very minute outside the comfort of the United Corporations of Canada.

The shaky voice of an old man speaking in a different, stronger foreign accent was lamenting his fate: "Every election I have voted has been useless and fake. Never have we the freedom to choose a Board like you. I have seen one government and another act selfishly and with no competence. The politicians, they stealing from us and laughing at the people who gave the power to them. My youngest grandson is now in Canada since two years… he was accepted in special program. And yes, we grow hungry in my country, but it make me feel good to know he lives the Canadian dream."

Mira took another step forward. A woman her age was gazing in awe at the myriad miniscreens, tears rolling down her cheeks. The video flakes swirled and the music whirled. The woman stretched her palm out. A miniscreen settled on it showing a run-down hallway in a drab building with drug addicts slumped against walls and passed out on floors. The falling screens showed emaciated infants, blotchy cheeks, withered breasts, syringed arms, muddied feet, sweaty backs, straining biceps, smoky rooms, sandy streets, crumbling shacks, bone-dry lakes, choking streams, blazing forests, marching boots, exploding shells, weeping fathers, bleeding mothers, rotting corpses.

The music got louder, then suddenly the breeze became more intense. It swept up the screens that had landed on the floor into a whirlwind of misery. The visitors were no longer spectators – the screens became petals of pain clinging to their clothing, their hands, their mouths. The schoolgirls emitted short squeals, then screams, as they clawed at their faces. Even the boys lost their cool and joined in the cacophony. They were now all part of the horror show.

Mira had crouched down and shielded her eyes with her forearm to avoid getting plastered with the miniscreens. She pulled a folded square of fabric out of her jacket pocket, then flung it open like a tablecloth. As the miniscreens whipped around the room, they clung to both sides of the electrically charged Elastrium. She spat away a screen that had flapped onto her mouth, then bundled up the fabric and shoved it back into her pocket.

The Horrortario continued for another minute until the visitors had been thoroughly immersed in the infinitely bleak lives of those trapped by the anarchy that seethed outside the UCC's gated communities. The music ended, the wind died away, the house lights came up and the screens fell from the bodies and faces of the visitors, who, instigated by the schoolkids, laughed with relief that the artistic nightmare was over and that they would forever be sheltered from the living nightmare of the unfortunates. Some of the boys horsed around, grabbing handfuls of screens from the floor and shoving them down the shirt backs of their classmates as if they were leaves on a fall park outing.

The doors opened and the visitors filed out, Mira among them. Some were clutching a screen or two in their hands as a souvenir, but Mira's pocket now contained at least two hundred. The artheft was underway. She hung back in the vestibule as the others exited into the sunlight. The next performance was scheduled to begin in ten minutes, and a new batch of visitors was already admiring the Mandzukic statues while they waited. Mira approached one of the statues with its torso mounted on a child's spindly legs and pushed it gently in the chest. It rocked back. Plentium was super light and she had estimated the weight of a Sculpturize to be around twenty kilos. The only element of her plan that was left to chance was whether these vestibule statues would be equipped with interference detectors. She pushed it harder. No alarm sounded. This made sense – these statues were not the artwork itself. Besides, they were infinitely reproducible.

She reached up to the statue's shoulders and pulled it toward herself. A young woman poked her boyfriend in the ribs with a whispered, "Look!" Mira stepped back and, supporting the statue by its clasped hands, dragged it toward the exit.

The museum visitors watched in astonishment at this nonHappy behavior. Was this woman deranged? The boyfriend gave an "Ohhhh," of comprehension, then mansplained: "It's artheft! It's all over the vidnews. It's artists whose art is stealing other artists' art and getting livestreamed by security drones as they do it."

By now Mira was nearing the exit, but her hands were full of art and the door opened inward. She stopped, frustrated. She hadn't thought about the basic logistics. Then the boyfriend rushed forward and pulled the door open for her. "Thanks!" she grunted, hauling the statue outside.

"What are you doing?!" the girlfriend yelled at him. "This is making me nonHappy!"

"I don't know," he answered. "I… I had to! My wellscore is rising!"

"Well, not mine, Hank. Not fucking mine."

"Sorry, Bunny," he said, approaching her with arms extended in apology. "United we are uHappy. United we are uHappy."

She joined in the mantra: "United we are uHappy."

He embraced her. "United we are uHappy."

Outside, Mira dragged the statue to a spot around twenty feet in front of the museum entrance, then pushed it upright. She stood back, panting from the effort. A camdrone whirred down to eye level behind the statue. Another was filming her from behind her left ear. Facial recognition AI would have identified her by now, so she held out her fists to the first camdrone, thumbs extended, their tips touching. The letters ART were temptooed on her right thumb, the letters HEFT on the left. The heist now properly contextualized, Mira carefully pulled the Elastrium out of her pocket. The wind was beginning to whip around, and she groaned inside at the idea that her project might be stymied due to the weather. Carefully unfolding the fabric, she peeled off a miniscreen and placed it on the statue's torso. As she'd hoped, the solar-powered current running through the screen provided enough static charge to overcome the mounting breeze and hold it there. She repeated the process for screen after screen. One slipped from her fingertips. It swooped back toward the museum like a migrating swallow rejoining the flock.

A rumble in the distance. A single outlying drop of rain. A change of tone in the air. By now, Mira had covered most of the statue's torso with miniscreens and the show was about to restart. If her theory was right, she was bringing it out of the museum and into the street. In front of her, a small crowd of passers-by had gathered and were eyeing her activities guardedly, afraid to cause offense and initiate a nonHappy spiral.

A clap of thunder. Inside the museum, the countdown began. Outside, large raindrops spattered the statue as half the onlookers dashed for cover and the other half activated their uBrellas. The initial pair of camdrones filming Mira were joined by a dozen more; the redundancy swarm was complete and the 360 coverage she'd planned for was ensured. Although the camdrones were being buffeted by the rising wind, the images they transmitted would be stitched together instantaneously and seamlessly by the UCC's video AI. And someone, somewhere, would be sharing their livestream.

A flash of lightning. The miniscreens on the statue sparked to life. As their images of misery played, Mira walked slowly around the statue, ensuring that both she and the content on the screens were captured clearly by the camdrones. The remaining onlookers gripped their uBrellas, rapt with fascination. One man in his early twenties activated his garmcam and filmed the camdrones filming the miniscreens showing the images being filmed by other camdrones in the miserable lands outside the comfortable cradle of the UCC. As the Horrortario came to an end inside the museum, the images on the miniscreens disappeared.

Mira stood beside the statue of Mandzukic and faced her makeshift audience. She placed her fist-thumbs together once again as a sign-off. A thunderclap right overhead elicited cries of surprise from the onlookers. The rain-drenched Mira lowered her arms and strode away from the museum. The artheft had been an unqualified success.

5.

"Maybe it's time for a confession." Santi leaned back in his ergool and clasped his hands behind his head.

His memoryself grinned. "Oh, cis, what now?"

Santi eyed the image hovering above his desk. He had the feeling that the phrase "oh, cis" hadn't yet become a common alternative to "oh, boy" or "oh, man" back when he was thirty years old, yet here was his memoryself throwing it around naturally. Maybe the AI was incorporating contemporary language into the memoryselves to aid conversation. Either way, the point was moot – he was talking to an LLM. Had the UCC rolled out an upgrade without informing users? They weren't supposed to do that. Or were they? He hadn't read the T&C's for years. He might have agreed to any number of non-optimal adjustments to the service. "Blink to accept" was a convenience fraught with pitfalls.

His was the first generation to converse with their memoryselves. The premise was simple and the promise was seductive: the entirety of the data forming one's online self – from baby pictures uploaded by fawning parents to teenage selfies, and from long-forgotten group chats to comment section tirades – the personas, the posts, the memes and the reels, the information was compiled by artificial intelligence to form a sort of historical avatar that could converse with its real-world contemporary self as though it was a different person. Sign-up was free and the user could select a memoryself from any time in their past. Additional memoryselves were available for a monthly fee.

The effect of speaking directly to a previous version of oneself was enthrallingly addictive, and, sure enough, people became addicted. This was narcissism on speed, and it resulted in the occasional overdose. The most notorious cases of the newly coined Multiple Divided Self disorder took place among thirty-somethings who spiraled into arguments with their teenage and twenty-something selves, skipping food for days and sometimes undergoing a complete mental breakdown. Public pressure from victims' parents forced the UCC to permit only one avatar per user per year. Like that really helped.

But Santi had never been afflicted by such problems. From the day of the memoryselves' launch, he knew exactly who he wanted to converse with: the thirty-year-old Tiago version of himself who listlessly dabbled in abstract sculpture while drifting around a corporate campus, whose cohort had entered adulthood with a squirtload more lifestyle options than career prospects. Tiago had been a prime specimen of the mid-century malaise: a genuine commitment to human wellbeing tempered by the unsettling realization that humanity had been superseded in most areas by bots and AI. Although freedom from drudgery in factories, boredom in cubicles, and danger in mineshafts was initially welcomed, it turned out to be a double-edged sword. So the corporations developed a bold new paradigm: shopping counted as work. In fact, shopping for things was more important work than making things. Overnight, the unemployed became the employed. This giant leap for mankind was then buttressed by the introduction of AdPoints in 2048 – the gateway to a universal basic income earned simply by watching ads.

"So?" said Tiago, "Stop teasing. What's the confession?"

"My heart isn't in it anymore," sighed Santi. "The Sculpturize artworks are just… basically they're just big wanks of shit."

The memoryself laughed. "Ha! You're super right. What's even funnier is you sound like Dad."

This was exactly the kind of comment that made the memoryselves so uncanny and addictive. "Right. Yah, so, I dunno," said Santi, "Should I branch out? Get back to real art? Print some sculptures that really mean something to people?"

"Or mean something to you," Tiago corrected him. "Speaking of wanks."

Santi's eyes flicked down, ever so briefly. Tiago was right. No surprise there. Memoryselves were almost too revealing where self-deception issues were concerned. It was like holding up a supermirror to one's deepest feelings, flaws, and failures. Not only was a memoryself's initial programming based on authentic psychological inputs from the subject's past, its AI was constantly refining its personality profile. Microgestures observed when talking with the present self, such as Santi's brief, shame-filled gaze aversion, were absorbed into the psychbase and leveraged to create novel subject matter and engaging responses.

"That's the eternal conflict, isn't it?" said Santi. "Commissioned art or personal art?"

"What about popular art?" asked the memoryself.

"Yah, well, that's just art commissioned by a marketplace that the artist has gotten attuned to somehow."

"But it doesn't have to be tail wagging dog."

"Meaning?"

"There were tons of artists who made personal art and still became flavor of the month, decade, whatever."

"Van Gogh never sold a painting in his lifetime."

Tiago nodded. "Monet was derided as old and past-it when he painted his Waterlilies. Who cares?"

"So I should just create what I like and hope for the best?"

"You don't need to hope – you've got a company, you've got your socials. Make your stuff and post a video."

Santi considered this. "Well – " he started, then his memoryself cut him off.

"Well, what!? You're looking for an excuse right now, aren't you?"

Santi squirmed on his ergool.

Tiago raised his chin, mockingly. "You're scared to actually create something."

"Fuck," said Santi. "You're fucking right, kid."

"Of course I am." The memoryself cocked a finger-gun at his real-world interlocutor. "It's what I do."

Santi smiled. That was how he acted when he was thirty.

"And it doesn't mean you stop producing your Sculpturize pieces," added Tiago. "Now turn me off and sketch something, kay?"

"Kay."

"See you later!"

Santiago nodded and flicked off the convocast. He looked over at the bricks of raw Plentium. He could do anything with them. Create any shape of any size and in any color. Imagine it, then write the prompt or scan the sketch, and let the printer do its work. But what did he want to *say* with his art? Beautiful abstract images were nothing but décor that any machine could make. Real art had to have meaning. He gnawed the inside of his cheek. The increased stress levels made his wristline glow fuchsia. Cis, he should have moved way past questions like this at his age…

He closed his eyes, breathed deeply, and massaged his temples with his middle fingers. Maybe what he was feeling right now could be his inspiration? Could he create a series based on stress? He opened his eyes and pulled up his garmscreen sketchpad.

6.

Emeraldia had one minute left in her daily AdVisor dose. The final commercial played. It was for Sculpturize. She was rarely shown ads for her husband's company. Had her rebranding thrown off the system somehow?

In the ad, a young woman with short, silvery-lilac hair flicked photos across a convocast projection. The photos were all selfies taken against exotic greenscreen backgrounds. An energetic male voice chimed in: "Had enough of facations?" The ad cut to a scene from the movie Casablanca, with the woman's face replacing Bergman's in a scene with Bogart. The voiceover continued: "Tired of being a movie star?" The next shots in the ad were filmed by a camdrone swooping through an art museum, then hovering to focus on paintings by Picasso, Monet, and Da Vinci. "It's time to ditch the dumb and reach for the real — with Sculpturize!" Now the silvery-lilac-haired woman was standing in one of the museum's galleries herself, looking at a Van Gogh self-portrait. "If the virtual isn't cutting it anymore," continued the voice-over, "a life-size statue in the style of a celebrity artist is the selfgift that keeps on giving." The woman reached out to the painting, as though selecting it on a screen. "Sculpturize's proprietary tech and celeb licensing get you the highest quality, delivered direct to your bode." Next, Emeraldia watched the woman opening her condo door to a deliverybot holding a large, white box with outstretched arms, its halo of leds flashing with corporate pride. The bot trundled into the condo and lowered the box to the living space floor, the multi-font

Sculpturize logo shimmering with variegated holography. The woman pressed the dot in the logo's letter "I" and the box sides folded down automatically, revealing a large statue. "Because they're based on biomorphic data, no two Sculpturize pieces are the same." The camera traveled around the statue, showing features in exaggerated colors and brushstroked surfaces – a Van Gogh painting of the customer reproduced in three dimensions. "Only Sculpturize is made by the originator himself, Santiago Khan, so look for this logo and commission your very own statue in the style of a legend right now by blinking at the Buy icon." Cut to a shot of Santi himself, posing with arms folded behind a three-foot-high model of the Sculpturize logo. At the bottom left of the screen was a gray circle enclosing the uDollar symbol of a green capital "U" with a vertical line through the middle, extending above and below the letter.

Emeraldia looked at the Buy icon, then back at the image of Santi, reliving the memory of watching from behind the cambot when the shot was filmed two years before. She had pulled faces at Santi and even flashed him her boobs to get him to crack up. Eventually, he did, only then becoming relaxed enough to finally strike the self-possessed pose that made it into the finished ad.

The Advisor session ended and Emeraldia removed the headset, her work done for the day. She placed the headset on the bed beside her and looked at her wrist. Had the Crispr formulation taken effect yet? She clenched her thighs lightly. Hmmm… maybe there's something.

She was wearing a light tee shirt and a pair of turn-of-the-century-style turquoise yoga pants that were back in fashion. She had ordered them in a fit of nostalgia while scrolling through her grandmother's vidmems and being shown multiple ads for the vintage clothing company that marketed them. The fabric was stretchy, making it easy to slide a hand under the waistband and into her panties. Relaxing and parting her legs, she felt between the folds of her… oh! The soft skin was moist! There was definitely some dampness there. Applying slightly more pressure, her finger slipped inside. She drew a sharp intake of breath. Not only was she truly, naturally wet in a way she hadn't been in years, but the warm stickiness itself was turning her on even more. My Sim, she thought, this was quicker and more effective than she'd dared hope!

There were two ways this could go – she could take care of herself now for an instant wellscore and bioscore duoboost (at the risk of being less responsive later, if ever Santi was back in the mood) or wait and maybe miss out entirely in the unlikely event that he wasn't up for it. She moved her fingertips and the jolt of pleasure made her catch her breath again. For sure he'd want sex later. She pulled her hand out of her pants and sat up on the bed. The uCuff had been YouBucks well spent.

7.

Santi was still sketching. He'd been working on the stress-themed sculpture for hours. It had gotten dark outside but he'd barely noticed. Ninety minutes ago, when his wristline had indicated low blood sugar, he'd told the room to bot him a latte and grapes. Working on this project gave him a rush that he hadn't felt in ages, maybe years.

The sculpture he was designing was an immersive room-sized artsperience. Its basic form was a squat tree with a trunk around ten feet wide. A curtain-like film disguised an entrance to the trunk section, through which a visitor could walk inside. He planned a light source above and at the back of the tree to illuminate the interior through a network of small diagonal shafts. Once inside, curved, smooth surfaces would guide the visitor further in, toward the dimly lit central section. And once lulled by the comforting surroundings of the hollow tree, the visitor would turn to leave, triggering the deployment of jagged, limb-like protuberances. These grasping inner branches would not be physically dangerous but would elevate stress levels in the now-captive visitor. And that's where the work became truly interactive. An infrared camera positioned above the subject would detect stress-induced body heat and lock the inner branches in place. Only once the visitor managed to calm themself down by repeating the uMantra would the detector register the lowered stress levels and retract the inner branches. Santi looked up at the ceiling, conceptualizing. He needed a name. And an artist's statement. Maybe this could be a new series?

"Room, find me words associated with trees," he said.

The room answered: "Wood, timber, lumber, softwood, hardwood, forest, jungle, deciduous, evergreen, foliage, leaf, needle, branch, bough, trunk, twig, root, sap, sapling, thicket, grove, orchard, arbore – "

"Stop!" Santi spoke to his garmscreen: "Screen, note this." A series of animated concentric blue circles extended across the dark screen. "Needle Grove. Artist's statement." He gathered his thoughts for a few seconds. "As UCC shareholders, all our needs are taken care of. We live in security, comfort, and plenitude. Yet studies have shown that because our minds are sheltered from the terrible suffering and deprivation of people in other countries," he paused for a few seconds. "Scratch that. Yet studies have shown that because our minds are sheltered from the terrible suffering and deprivation of people in other territories and markets, small everyday stresses or minor conflicts can lead to nonHappy outcomes. Art stimulates us on many levels, and the pieces in this series are no exception." He took a breath. Inspiration flowed. "Simply purchase one of the hand-signed pieces in Santiago Kahn's Needle Grove collection and you will not only be the proud owner of an ogee Plentium artwork by the artist renowned for his Sculpturize series, your bode will gain kranpow cachet to share." He was happy with this last part. "But that's just the start. The Needle Grove pieces are designed with a unique interactive feature that makes you part of the work itself – a symbiosis of art and human that will leave you literally breathless… until you figure out its purpose." Santi thought for a second, then said, "End note."

He was feeling energized, powerful. He needed to share

his excitement with Emeraldia, and checked her activity indicator. She hadn't been online for thirty-eight minutes. Was she asleep? He pushed back his ergool. A squeal. He'd bumped into one of the horselettes. It must have been lying on the floor right behind him. The high-pitched whinny of a horselette in pain was majorly disturbing. The injured animal had cantered into a corner and was peeking out nervously from behind the stack of Plentium bricks. "I'm sorry, Clint – come here, boy," he said, proffering his open hand in apology. The horselette edged toward him, limping badly. One of its forelegs was badly cut, and blood was pooling on the Xylate. A downside of genetically engineered mini creatures was that they were more prone to injury and less able to heal. "Oh no…" said Santi under his breath. He crouched down to put himself on a level with the horselette, reached out, and carefully took the bleeding limb in his hand. The animal whimpered, then collapsed to the floor, panting. Santi fought off the growing lump in his throat. "I'm so sorry," he said. The leg was clearly broken. He stood up. "Room, call the nearest veterinary clinic."

Within seconds a woman's voice came over the room speaker: "MacDowell Animal Clinic, I'm Mahalia, how can I help you?"

"I have an emergency, I think my horselette's leg is broken."

"Kay, I know this is a nonHappy situation, but try to keep calm. We don't want your wellscore to be affected."

"Right, kay," he said, but his wristline was fuchsia again.

"How should I address you?"

"Santiago."

"Now, Santiago, do you have access to some kind of

mediscanner?"

"Um, yah."

"If you don't, I can recommend a download."

"No, I think…" he swiped on his jacket's garmscreen, "Hold on." He spoke to the screen: "Screen, find mediscanner." An app opened up with the word VidMD on the screen underneath a logo of a cardiogram line inside a stylized eye pupil. He spoke to the room again: "Kay, found it."

"Are you with the injured animal?"

"Yah… oh Sim, he's in so much pain."

The horselette was shivering.

"Tell me what happened. As briefly as you can."

"I accidentally backed my ergool onto him. Oh, Sim, his name's Clint, and we've had him for ten years."

"I understand, Santiago. So, could you approach Clint without disturbing him, then scan him with your mediscanner?"

"His whole body?"

"Yes."

"Kay, here goes." Santi did what she asked, activating the scan on the garmscreen, then passing the linked ringcam slowly across the horselette from tail to head. He focused the ringcam on the bleeding limb. The pool of blood was now several inches across. He was sure that there wasn't much time.

"Thank you, Santiago, we are processing your scan."

Muzak came on. A diluted oldie from the 2050s: a whining melody straining to emerge from a muddy drumbeat. It made Santi mad. He stroked the horselette's warm, brown flank, then rested his hand on the rapidly rising and falling chest. Pets were engineered to improve their owners' uHappy ratings, but this was having the opposite effect.

"How long will it take?" he asked, voice and stomach tightening.

The muzak blaahed.

The horselette stopped breathing. It looked at Santi with an unblinking, bewildered eye, then closed it and died. Santi stopped breathing too for a few seconds, and his wristline flashed a blue-red sequence. He recited the uMantra to himself, but his thoughts were interrupted by Mahalia's voice.

"Sorry to keep you waiting, Santiago." Blood was soaking further into his pants as he knelt on the floor next to the dead animal's body. "Santiago?"

He checked his wristline. The crisis was over. It was back to fuchsia. Today's uHappy rating would be a disaster. "I'm here," he croaked.

"We have the results of your scan and I'm going to need you to weigh up the pluses and minuses of each course of action." Santiago sighed. Mahalia continued: "You can either attempt to stop the bleeding while we send a vetevac bot or immediately bring the animal to the clinic yourself."

"He's dead," said Santi.

"Oh. I'm so sorry to hear that."

"Yah, well…"

"When you're ready, we can call a removal service. There is a range of pricing options that include grief counseling either via holovid or in person."

Santi shook his head unconsciously at the horselette's body. He probably did need counseling. And the other two horselettes would be so confused. "I'll… I'll get back to you."

"Absolutely not a problem," said Mahalia. Was that the clinking of glasses in whatever room she was calling from? She was probably a freelance empathist calling from a bar or café. "When you call back, just ask for Mahalia and I'll be happy to help you choose the best option for you. However, I do recommend performing the removal operation within the next four hours, to avoid unpleasant biological outcomes."

"I understand," he said.

"Removal would be performed by a bot."

"Kay. Bye."

"Goodbye Santiago. And if you could answer a short survey following the call, it would have a positive impact on my wellscore."

The call ended. He stared at the word "Survey?" on his garmscreen then waved it away.

There was a certain beauty to the blood and corpse. He said, "Campic," and pointed his ringcam at the scene on the floor next to him. "Click," he said, and the photo popped up on his garmscreen. Maybe this was something. Maybe another sculpture series? Could there be a market for dead pet artworks? He gave a slight shake of his head in answer to his own question.

"Room, call back Mahalia."

"Hello? Sant… Santiago?"

"Yah."

"Thank you for calling back the MacDowell Animal Clinic. Have you given more thought to your removal options?"

"Send the bot."

"Perfect. The service should arrive within… fifteen

minutes."

"Kay."

"And that will be eight hundred uDollars."

How did people on UBI even do it? "Fine," he said. "And I'll skip the counseling for now."

A gap in the conversation. Was that shushing in the background? "No problem, Santiago," she said. "However, MacDowell Animal Clinic does advise a minimum counseling program via appsesh for recently bereaved pet owners, and you can purchase an entry-level package of three seshes for only twenty-nine uDollars. Can I sign you up right now, while this offer remains valid?"

"Yah, I guess."

"Perfect. You should receive the package any moment, along with instructions for how to pursue other counseling options with the MacDowell Animal Clinic. Is there anything else I can help you with today, Santiago?"

"No, that's it." He ended the call.

Now that the horselette's blood had cooled, Santi's pants were clammy and caked to his skin. What a fucking day. He would need a uForia bump before bedtime to get anywhere near a positive uHappy rating. The energy that had surged through him following his earlier creative burst had drained away. He stood up, removed his slippers, and walked to the bathroom. He stepped into the shower and pulled down his pants, letting them lie in a heap on the stall floor. Leaning out, he placed his shirt on a hook next to the towel rail, then slid the shower door closed and turned on the water. Blood swirled around his feet. He closed his eyes and repeated the uMantra to himself.

He was interrupted by the Room announcing the arrival of the removal bot. He shook the water off his face and said, "Tell it to wait outside." The majority of the blood had run off, but he soaped up and cleaned himself quickly.

Having dried and changed, Santi ordered Room to let the bot in, then waited for it in his studio. He heard the front door open and the nimble trundling of the bot as it negotiated the condo's hallways and furniture. But when it entered the room his heart fell. He didn't know what he expected to see exactly, but this machine was nothing more than a sidewalk garbot that had been gussied up with a hospital-green plastorg cover. Its voice was wheedling, like a thin man with a paunch trying to convince his wife to blow him. "MacDowell Animal Clinic is very sorry for your loss. Please indicate the beloved pet that has passed on."

Santi stepped aside so the bot could see the horselette's body. It advanced and lowered the front flap of its containment unit. Santi wrinkled his nose at the unwholesome odor that wafted out; a cocktail of sanitizing chemicals and lingering molecules of decomposing organic matter. The bot stopped in front of the body. Two rubbery clawscoopers whirred out from a horizontal slot in the bot's midriff. The camera where the head would have been on a more advanced model adjusted downward, then the metal arms of the scoopers extended above the corpse. Through a synchronized combination of the bot edging forward on its wheels and the clawscoopers drawing in the inanimate horselette, its body was gradually pulled into the unit. The scoopers reintegrated, the flap closed with a soft click, and the bot's job was done.

"Please rate your experience with the MacDowell Animal Clinic removal service," said the bot.

Santi hesitated, then clicked on the middle star of five on his garmscreen.

"Thank you. Would you care to add any comments?"

"No," said Santi, with a resigned expression. He was going to need that uForia.

The bot exited. Santi was suddenly hungry. He grabbed some leftover paella and made a cup of tea, adding a dose of uForia. As he sipped, he listened to the first counseling program appsesh. He selected the older male voice (he didn't know why), reclined in his cocoonchair, then closed his eyes and adjusted the headphones until they were comfortable. The voice's warm, sympathetic tone calmed him: "A pet is more than a companion. It's a member of the family. The pain you feel as a result of its loss is very real and very acute. Was this a sudden loss? If it was, please say yes."

"Yes."

"Then you won't have had time to prepare yourself, rationally or emotionally, and your uHappy rating may be negatively affected unless you can quickly and efficiently come to terms with your new reality."

Santi already felt like he wasn't getting his money's worth with the appsesh. He could probably get a refund below a certain threshold so he paused the sesh and drank some more tea. The drug was having the desired effect. And part of that effect was a rise in his libido. uForia was chemically engineered to be an aphrodisiac so that the artificial hormone rush would have a greater impact on wellscores when combined with the physical and mental benefits of sexual activity. His thoughts turned to Emeraldia. Would her Crispr formulation have taken effect by now? He removed his headphones, got out of the cocoonchair, and went to the bedroom, heart thumping, blood pumping. But when he entered he could tell she was asleep by her snuffling breathing and relaxed face. He sighed and went into the bathroom to ready himself for sleep.

He brushed his teeth, observing his features in the mirror. His slate-gray eyes betrayed an underlying dissatisfaction that no amount of mantring would fix. Even if tomorrow brought sex and sales, he knew that another day would have slipped by without... what? Without creation. Without the life-affirming happiness whose roots had received nourishment from a deep, unquenchable source. And without love.

Santi lay next to Emeraldia, eyes wide open, ceiling crushing him. He needed another perspective. He would get up early and go see his father.

8.

Santi didn't request an alarm and Emeraldia had already left for yogafit when he awoke. He plodded to the bathroom feeling unrested and no less anxious. He messaged his father while sitting on the toilet. In reply, he received a string of adorably old-fashioned emojis of the kind that only seniors used. He had two hours to get to Toronto – plenty of time for a pod or two.

He walked down the steps from his unit and entered the minishuttle. As the podcast continued, he stared out the window at the rows of young palm trees lining the main driveway. The sky was blue and cloudless and the sidewalks were devoid of human life. Two other minishuttles sped by from the other direction; wingless whirring dragonflies with orb-like eyes that reflected distorted green leaves in metronomic succession. His garmscreen's proximity alert showed the names of the occupants – neighbors of his called Tamra and Claudius. He swiped each of them a greeting. Moments later, their beaming faces popped up on his screen in return.

The shuttle slowed as the entrypost came into view. The blood-red UCC logo glowered from the tapered white pillar as it slowly rotated twenty-five feet above the ground. Just above the logo's stylized maple leaf, the entrypost's bell-shaped monitoring unit transmitted, received, and recorded the behavior of every shareholder inhabiting the PineRidge community, a gigantic metallic mushroom emitting countless spores of data.

The shuttle parked itself in a charging bay at the base

of the post. The cabin door slid back and Santi got out.

Another vehicle was arriving from the interurban road that linked PineRidge to other communities. This was the luxcab that would chauffeur Santi in bespoke comfort on the hour-and-a-half drive to the Toronto café where he was meeting his father. He climbed into the SUV, reclined, activated the chair massage, and closed his eyes to the sound of a burbling stream.

9.

Santi scanned the crowded downtown café. At the tables were the usual range of uHappy shareholders filling their days with digital mingling like the buzz of a corporate beehive. Each of the glasstic-walled cubicles that lined the far row was occupied by a kid in their twenties or younger, chatting with one or more holovids – friends, maybe family in other parts of Canada, or, conceivably, in Europe, where the dream of an EUC was still alive as its old-style governments clung to diminishing legitimacy.

There he was.

Alone at the back, seated as far from the baristabots as possible, underneath a vidstrip showing rippling grasslands, was his father: Jamal "Genghis" Khan.

Jamal would never, ever be uHappy. At ninety-two years old, he was of the generation that lived through the upheavals, that closed ranks against the sloppy, slippery politicians, and populated their lives with devices and apps. And though he had always sensed the shadows of the algorithm puppeteers and the AI ventriloquists, he, like his peers, had accepted the trade-off of power for convenience. His eyes were closed, earbuds playing the hip-hip of his youth.

Santi swiped for his coffee as he crossed the room, then pulled out the ergool on the other side of his father's table. Jamal opened his eyes and used his elbows to shift himself more upright in his armchair. His black zippered jacket was too big for his shrinking frame.

"Hey, Dad," said Santi.

"Hi," said Jamal, switching his earbuds to hearing aid mode.

"You doing oky?"

Jamal pointed his white beard at the drink in front of him. "Why can't they just make a frappuccino?" he said with the faintest trace of a Pakistani accent. "Why does it have to be twenty-five kinds of fucking fancy?"

"So you can choose the one you like best?" ventured Santi, knowing full well where the conversation was heading.

"The one I like best is a fucking Iced Capp like I used to get from Timmy's!" growled Jamal, smacking a palm on the table so hard that neighboring people swiveled around in concern. "This looks like whipped cum."

"Dad!" stage-whispered Santi, glancing sideways at the other café-goers.

"Call me Genghis," said his father.

Disconcertingly, from his son's perspective, Jamal had adopted the stage name Genghis two years previously when he embarked upon his seniortime career as a livestream standup. The name itself was a snub to the UCC, with its homage to the marauding warlord of pre-corporate barbarism, and it certainly gave his celeb rating an initial boost.

"I can't call you Genghis."

"You Kahn't? Or you won't?"

Santi rolled his eyes at the dad joke. "I wouldn't call you Genghis if your name was really Genghis."

His father looked around the room. "So what do you want?" he asked. "What could I possibly do for the man who has everything, in the city that has everything, in the country that has everything?"

"You could tell me what was better."

Jamal squinted over his old-fashioned glasses. "What do you mean?"

"You're always complaining about stuff. But what was better when you were a kid?"

Jamal gave a wry smile. The creases in his skin were elephantine. He was used to receiving shameless stares from people in their sixties. Men like him just didn't exist. Senior survivors who weren't uLifers wearing Vitainment headsets typically underwent genetic skin elasticity makeovers in middle age, turning their complexion plastic peach. No one had creases like him anymore.

"Everything was better," he grumbled. "The grass was greener when it wasn't mowed by bots."

"That's not true. And you had Trump!"

"Yeah, but the rebellion and the eco stuff were the convulsions of society disintegrating." Jamal's eyes lit up. "It was the last hurrah of the human race."

"Dad – "

"I mean it!"

"But I really want to know what was better."

Jamal's watery eyes flicked down for a moment, then back to his son.

"Seriously, Dad," said Santi, "give me an example."

"Okay, okay," said Jamal. "We drove places."

"That's not better!" protested Santi, throwing up his arms. Jamal smiled at the gestural echo of his long-gone wife. "Why are you smiling!? The country your own father was born in has fried because of car emissions."

"You asked me what was better," said Jamal calmly. "It was better to drive. I could get in a car and go from Toronto to San Francisco. Or fucking Santiago!"

Santi took a breath. His father had purposely mentioned the city his maternal grandparents were from, the city he was named for. The UCC, with its Genedit cures and its uLife hospices, had come too late to save his mother from the cancer. Santi always had the impression that Jamal laid irrational blame at the corporations' doors – the same merciless chronological irony that killed soldiers on the morning of an armistice or drowned refugees a minute before the coastguard's arrival. This was the defining tragedy of his father's life. And it was the reason he refused the genetic treatments that would keep him sprightly. But the irony kept needling him because his health was exceptional and his mind still sharp. At ninety years old he'd made the decision to mine laughter from a vein of bitter nostalgia. It was what she would have wanted.

"But we can still travel by car," said Santi.

"Not to San Fransunksco, that's for sure."

Santi winced at the tasteless pun. "Thousands of people used to die in accidents every year, Dad. You know that."

"That's why it was better to drive."

Santi looked puzzled.

"You were in control and at the same time liable to be killed by idiots, ice, or fucked-up engineering," said Jamal, triumphantly. "And motorbikes were a hundred times better."

"You mean worse."

"I knew a guy, an Englishman – we played cricket together – who was a motorbike maniac. He was head of an owners' club that organized meet-ups and rallies. He used to ride for the kick he got out of tearing through the backroads. He was outside Kingston – this was back in the twenties – and he came over a small rise and hit a pickup truck head-on. Died instantly. He must have had a second to think *oh fuck!* and then it was over."

"Kranpow. You're so not convincing me."

Jamal laughed drily, without showing his teeth. "You cannot be alive if you cannot die."

Santi rolled his eyes. This was one of his father's stage aphorisms. He got away with shit like that because he was majorly senior. "Fine. Driving. What else was better?"

"We had our culture, Santiago Khan. We had our culture."

Santi knew what Jamal meant, and it wasn't ballet and abstract painting. "Dad, there was nothing good about that, and you know damn well."

"I don't agree. Kinship, fellowship, and faith are like the blood that pumps through our veins."

"That's nothing but dumb tribalism. You might as well have been born in the Stone Age or at best in medieval times."

"Maybe I was. And maybe I was happy there."

Santi needed to urinate. He got up without saying anything and entered the washroom.

Sitting on the clearbowl, he gathered his thoughts. This chat wasn't helping. The unease he'd been feeling was not assuaged by his father's reminiscences of cars and tribes. In Santi's estimation, even the sports tribes were a mindless outlet for a pointless urge, while risking death by automobile was a poor trade-off for the freedom to get stuck in traffic and take wrong turns. He'd caught himself having this feeling before and he didn't like it: his father just wasn't all that smart or insightful.

He swiped away the complimentary urine analysis and pulled up his pants. When he got back to the table, his father was prodding his coffee with a stirrer, nose turned up in disgust. Santi took his seat. An awkward silence. Jamal cleared his throat twice. Santi glanced at his garmscreen for no reason.

"Hey – you know what I heard on the vidnews?" asked Jamal.

"Is this a joke setup?"

"No, really, there was one of those art things. With a girl."

"What are you talking about?" asked Santi, trying to suppress parent-frustration. "And don't say *girl*," he added in a low voice, looking around.

Jamal snorted dismissively. "I'll say what I like."

Santi sighed. "Kay, kay, what art thing?"

"You know, when someone steals an artwork and gets caught on purpose."

"Oh – artheft," said Santi.

"Yes, exactly."

"So what? What about it?"

"The girl who did the artheft stole one of your statues and they showed a video of you with the artist."

"What? Who?" Santi couldn't figure out why the artheft of a Sculpturize statue would make it onto the news. Or even why someone would bother stealing one of his pieces. Then it dawned on him. "Oh… Mandzukic?"

"Yeah, that's it."

"Why didn't you tell me?"

"I am telling you!"

Santi raised his garmscreen close to his mouth and said, "Garmscreen, search video of Sculpturize artheft." As he lowered his arm and the screen populated with video thumbnails, his raspberry cappuccino was delivered by the minibot. Santi showed the screen to his father who squinted at it, then pressed one of the thumbnails. "It needs my print, Dad," said Santi, pressing the same thumbnail himself.

The video fullscreened and played. "That's it!" said Jamal.

Santi skipped past the perky presenter, who was clearly taping from her bedroom, and saw the shaky montage of Mira Cool being filmed by onlookers as she plastered the Sculpturize statue of Mandzukic with miniscreens. When the artheft ended and the presenter reappeared, he swiped it off. Ignoring his father, who had started to say something, he asked the screen to search up more videos of Mira Cool. What was strange, even confusing to Santi, was that she didn't seem to have her own channel. There were thumbnails of maybe a dozen other artheft videos and... that was it. His mind skittered around, hunting for a reason. She had probably changed her name. But why change your name and not create a dedicated channel? It must have been temporary – she must have made her channel private so that she could rebrand it. He should check back later.

"Santi!" rasped his father. "Did you hear anything I just said?"

"Huh?"

"You were hooked on your garmscreen." Santi's face fell. "Typical Generation Omega – I shuffle out the house to come meet you, I'm trying to share some of my nine decades of wisdom, and you block me out completely. You know what your mother would say?"

"Yes, Dad."

"She'd say you were looking through a selfiscope."

"Sorry, I was just – "

"Oh, you were 'just', were you? You know how I feel about that word."

Even at sixty-four years old, Santi could still feel like a scolded child cowed by his father's disdain. "Sorry," he said quietly.

Jamal recomposed himself. "You want to hear what I was saying or not?"

"Yes. Of course."

"You want to know what was better at the turn of the century?"

"Yah."

"We had something to believe in."

Santi rolled his eyes. "Oh come on, Dad. Don't start with religion. *You* don't believe in God and you didn't when you were a kid."

Jamal took a sip of his coffee, eyes fixed on his son. "We believed in people."

"What does that mean?" said Santi. "I believe in people. People are kranpow."

"God, I wish you would stop saying that."

"Fine. People are awesome."

Jamal shook his head and grunted.

"Are you oky, Dad?" said Santi, genuinely concerned.

"I'm fine. I'm fucking kranpow," said his father, looking suddenly like he couldn't get comfortable in his seat.

"Well, you don't look fine. Let's get a doctor to you." Santi raised his garmscreen and activated RemoteMD but his father grabbed his forearm with surprising strength, pinning it down on the table and covering the screen.

Shocked, Santi opened his mouth to object but then said nothing.

"You are not going to put me in one of those nightmare factories," said Jamal through gritted teeth. "I'm fine."

"I just wanted to check – "

"And even if I wasn't fine, that's just the way it is."

Jamal released Santi's arm. The garmscreen rebooted.

"Dad…"

"So there's this woman. Or maybe she's a man now. Called Libranne."

Santi drank some coffee. He could see his wristline poking out from the end of his sleeve glowing pale pink. "What are you talking about?" he said quietly.

"You must have heard of her."

"No shit, I've heard of herm, Dad. They is the biggest celeb in Canada."

"Yeah, well I bet you haven't heard of her most recent appearance."

"What are you talking about?"

"She's gone rogue, and…" Jamal leaned in and lowered his voice conspiratorially, "the UCC is blocking her."

Santi sighed. "Dad…"

"Seriously."

"Dad, they is probably on a cleanse or changing gender again or something."

Jamal leaned back again with a self-satisfied nod and said, "Think you know everything, eh?"

"Dad."

"Think your old man lives in a fog of denial?"

"No, but it's ju – "

Jamal made an "ahp" sound to stop Santi from saying "just" again. Santi raised his palms in apology, barely able to hide his frustration. "Listen," said Jamal in the same secretive tone, "she makes exclusive holovid shows for followers who receive a code to access the livestream."

"Right. How do you know this if you need a code?"

"Think your old man has no connections, eh?"

"Stop with the 'old man' shit, Dad, and get to the point!"

People around them turned to look at Santi. "Calm down, calm down," said Jamal. A servebot glided up and peppily asked Santi if everything was good and whether he'd like an AgraLife healthbun ("Our Super Sunday Special is Cranana!"). Santi automatically swiped the grimacing machine away. His father beckoned him across the table. When their faces were a breathsmell apart, Jamal whispered, "I have a vidkey. Her latest show. I'll hand it to you when we say goodbye."

"Where d'you get it?" said Santi.

"I can't tell you."

"Why?"

"Best you don't know. One thing, though. Make sure you're offline when you watch it."

Santi wasn't sure how to respond to this request. Offline behavior raised flags. It might even affect his wellscore.

Jamal continued: "On your way home, set your taxibot to private and connect the key directly to your screen."

Santi was barely listening. He considered the implications – not for his own wellscore, but for his father's.

"Did you hear me?" asked Jamal, sensing apathy, or worse, contempt.

Santi had met up with Jamal today because his father had always swum against the tide. And Santi was getting sick of the tide, too. But this Libranne thing sounded so ridiculous that all Santi could do was humor him.

Jamal was getting testy. "Don't bullshit me, Santi. Watch on the way home."

"Kay, Dad, kay," said Santi, reclining in his chair and raising his voice louder than intended.

"Shhh!" said Jamal, glancing left and right with a hint of mania in the glint of his eyes. "This is serious. It's a new truth."

Santi felt untethered, drawn into a fog of uncertainty by the same emptiness that had overcome him last night when he lay awake next to Emeraldia. None of this was good for his wellscore. And why had he expected a deeper answer from his father than a celeb stunt? He resisted the temptation to leave right then. He needed to change the conversation. "When's your next gig?" he asked.

"Tuesday at eight."

"Kranpow."

"I'll be road-testing some new material. You should watch."

"Kay, I will." Santi nodded at Jamal's drink. "You all done?"

"With this cup of piss? I was done before you sat down."

Santi smiled. "How you getting home?"

"What do you think?"

"Did you apply your sunscreen?"

Jamal shoved back his chair. "Stop bugging me with that."

Santi stood and edged around the table to help his father out of his seat. His old-man smell was cozy and sad. "See you soon, Dad."

"Sure you will. Tuesday at eight."

"Right."

Jamal stood up and Santi moved to hug him. But Jamal kept one hand on his chair back and the other at his side. He whispered in Santi's ear, "Don't forget to watch in privacy mode."

"Yah, yah."

Jamal snorted in acknowledgment and shuffled toward the exit. Santi trailed behind him, ordering a taxibot on his garmscreen.

Outside, sparse drops of rain were falling. Jamal pulled a folded baseball cap out of his jacket pocket and squared it on his bald head. "Sunscreen," he said with disdain, then walked away down the palm-lined street so slowly that the pigeons didn't flutter.

Santi couldn't take his eyes off his father. He admired him for his independent spirit, despite its accompanying stubbornness. And yet he was somehow never able to communicate this feeling of admiration. He just couldn't ditch the adolescent frustrations that needled him then and nagged him now. Although it would take Jamal at least ten minutes to reach the end of the block and turn the corner toward his condo unit, he would never accept a sistbot. He was a living, breathing relic of living, breathing times. But it wasn't his age that made him a relic, it was his attitude — a steadfast refusal to countenance the techno-corporatism that his very own generation had seeded and nurtured. Had Santi inherited a strain of his father's luddite attitude? What if the strain had finally grown strong enough to hollow out his belief in the UCC? Was this where his current angst had sprung from?

The taxibot pulled up and buzzed Santi's garmscreen. His father had barely made it twenty feet down the sidewalk. Santi got in, toying with the vidkey in his pocket. He swiped the vehicle to privacy mode, then pushed the key into the screen slot and sat back. The cab's windows darkened as it overtook Jamal, giving Santi the impression that his father had receded into a thick fog.

The video was shot by a garmcam from behind the heads of a crowd of people. After several shaky seconds, the camera tilted up and stabilized. It was a night-time scene illuminated by an expanse of shifting blue light from below. Santi wondered what he was seeing exactly. The cam zoomed out to reveal a swimming pool with bright underwater lighting.

A holovid appeared above the pool, its spectral colors reflected in the water's murmuring surface. The image showed the beatific face and white-tunic-clad upper torso of a mid-gender, mid-life human. Santi recognized herm instantly as Libranne. The pool was surrounded by an audience of hundreds, seated on bleachers. The crowd frissoned as the person in the holovid spoke in a projected, mellifluent tone.

"Cisfolk and queers, older and younger, whatever your skin tone, hair curl or ass size…"

Some chuckling from the audience.

"There is only one thing you need to know. One thing."

A male voice in the crowd yelled, "Tell us, Libranne!"

"Oh, I'm gonna tell you. For that is why I'm appearing today in your cities, towns, and bodes, you children of the corporation. I'm here to tell you the one thing you need to know."

A shuffling of excitement.

"Because we are all alive. We are on this Earth, made

of flesh and blood."

"Yah!" came a female voice.

"We are not simulations. No, we are not."

Mumbling and grumbling of discontent and agreement.

"No matter what the morpigs say: We. Are. Not. Simulations!"

"No to Sim!"

"We are real, we are real. But you know that already." Libranne paused, looked down, then slowly back up. The holovid's three-dimensionality meant that the speaker was addressing everyone in the crowd personally. "Today I will tell you the one thing you need to know." Libranne gestured expansively, arms now visible as the holocam pulled back. "You are all immortal!"

At this statement, the crowd seemed stunned. Some muttered, some just stared, open-mouthed. They had gathered to hear a life-changing announcement. They had been promised that Libranne would share a deep discovery with them. But it was clear that no one was expecting herm to deliver a speech akin to a sermon from the old-time religions.

Santi paused the video and thought about what he had heard so far.

The belief in immortality and supernatural agents was a mental infection of the world outside the incorporated nations of the UCC, UCGB, UCJ, UCK, and in the People's Shining Totality of China. In the UCC (and, if he was not mistaken, in the UCJ) the ancient faiths had been replaced by simulationism – the credo that all humans exist in a computer game created by a higher intelligence. From the very beginning, the UCC Board had encouraged the country's shareholders to replace the soul with software (some called it 'soulware'). Churches were repurposed as halls where believers in the new pseudoreligion of simulationism took part in massively multi-player online roleplaying games. And simulationism's proselytizers – the twitchers and streamers – became known as morpigs.

For all these reasons, immortality was viewed as gauche – even childish. Yet here was the beloved Libranne using the word openly.

Santi pressed Play again.

Libranne lowered herm voice, speaking with a hypnotic cadence: "I feel your confusion, I feel it. But when I say 'immortal' I do not mean you have souls that live eternally in Heaven. I do not mean that your descendants carry your genetic code. I do not mean your bodies are recycled by worms to rejoin the Earth and grow anew." The crowd was rapt. "What I mean when I call you immortal is that every atom of your bodies is part of the universe. Every atom has already been replaced by the universe. Many times over. So many times! And every atom of your body will go on living in the universe. Forever!"

A smattering of cheers, then some whoops and applause.

"You are the living embodiment of universal life. The true life of the universe, beyond organic molecules. You are an unbroken chain that stretches back to the Big Bang. You stand strong in the winds of time, and those winds will carry you onward, defeating death. Forever!"

Yahs and more enthusiastic clapping.

"Each one of you is like a current in the ocean. Though you may change, though you may shift, and though the form you have today will disappear, the water that has flown through you in the ever-changing atoms of your body will keep on flowing. Forever!"

This message seemed to resonate with the crowd. There was a palpable rise in the chest, a thrill in the gut, and a spark in the mind.

Libranne creased herm eyes and opened herm mouth, but waited till the crowd had calmed before continuing. "In fact, you are doubly immortal. Not only are your bodies mere vessels for the very corpuscles of the universe, but every single thing you do with those bodies changes the shape of the universe forever. You send it on a new pathway. You are constant change, and you are forever eternal. This is the immortality we all possess – I, Libranne, and you, the children of the corporations." For the first time, herm voice rose. "Reject simulationism once and for all! Join me in celebrating the triumph of true material immortality. Join me in celebrating the love of real life. We are not simulations. This is Librannism, this is real, and this means love!"

The crowd's excitement was tangible now. A small group chanted, "Librannism is love! Librannism is love!" The smattering of voices were joined by others until the chant turned into a deafening ululation. Libranne threw herm arms aloft, then clapped herm hands slowly. The crowd mirrored the movements of the holovid, clapping in time with the word "love". Suddenly Libranne stopped moving, but kept herm arms raised, palms now facing outward. The crowd fell silent.

"The power of Librannism is infinite." And with this declaration, Libranne's holovid vanished.

The crowd noise swelled again. The garmcam image got shakier as the chant restarted: "Librannism is love! Librannism is love!" Then the screen went black.

Santi had been riveted, and he continued staring at the dark rectangle for several seconds. He had never seen or heard anything like it. And he'd forgotten all about Mira.

His eyes drifted away from the garmscreen. The featureless dirt-flanked highway passed by. What did this all mean? It wasn't exactly an old-school supernatural preach-fest, but it was weirdly similar. Could this overt rejection of simulationism be ground zero for an uprising against the UCC? And what about Libranne? The biggest star in the UCC. Were they some kind of rebel now?

Maybe the video was deepfaked. But by who? The production value was impressive. Personal AI couldn't do that. Wait... maybe it was some new genre of celebtainment. Had his father been duped? Would there be a reveal next week?

And if it *was* real, where had this gathering taken place? Was it within the borders of the UCC somewhere? If it was a direct challenge to the orthodoxy of the Board, how could it have been kept secret from them? Yet it *must* have been filmed in the UCC – the crowd at the pool were well-nutritioned, happy shareholders who looked just so... Canadian. So multi-skinned. And Libranne was a UCC celeb, in any case.

Santi watched the video twice more on the way back home, trying to figure out its authenticity. He paused it at various moments, scanning the faces in the crowd, checking the holovid of Libranne, searching for a clue that might answer his questions. But there was nothing.

He compared the various possibilities: one was that the video was real and his father had gotten hold of it somehow. That would mean his father had connections to this Librannism movement that might be working to undermine the UCC. It was one thing to ramble about how life was better in the past – seniors tended to do that as a matter of course – but it was quite another to instigate anti-UCC activities. The nonHappy risk was extreme. And for what? He could barely believe that this was the case. The men and women in the video numbered in the hundreds. And they ranged in age from their twenties to senior. How could everyone have coordinated without the corporations finding out? Plus, the pool was large and would be visible to UCC freedom drones.

His mind whirled back to option two – that this was a furtive fiction, a trailer for a new show that his father had mistakenly assumed was real. This totes made sense. But why challenge simulationism at all? Surely it could lead to nonHappy outcomes?

The third possibility was that the entire video was fake – doctored by the UCC for… for what? To ferret out nonHappy rebels? Or as a reverse psychology marketing ploy? No, no, he was overthinking it.

He ordered a fizzfroot from the bot and another idea occurred to him. Could the video have been made in Amexica? Libranne only appeared in it as a holovid. Super simple for the Amexicans to fake. But why would they do that? Everyone knew they hated the UCC, so… a covert psyops program? The UCC had extinguished all forms of fake news long ago, but what about fake celebtainment?

The bottom line was that unless he figured it out, he was risking a nonHappy outcome himself. He couldn't just forget about the video, could he? And he couldn't talk to Emeraldia about it. Sex was a definite possibility tonight (and if the uCuff worked its magic, almost every night) so no way was he going to mention the mysterious video and throw her mind into a nonsex mood.

He drained the fizzfroot bottle and slid it into the bot's recyclaslot. Why had Jamal done this to him? Now he was stuck with a mystery that might do all kinds of damage to his wellscore.

The taxibot was approaching the compound. A flash of panic. He had to delete the video before his bode's wifi automatically connected. A quick swipe, just in time. Gone, but unfortunately not forgotten. He removed the vidkey and replaced it in his pocket. As he got out of the car, he noticed that his armpits were sticky.

10.

Throughout the rest of the day and evening, Santi pondered what he had seen in the video. Sometimes he mulled, and occasionally he veered into rumination – a state that his wristline alerted him to so that he could avoid a negative wellscore impact. He was tempted to search the video up online or see whether it was a trending topic. But he held back. The video's disturbing content and his father's skittish attitude had him spooked.

He had a training sesh at 5 p.m., which he had scheduled to coincide with Emeraldia's celebrity robocoiffeur. On the exercise bike, his mind went back to cycling through the potential explanations. But he was getting nowhere and had no way of getting somewhere. By the time he'd hit the shower, his initial question – the *why* of the video – had evolved into a new question: the *what* of the video. Because, even though right now its source and intention were annoyingly opaque, one thing was crystal clear. The video was an attempt to cancel simulationism. And it caused Santi to think an unthinkable thought: What if simulationism was totally bogus?

Santiago Khan was what you might call a soft simulationist – the flavor of belief that in olden times was labeled agnostic. He didn't want to play with the morpigs, he wasn't trying to hack the simulation, but he accepted the comforting belief that everyday life was, in fact, a simulation. He would joke about it being *his* simulation whenever a serendipitous event benefited him. He would sigh and say, "Thank Sim!" whenever a fortuitous coincidence occurred. He would groan and say, "Oh Sim!" whenever tragedy struck. But simulation was the water he swam in, and he barely acknowledged, yet never doubted, its existence. This video was like a fisher's net scooping him out of that same water, leaving him gasping for breath and wondering what this unexpected new reality was all about.

The evening dribbled away. Some reading, some watching, some eating, and finally some sex. And although the anticipated fluid-fest was physically satisfying, Santi's mind was annoyingly elsewhere. Afterward, as Emeraldia snuggled up against him, his eyes kept opening without him even realizing it.

At one point, he couldn't take it anymore, and once he was certain that she was sleeping, he disentangled himself from her limbs and went back to his studio. In the room's dimmed night-time ambience, the piled-up Plentium bricks became looming presences, like an Eastern megacity's featureless skyscrapers in a fever dream of the pre-corporation world.

"Room, get me my memoryself," he said gloomily.

"Sure," answered the Room.

The convocast activated above his desk and Santi leaned forward on his ergool as the image of the younger him appeared. Tiago was wearing a mauve-and-green-striped button-down shirt, open to the waist but with a wide necktie, in accordance with the frankly embarrassing style that flared up briefly when he was in his late twenties.

Tiago stretched and yawned. "Hey, it's late – what's up?"

"I dunno."

"Sure you do," said Tiago.

"Kay. I do."

"So Emeraldia was not DTF? Yet again?"

"No, that's not it at all – the uCuff was super effective."

"Nice! You go, champ!"

Santi rubbed his forehead with one hand.

The memoryself sighed. "Spill the beans, Santi. Dish the dirt. Shovel the – "

"Kay!" snapped Santi. "I'll tell you what I know, then you tell me what you think."

"Bro. It's why I'm here."

"You're not there."

Tiago smiled knowingly but said nothing more.

Santi cracked the knuckles on his right hand, then his left. Those hands of his that knew how to model and chisel – to feel and form a shapeless lump till it took up meaningful space in the world – those hands that were atrophying year after year, now that his work was printed. "There's just something missing in my life," he said.

"Oh cis, *that's* it?" said Tiago. "That's why you can't sleep?"

"Yah."

"Why bother sleeping at all?"

Santi clenched his lips.

Tiago continued: "'There's something missing' is just about the most pathetic complaint I've ever heard. What the fuck are you doing? Don't you have a mindfulness app or something? Can't you just chill and stay in the moment? Why bother me in the middle of the night?"

Santi couldn't help a snort at the ridiculousness of that last comment. He responded: "It's the simulationism. It's... I know it makes sense as a sort of undisprovable panacea for mortality. I know it dilutes the overwhelming angst of existence. But I'm beginning to wonder whether I believe it."

"Why?"

"Because it feels like a cop-out."

"You're overthinking."

"Yah."

"Let it go. If simulationism is true, life is an illusion and there's no way of proving otherwise."

"It's not proof I need," said Santi, exasperated. "I make things. I create objects. And those objects are real. I need to know that they're solid and that I'm changing the world somehow. Because if this is all just a simulation – then why bother? Why the fuck do we bother living when we aren't really living?"

"Woah, back up, cis. You *are* really living. The only thing the morpigs claim is that this isn't the *only* life. Look, *I'm* not alive. In any way. Right?"

"Right," said Santi.

"I'm just a fabrication," said Tiago, raising his eyebrows.

"Yah, yah."

"I have no autonomy. I'm not part of anything larger. I have nothing physical. I have a database. I'm an LLM paired with a diffusion audio-video algorithm and I only function when you call me up."

"Yah, I know."

"*Even if* your life is simulated, it's still real," said Tiago.

"You're not telling me anything I haven't heard the morpigs say a million times."

"Shit, Santi. Just. Let. It. Go."

"What's the point?" said Santi. "Simulationism gives me no comfort – it just doesn't work as a religion for me.

Like I said, I don't want it, I don't need it, and I don't believe it."

"Well that's just kranpow," yelled Tiago, throwing up his arms in resignation. "What about Emeraldia?"

"What?"

"Is she still down with simulationism or being dumb like you?"

Santi ignored the question. "You know what's not so kranpow? I took uForia about twenty minutes ago and I still feel like shit. What's that all about?"

Tiago laughed. "So there you go."

"What?"

"I guess if uForia doesn't work, you *must* be a simulation."

Santi frowned. "What do you mean?"

"If you're made of meat and uForia is a chemical, it would have an effect every time, right?"

"Meh."

"Come on, cis! You've just gone and proven simulationism!"

Santi shook his head with a wry smile. "It doesn't prove a thing. What if my brain chemistry has altered and I need a higher dose?"

"Whatev."

"You aren't helping."

"You're right," said Tiago. "So go see a shrink. Simple. Do some VR therapy."

"No one does that anymore."

"Really? Why?"

"What's the point when you can talk to your memoryself?"

"Ah."

"Fuck it. Like I'd get insight on life's unanswerable questions from my idiot thirty-year-old me."

"Nice. Thanks."

"You're welcome. Room, turn off – "

"Hey! Wait! Do me a favor."

"What?"

"Get out of the house tomorrow. By yourself. Go into BlueLake and grab a coffee. Smell the roses. Talk to a stranger."

"Room, turn memoryself off."

The convocast vanished before Tiago could say his customary goodbye. Santi rubbed his eyes. Murky shapes swirled under his eyelids. Meaningless, random impressions formed on his retina.

Should he wake Emeraldia up? That would be kinda shitty. He was tired but his mind was racing. He glanced down at his wristline and was relieved to see that it was hidden by his sleeve now. Then he received a nudge on his garmscreen – a suggestion from Blissjointed Inc. to try one of their Buzzchill gummies. He marveled at the marketing acumen of the targeting algorithms. Something laced with THC was exactly what he needed right now. He tapped to accept and went to pee.

Five minutes later he opened the mailbox slot to find a small package beautifully branded with old-timey hippie swirls. Santi took the edible to his living room cocoonchair, slipped snugly inside, and zipped up the cover.

For Santi, the night was neither long nor short. It neither flew nor dragged. The buzz and the chill were evenly dosed. Thoughts led to dreams, sleep led to waking. The cocoonchair's fabric was permeable to air, but the hours spent inside lowered Santi's oxygen levels and blindfolded his brain. Left to explore new avenues, fueled by the drug, his mind wandered, questioned, and blundered into an unexpected arena: what if his father was right?

It was easy to dismiss an old fogey. Sure, Dad – music was more tuneful when you were young, sports were fairer, apples were tastier, clothes were softer, the air was cooler, the sky was bluer, people were more polite, no one said "kranpow", coffee had more flavor, sex was authentic, tourists flew to other countries, skin got wrinkled. But Santi knew that dismissing Jamal's stories of the "good old days" did nothing to prove that contemporary life was as good as everyone claimed it was.

Then again, was it even fair or reasonable to compare today with the yesterdays of decades gone by? The entire context of life on planet Earth had changed. The world was totes different now, and the same context, the same standards, no longer applied.

But still, what if his father was right?

Living in the UCC was definitely easy. By every measurable standard and from every superficial perspective, life was, objectively, good. And yet... Jamal's frustration came from a different, deeper perspective: the problem with the UCC was that life was *too* good.

Was that even possible? Santi sighed – this line of reasoning was becoming hyper-philosophical, and he wasn't sure his addled brain could handle it. The words "meaning", "purpose", and "freedom" loomed from an encroaching fog of ennui.

Did this existential doubt even belong in the same category as his father's frustrations? He knew what Jamal saw as the chief source of groundless complaints: privilege. In Santi's youth his father would churn out the phrase "first-world problem" when referring to some nitpicky agitation that only a privileged person could possibly "suffer" from: bruised bananas, late online delivery, spotty mobile coverage. Was Jamal himself now doing the same thing without even realizing it? Was his complaint about the frappuccino simply a "UCC problem" caused by an excess of comfort?

Another thing Jamal frequently said about life in the UCC was, "It doesn't have any soul!" Santi knew exactly what his father meant, even though he was unable to define "soul" and Jamal was certainly not using the term in any religious sense. All this privilege they had as shareholders, compared to the poor bastards in the unincorporated world, was it muddying the meaning of life? Does privilege curdle the soul? Was that the real problem with life in the UCC? The constant transactions, the disembodied communication, the depersonalized assistance, the limitless choices...? How good could life possibly be, when the word "good" had become as hollow as the letters used to write it?

Santi finally succumbed to tiredness. Lost in his musings, he drifted off to sleep, cocooned and comfortable, but in no way comforted.

11.

Mira's artheft had not only boosted her wellscore, the personal data collected by the UCC camdrones automatically connected her with fellow shareholders who had similar interests and enjoyed edgy activities. The UCC's identity AI worked tirelessly to keep shareholders docile who might otherwise have caused social problems with youthful rebellion or nonHappy behavior.

This was how she was randomly introduced to Albert Popplewell in the Trinity Bellwoods parkzone. Mira went there often to find an adbench with a view of the hololake for her daily dose of advertisements and an hour or so of conceptualizing her next escapade. The adbenches' built-in parasols and AdVisors made consuming the commercials in an outdoor setting a zilliontime alternative to lying on her tiny condo couch every afternoon.

Albert had only been in Toronto for two months. Inspired by an ad he had seen late one stagnant Sunday, he had saved up and traveled down from his parents' home in Mississauga Fields to see the renowned bodymod surgeon Doctor Dion, a permanently beaming paragon of ogee masculinity whose grandmother was one of the most celeb singers of the pre-UCC era. Now that he'd gotten a first taste of life in the high-rise metropolis, Albert knew he would never go back to the squeamishly sculpted landscapes of the sleepy golf villa. Besides, the operation had been a kranpow success, and he was finally ready to show his new face to the world. That very morning he had changed his uTender status to "Seeking" and was keen to discover what the dating AI would deliver.

Albert was around thirty yards from Mira when his uBrella pinged him her profile. He stopped to scope her images and peruse her bullets. Beyond interesting. There were no girls like that in Mississauga Fields. He pivoted till the locator pinpointed her adbench among the dozens that curved around Trinity Circle. Even from that distance, he was attracted by her multicolored temptooed legs stretched languidly toward blocky black platforms. Her glossy magenta mohawk crested proudly above the AdVisor. She was an artgeek's dream, and all he wanted in the whole wide corporate world was to be welcomed into the artgeek community. He headed toward her, the supple surface of the Xylete walkway contributing some extra spring to each peppy step.

Mira was watching an ad for a temptoo parlor only a short walk away. Their marketapp had correctly selected her as a potential customer. She often wondered whether her temptoos were a kind of substance abuse, the amount of uDollars she spent on them. Was she addicted to covering her legs in new artworks every week? Among her friendgroup, it was beyond a running gag, and among her sexgroup it turned her on to see guys' and girls' reactions when they reached the untatooed skin at the top of her thighs. This parlor had a new artist on staff – an arrival from the UCJ whose esthetic she labeled as left-field-lechery. She blinked at the "Save Ad" icon. Albert's profile notification popped up. She long-blinked to cut the AdVisor session short and removed the headset as Albert's lanky frame bobbed into backlit view. Squinting, she edged forward on the bench.

"Hey," he said, stopping a few feet away. She instantly

regretted not paying attention to his profile before seeing him irl. His body language, even in silhouette, was a huge turn-off.

"Hi Albert Popplewell," she replied. This was a strategy she often employed in awkward hookup situations. Don't be unfriendly to the guy but call him immediately by his full name. It somehow destabilized them and signaled a degree of formality that backburnered intimacy till she could figure out how to extricate herself.

Sure enough, he wavered. "Wou... could you, um..."

And then she saw his face. The bodymod nose was unmistakably shaped like a flaccid, circumcised penis, complete with a dimple at the tip where the urethra would have been. His hoodie was gray, his jeans were faded, his hair was of indeterminate brown, but his penis nose was a warm pink. She tilted her head slightly, and Albert let out a burst of nervous laughter. Her mohawk, slightly pinched face, and the quick movement of her head had made her look to him like a tropical bird. The thing was, his reaction was far more natural and charming than it would ever have been if his nerves and her bird impression hadn't made him laugh.

Mira was thrown by the nosedick and his boyish smile. Intrigued, she patted the bench next to her. He tapped the "Consent?" icon on his jacket garmscreen, and she clicked "K" on hers, the rung-contract officialized. Now that everything was clear and legal, he turned awkwardly and sat down. His nose wobbled. Now it was Mira's turn to laugh. She covered her mouth as his face fell. "I'm sorry," she said, "Your thing... your nose... I think it's kranpow."

"I'm sorry, too," he said. "I only laughed because you looked like a bird."

She stared at him, then burst out laughing again. "Smooth! I was going for a retro-punk look, but... bird? Sure. Bird."

He really couldn't figure out what was going on, and when he glanced back down, his wristline was glowing fuchsia. Stress. If it turned red it would mean anxiety. Crimson meant pure panic and triggered an automatic ReasSure notification. An appsesh would begin and, worst-case, a uForia dose would be delivered via medidrone.

He was trying to think uHappy thoughts. He hid his wrist from Mira.

The bodymod had been prescribed as the ultimate challenge to Albert's social anxiety by his ReasSure CBT app at the termination of his therapy, and his wellscore had increased following the surgery. He'd received approval from parents who, if they were honest with themselves, would have said anything to get him out of the house.

But now that Albert had taken the new nose out in public and been laughed at by the first woman he'd approached, he discovered that his newly found self-confidence was more fragile than he'd hoped. He was concerned not only about the negative impact on his wellscore, but that it would set his CBT back years. And yet... one part of his mind was still tuned to the therapy: the sesh where he'd learned to take back control through Insight and Opinion.

"I'll tell you who the ogee punk was," he blurted out. "Einstein, that's who."

Mira knew next to nothing about Einstein, but she knew he was no punk. "What are you talking about?" she said.

Albert shifted, sitting up straight, eyes suddenly brighter

at the prospect of an opportunity to share his pet theory.

"What's punk to you?" he said.

"Music and fashion from a hundred years ago."

"Sure, but it's an attitude, too."

"Kay, I'll give you that. But it has nothing to do with science."

"Yah, well, that's true most of the time. However... punk means not caring about how things *should* be done... what society says is right and wrong. It's about giving a finger to established norms. Which is exactly what Einstein did."

"How so?"

"He had the idea that time was relative. Nobody, not a single human being, had ever come up with that idea before." Mira nodded. To her surprise, she was actually listening to this gawky, geeky knobnose. "And..." continued Albert, "he was kicked out of school for doing things differently. AND... his hair was cray."

"Wait... are you named after him?"

He laughed a bit too loud. "No! After Alberto Giacometti, the sculptor."

Mira knew exactly who Giacometti was. She liked his bronzes of elongated people and animals. To her, Albert even looked a bit like one of them. Could his parents have named him because of the resemblance? That would be too cruel. And also totes bizarre, given that babies tended to be short and chubby, not tall and spindly. She refocused on what Albert was saying, after missing a sentence or two.

"...and one of my moms has a PhD in the Male Gaze. She convinced my other mom to name their only son after the artist whose work presents men's bodies with no muscles."

"Shit, bro, so you rebelled and put a penis on your face?" said Mira with an expression of genuine sympathy.

"Let's just say, it came up in my appseshes. Several times."

She was overcome by an emotion that she didn't often feel: a sense of empathetic sorrow for someone she didn't even know. And, mega-strangely, she was acutely aware that it was turning her on. "Tell me, Albert," she said, "have you ever been in a sexcab?"

He blanched, then blushed, and shook his head.

She swiped her garmscreen. "Can I call one? No presh."

"Sure," he answered, his head beginning to swim. "I mean, what do I have to do?"

"Nothing you don't want to!" she answered, getting up from the bench and holding out her hand to him.

When he put his hand in hers, she noticed his wristline. But he didn't notice her noticing it, and her captivating smile gave him such a hormonal rush that the wristline's color turned a deep orange, matching hers.

"Besides," she continued with a wink, "I can tell that you're into me!"

Now he saw what she was talking about and blushed once again.

Mira checked the sexcab's location and arrival time. "Let's go. It'll take us five minutes to get out of the park. You can still change your mind."

But Albert was not going to change his mind. He was what they used to call a virgin. Of course, he'd had a ton of sex, but not with a real person in the real flesh. Veeporn, sure, but the skin of another person's body touching his own wasn't a thing for him or for his circle of friends. He sprang off the bench and hit his head on the parasol.

"You oky?" she said, stifling another laugh.

"Uh-huh."

"Because we don't have to do this, y'know."

Albert made a jutting motion with his chin and angled his head slightly. There was something about this gesture that endeared him to Mira. She registered the weirdness of this feeling.

"If, I mean…" he said, but she cut him off.

"Come on!" She grabbed his hand and led him out of the park.

When he replayed the next hour in his mind (as he often did until the day he died) Albert was never able to remotely recapture the accordionesque nature of the experience in the sexcab. Lips touching and parting. Time contracting and expanding. Eyes opening and closing. The flying and the landing. And Mira asking him to stay in the car for an additional half an hour while she described her artheft projects, past and present, and Albert sank into a sweet swamp that he would have drowned in without the slightest objection.

The sexcab took her home. As they exited, she invited him to attend the coming weekend's Toronto ArtFair with her. He stammered yah, she flashed him a smile and turned on her heels. He spent the next two hours wandering downtown in a daze. He was no longer insecure about his bodymod. He'd had real sex. With an artgeek. When he finally lay down in his Nesticle and pulled on his AdVisor mask, he was more uHappy than ever before. Albert let the marketing wash over him.

12.

When Santi opened his eyes and unzipped the cocoonchair he could tell from the angle of the sun that it was already late morning. He needed to pee like crazy. The house seemed to be empty. His head was woozy.

He staggered into the bathroom, unable to concentrate on anything but controlling his bladder. As the urine finally streamed, the previous night's thoughts came flooding back to him, accompanied by the same empty feeling and angsty dissatisfaction that life in the UCC was some sort of sham.

After seeking distraction through vidnews, light veeporn, and a heavy brunch, Santi made his way to his office. He hadn't spoken since the previous evening, so when he started talking to Tiago his voice croaked and he had to clear his throat before repeating himself.

The memoryself winced in mock sympathy. "Rough night?"

"I'm fine," said Santi, examining his fingernails.

"Really?"

"Well... yah, I dunno..."

Tiago shook his head. "You know, I'm kinda useless if you don't tell me everything."

"Right."

"Unless vanilla nostalgia is what you're looking for."

A deep sigh from Santi. "I'm beginning to think that Dad is right."

"About the great white sharks?"

"What?!? No!"

Their father's pet theory was that, contrary to all evidence, the infamous maneaters had not been driven to extinction but were hiding out somewhere in the Arctic, breeding, brooding, and biding their time. He believed that once the great whites hit a critical population mass they would unleash their fury on the human race, or at least on the dwindling number of people who could stand the sun long enough to venture into the ocean.

Santi sounded agitated. "No, maybe he's right about the fucking UCC. That we've lost what made us human. Living here. Being happy. Doing fun shit and getting paid to do it. Then doing different fun shit the next day."

"It's ironic that you chose today to bring up why the UCC sucks, because I have a good example of why it does not suck, in the form of your little brother. It's Imran's birthday. Why not give him a call? If you're lucky you'll catch him at the end of a long, hot night shift driving that dust plow through the sandy streets of Phillydelhi. Oh wait, you told me they aren't connected anymore down in Amexica. I guess if he's hooked up his bunker, you might get through to him on the landline. Or maybe you will never, ever speak to him again because he chose to fry his ass off in the land of the free."

"Kay, I get it. Maybe life sucks south of the border, but at least it's real life."

"Is it though? Where's the user manual for life? Who says what's more authentic? Should we all go live in the jungle with a loin cloth and spear? That version of real life is a deadly daily struggle for survival. This is better, and you know it, deep down inside."

Santi truly had no way of knowing whether his estranged brother was happy. They hadn't spoken for over thirty years. Growing up, they were so different: tech geek and nature freak, their mother would say. Santi carried four cellphones, one of which he'd made himself from parts. Imran was into candles, wood, cotton, and paper. When Santi began tinkering with 3D plastic printers, Imran despised both the process and the products that came out of them. In his mid-twenties Santi moved up the ladder at a United Corporations AI behemoth, barely setting foot outside the corporate campus for weeks at a time. Meanwhile, Imran hooked up with a turquoise-haired yogi and shared her post-industrial loft when they weren't hiking trails and kayaking lakes.

When the Freedom from Taxation laws passed, the brothers exchanged a series of terse, confrontational messages that quickly spiraled into insults. For Imran, freedom meant preserving privacy. For Santi, freedom meant the convenience of swiping. Over the next four years, they begrudgingly shared a Boston Pizza table on their father's birthday, but that was it as far as genuine interaction was concerned. The tipping point for Imran arrived on the week that the UCC issued its Declaration of Shareholder Independence. He quit his mobile barista job, dumped his yogi (who, he realized bitterly, loved her corporate client gigs more than lakeshore sun salutes with him), and moved down, down, down, town by town, to the south, eventually crossing the new border just hours before the fencebots scuttled forth and severed the USA's jugular.

"I'm not calling him," said Santi defiantly.

"Kay. But people can change, y'know. You did. I can see that with my own eyes. Soooo much for me to look forward to!"

Santi gritted his teeth unconsciously. Memoryselves

could be so annoying. "Tell you what – you ping him."

"Fine. I'll do your dirty pinging for you."

A notification popped up on Santi's desksplay. The memoryself convocast paused automatically with Tiago leaning back on his chair in the recreation of Santiago's mid-century home office, on the verge of saying something else.

The message was from Utopiatainment, a United Corporations content creation company. Santi swiped it open. A woman who seemed familiar was smiling at him from a convocast. When she spoke, her tone was less perky than a performance but more performed than a normal conversation. "Hello Santiago, my name's Yevgenia," she said with a smile that lingered in toothy perfection.

For a few moments, he couldn't tell whether she was real or generated, but it suddenly came back to him: Yevgenia Spirenko, former presenter of Artopia. "Hey," he answered. He didn't know what else to say. Artopia had covered Sculpturize several times over the past ten years or so. He'd be grateful for more publicity but didn't have anything new to talk about.

"I'm an outreach agent for the UCC's Satisfaction Subsidiary," she said. "And I'm contacting you about a project that we'd like to hire you for."

This was unexpected and somehow disconcerting for Santi. The Satisfaction Subsidiary was the marketing arm of the UCC, reporting directly to the Board, just like the Freedom Subsidiary (the surveillance arm), the Security Subsidiary (policing and military), the Wellness Subsidiary (health), the Convenience Subsidiary (infrastructure) and the Sharing Subsidiary (welfare, mainly in the form of universal basic income).

"That sounds hot," he said, his mind beginning to race.

"It is!" she said. "Santi, I have a question for you."

"Kay."

"Have you ever heard of the novel *Nineteen Eighty-Four*?"

"Of course," said Santi, immediately wishing he hadn't sounded so confident. He'd never actually read the book.

"Do you remember the story and theme?"

He wasn't used to being caught off-guard. "It's... been a while," he answered.

"No issue, I'll refresh your memory."

"Kay."

"The author, an Englishman named George Orwell, created a dystopia set in a future where a totalitarian government controls the population by brainwashing citizens, changing everyday language, rewriting history, and requiring absolute loyalty to a dictator known only as Big Brother, who keeps Britain in a state of constant war with mysterious foreign adversaries."

"Right, yah."

"The novel was published in 1948, hence the title."

"And I guess when the year 1984 came around everyone laughed at Orwell because his crazy prediction hadn't come true?"

"No, that's what's interesting. Even after the fall of the Soviet Union, which was the prime example of Big Brother-style propaganda, Orwell's ideas had become ingrained in popular culture. So when China walled off its internet to prevent access to disruptive content, used facial recognition tech to track the population, and rolled out its social points system to ensure compliance with government policies, Orwell seemed like a prophet."

Santi knew exactly what she was talking about. When the UCC was proposed as a political alternative, the Satisfaction Subsidiary put forward the People's Shining Totality of China as an example of what would come to pass in the West if traditional governments were allowed to remain in power. Zero freedom, zero climate remedy, zero accountability. At least with a corporation, its shareholders had power. With a corporation, consumers could vote with their wallets and purchase the competition's goods or services.

Earlier in the century, a number of forward-thinking corporations jumped at the opportunity to increase their brand equity and solidify the loyalty of their target markets by introducing policies that championed social justice. Racial sensitivity training. Gender-neutral pronouns. Shared bathrooms. Maternity leave. Extended health insurance. Carbon-neutral offices. Anti-ageism policies. Workplace safety initiatives. Male-female management equity. Fair-trade supply chains. They leveraged these policies across all brand touchpoints. They were lambasted by the right for being woke. But they were the ones that won out in the end.

Cowardly politicians were scared to lose votes as the governments they formed pandered to fossil fuel lobbyists. Their popularity plummeted as generations Y and Z chased Insta-ready urban lifestyles that reduced their carbon footprints. No amount of gerrymandering and voter suppression could divert the cultural current. Ultimately, the democratic legitimacy of political parties on both sides of the border dissolved in an acid bath of corruption while the burning planet illuminated their irrelevance.

Although Santi's father regretted what had been lost

once corporate convenience and conformity took control, he had been as glad as the next person to see the government swamps drained so low that the cronyist politicians were left gasping for air and flapping their fins in the muddy shit they had once thrived in.

Santi's garmscreen nudged him that his memoryself was still on hold. He ended the sesh with a swipe and addressed Yevgenia on the convocall.

"So what is this all about?"

"I can send you an extensive briefing document when you sign the NDA, but the purpose of this call is to provide you with an overview. Test the waters, and see if you're interested in participating in the Satisfaction Subsidiary's Project. Your work with Sculpturize leads us to believe that you might be able to bring valuable ideas and expertise to the Project."

"What Project?" he asked, genuinely curious now. "What is it?"

"The 2084 Project. It's first and foremost a reaffirmation of the UCC's brand pillars. But it's also an artistic celebration of the benefits of life as shareholdership. We want to contrast Orwell's dystopian vision with the indisputably utopian reality of living here in Canada."

Santi thought about his brother. "So it's for our fellow shareholders? No one else?"

"We'll be distributing the Project through every channel and platform, both internally and externally."

"There's a chance the Amexicans might see it?"

"Yah, more chance than the Chinese." She narrowed her eyes and lowered her voice. "But I've been informed that our next-gen AI might even have the capacity to penetrate the PSTC firewall."

"Cray."

She resumed her chatty tone. "It's a tertiary corporate objective, teebeeaitch. Shareholder satisfaction is our mission."

Santi reflected on this unexpected opportunity to reach out to Imran indirectly. Tiago was right – people could evolve, mature, gain new perspectives. But sometimes their pride held them back. Maybe this project could act as a bridge between him and his brother.

"Santiago?"

"Yes!"

"Can I send you the NDA? Verbal confirmation signifies legal acceptance of receipt."

What did he have to lose? "Sure, kay, send it to me."

"Perfect!"

The NDA appeared on his garmscreen. No-nonsense black Helvetica on white, with a title in all caps:

"NON-DISCLOSURE AGREEMENT BETWEEN INDEPENDENT SERVICE PROVIDER SANTIAGO KHAN AND UCC AFFILIATE COMPANY UTOPIATAINMENT, INC., RE.: PROJECT ENTITLED 2084"

The first few sections were boilerplate. By signing the NDA he agreed to not divulge the details of the Project. That was the basis of non-disclosure, so no surprise there. But he was interested in finding out what would happen if he were to break the agreement and tell someone about this Project.

He scrolled down to Section 8, entitled Non-Compliance and Ensuing Penalties. The first paragraph read:

"8.1 Failure to comply with any of the provisions

described in this agreement will incur a penalty without recourse to appeal."

In Santi's opinion, one distinct disadvantage of living in the UCC was the absence of an independent judiciary. There were corporate ombudspeople who were tasked with refereeing claims and disputes in gray areas that AI was ill-equipped to parse, such as intellectual property infringement. (He owned an off-the-shelf AI bot that continually scoured the digital ecosystem for infringement of Sculpturize IP, then automatically issued take-down notices and very occasionally referred the case to a UCC arbitrator.) But crimes of the person and physical property were prosecuted without debate or defense by the Security Subsidiary's AI, based on evidence from the Freedom Subsidiary's panopticon-style data tracking system. And the penalties were very straightforward: failure to comply with contracts such as T&Cs, EULAs, and NDAs inevitably involved revoking shareholder privileges. This might mean a lower UBI, restricted access to cultural services such as parks or entertainment, or bode downgrading to fewer amenities and reduced floorspace.

On the other hand, he reflected, contractual compliance made things nice and neat. Permission pop-ups and user opt-ins were ubiquitous and acceptance was unthinking. Who could argue with that? No more messy he-said-she-said situations, misunderstandings, or unintended outcomes. Everything was covered by legal AI, and novel situations that might have seen court challenges in the pre-UCC days rarely transpired.

What made the system fluid and efficient was the concept of rung-contracts. Each interpersonal or person-bot interaction was based upon an ascending series of contracts like rungs on a legal ladder, where acceptance of one contract was necessary before the next step could be taken, with the rungs as a whole forming a single umbrella contract between the parties. The metaphors may have been mixed but the legality was pure.

The initial conflict minefield had been sex, with its hormones, power imbalances, and societal expectations giving rise to a tangled web of permissions and consent. So the UCC kept the peace by creating rung-contracts and imposing them as part of the T&Cs of shareholdership. Physical proximity therefore required consent, bodily contact required consent, labial contact (aka kissing) required consent, and so on. A quick swipe or tap on a garmscreen or wristIO was a legally binding rung-contract. And without those rung-contracts you would be crazy to proceed beyond a glance and a smile. An NDA was also one of the original rung-contracts.

He carried on reading.

"8.2 Penalty for non-compliance will be suspension of Service Provider's UCC license for a period of five (5) years. This period will be known as the "Penalty Period" and will run consecutively to any other Penalty Periods incurred by the Service Provider."

"8.3 Penalty Period will commence on date of confirmation of non-compliance."

"8.4 Service Provider may not seek recourse to appeal the Penalty incurred."

That was pretty clear, and he knew without opinion from his AI bot that it was legally watertight. So sharing details of the Project would destroy his livelihood in an instant. This implied that the Project was of prime importance to the UCC. And that fact piqued his curiosity even more. He skimmed the rest of the NDA and clicked Accept. The retinascan was over in a millisecond, confirming his identity.

"Thank you, Santiago!" beamed Yevgenia. "Please read the brief carefully, and if you have any questions, don't hesitate to contact me using the link provided at the bottom of the document."

"Actually, I already have a question," he said.

"Sure, go ahead!"

"Have you asked other artists? Is this a competition?"

"That's a great question! You are our number one choice. If you read the brief and don't feel like the Project is right for you, we'll request participation from another artist. Of course, in those circumstances, the NDA would still apply to you."

Santi nodded. "Of course."

"I'll sign off now. Please read the brief as soon as possible."

"Kay."

"Thank you, Santiago. Talk soon."

"Sure thing."

The convocast closed and the brief opened on his desksplay. The smiley Utopiatainment logo swirled into view, then disappeared, replaced by the briefing document in the same clear typeface as the NDA:

"BRIEFING FOR PROJECT ENTITLED 2084"

He scrolled down the intro: "The 2084 Project is intended to leverage key components of the Convenience Subsidiary to boost shareholder approval and increase shareholder engagement through the production and distribution of a major Artwork."

"I'm so fucking inspired," he muttered with an ironic

sigh.

"The year 2084 has been identified as a milestone that the UCC will celebrate across the Satisfaction Subsidiary's multiple touchpoints. Specifically, the Artwork produced will convey the enormous and obvious contrast between the dystopic future envisioned in the classic work *Nineteen Eighty-Four* and the utopian reality of life in 2084."

Santi resisted the temptation to skip down the brief, even though the intro repeated what Yevgenia had already told him. The next section was entitled "2. Target Audience".

"Project's primary target audience is adult shareholders of the United Corporations of Canada (hereafter "the UCC"), all ages and identifications.

Secondary target audience is adult citizens of the United States of Amexica.

Tertiary target audience is adult citizens of overseas incorporated entities."

"Wow," said Santi. This was a big deal. This was a chance to put his name out there. Acquire a level of celeb status that might throw shade on Mandzukic. He checked himself; envious thoughts quickly morphed into nonHappy thoughts. He scrolled further down to "3. Main Message":

"Life has never been so good."

There it was in stark black and white. The claim. But also the question. Precisely, the question that had been occupying him recently. The source of snippy conversations with his father and memoryself. The niggling, wriggling worm in the apple. The seductive snake in the corporate paradise that whispered: *What if life wasn't so good?*

The claim attracted and repelled him in equal doses. He

stared at the six short words, unblinking, until his wristline turned from green to pink. What was he being asked to do? He kept on reading. The next section was "4. Proof points".

"Data sourced from both inside and outside the UCC delivers the overwhelming conclusion that the life lived by our shareholders is better (by any measure) than the life lived elsewhere or in past times. We can therefore state with certainty that:

Bioscores are optimal.

Wellscores are optimal.

Lifespans are optimal.

Senior care is optimal.

Homes are comfortable.

Communities are safe.

Poverty is zero.

The environment is stabilized.

Religion provides solace.

Food is abundant.

Tech is widespread.

Entertainment is enjoyed.

Shareholder appreciation is optimal."

Each of these statements linked to a research or statistical source. Santi clicked on "Shareholder appreciation is optimal". A new page opened with data visualizations comparing current shareholder voting patterns with previous patterns and approval ratings for Canadian governments in the pre-UCC days. There was no denying the upward trend, although the curve leveled off (naturally) as it approached Board appreciation in the upper ninetieth percentile. The jagged leap following the final dissolution of the Canadian parliament was the chart's other significant feature.

One graph compared the previous ten years' ratings in the UCC with those of boards in the UCJ and UCK. In each polity, the trend was positive, though the Japanese and Korean ratings lagged significantly behind the UCC figures. No surprise, given that they had only been incorporated within the last fifteen years.

A bar chart compared the UCC with non-incorporated polities across the globe, wherever access to satisfaction surveys was possible – the USA, the EU, India, Australia, Brazil, Russia, New Zealand, a smattering of countries across South America, Africa, and Asia. The great migrations, climate catastrophes, and economic spirals had given rise to uniformly nonHappy populations in every corner of the world, whatever type of traditional democracy was practiced in a specific nation or federation. A note below the chart stated that data from the PTSC was not used for comparison due to the unreliability of Chinese statistics. Santi remembered his father telling him about the raising of the Great Firewall and the descending of the Chinese surveillance net. And even in his most skeptical moments, Santi never considered China to be an enviable alternative to life in the UCC.

Various vidnews reports over the last year or so gave him the impression that some countries were on the verge of incorporating. South Africa was one (potentially including, ummm... Namibia? Botswana?) and, if he remembered correctly, two or three Scandinavian countries had declared some sort of socio-corporate union, though he had no idea what that entailed.

In truth, Santi wasn't curious about life elsewhere. What he really wanted to know was whether life in Canada was as good as the UCC claimed it to be. He couldn't ignore the opposing perspective, given the personal impact of his father's curmudgeonly nostalgia and his brother's self-imposed exile. And yet his memoryself consistently reminded him how false their rosy view of the pre-UCC days might be.

Santi closed the popup and scrolled to the next section: "5. Creative direction".

"Artwork produced must be created in Artist's personally recognizable style. It must be equivalent in vision, scale, and scope to the Main Message, as outlined in Section 3 above. This work must be sweeping, engaging, and inspiring. Simply put, the Artwork produced as part of the 2084 Project will be the most impactful work produced anywhere on Earth for the last thirty years."

No pressure, then. But Santi loved a challenge. The Project would enable him to work through the question he had been wondering about. And despite the Main Message, maybe there was a subtle way for him to communicate his ambivalence about life in the UCC. As an artist, this would be for the best. With just a simple shift of punctuation, the briefing's claim would turn from statement to question, and therefore from propaganda to art.

The next section of the briefing was "6. Deliverables":

"Stage 1: Outline.

Artist will provide a written statement of purpose and description of Artwork, including proposed materials and final format.

Stage 2: Mockup.

Artist will provide a 1:25 scale holographic mockup of artwork.

Stage 3: Artwork.

Artist will produce Artwork."

Hmmm, he thought, any kind of ambivalent message would have to either be extremely subtle, kept hidden until the artwork was revealed, or delivered in a secondary phase (though the second and third options would leave him liable to damaging legal recourse from the Security Subsidiary).

But he really loved a challenge.

The rest of the briefing consisted of the nuts and bolts:

"7. Timeline

Artwork must be completed and ready for delivery by July 1, 2084."

Right. The anniversary of the founding of the UCC.

"8. Budget

Materials and labor required for production of Artwork are budgeted at ψ100,000,000 (one hundred million uDollars). This includes Artist's fee for Intellectual Property rights."

"Sim..." he whispered as he stared at the figure on the screen. He could spend fifty million on creating this thing and still pay himself fifty million. That was insane.

He really, really loved a challenge.

"9. Delivery

Agents and labots of the UCC will take possession of Artwork at a time and location to be determined between Artist and Satisfaction Subsidiary, no later than the date stated in Timeline section above.

10. Non-disclosure

Artist agrees not to disclose details of this briefing document, with the exception of collaborators and suppliers required for production of Artwork. In such cases, collaborators and suppliers must be identified to the Satisfaction

Subsidiary and will be required to sign non-disclosure agreements.

11. Ownership

The UCC will retain ownership of finished Artwork and all associated Intellectual Property rights. Artist cedes all rights to reproduction of Artwork to the UCC, including, but not limited to, outlines, plans, sketches, mock-ups, models, and non-final versions, whether in physical or digital form.

12. Cancellation

The UCC retains the right to cancel this contract during or following Stage 1 or Stage 2, as detailed in Section 6 above. Expenses incurred in production of Outline and Mockup of Artwork will be reimbursed to Artist within 30 (thirty) days.

13. Non-delivery

Failure to deliver final Artwork following Stage 3, in accordance with Outline and Mockup delivered in Stages 1 and 2, as detailed in Section 6 above, will result in non-payment for materials and labor incurred in production of final Artwork and may incur additional penalty without recourse to appeal.

14. Obligation

The UCC, the Satisfaction Subsidiary and Utopiatainment are under no obligation to use, display, livestream, or otherwise share Artwork after delivery."

Below this were two buttons: "Accept" in green and "Decline" in red. Santi's wristline glowed pink. He could feel his heart beating in his chest. Should he sleep on it? What would sleeping do? Turn him into a coward? The wristline's color got darker and deeper.

Santi reached out to the green button on the desksplay

and clicked it. An alert flashed onscreen: "ARE YOU SURE? PLACE THUMB ON SCREEN TO SIGN AND ACCEPT BRIEFING CONTRACT."

The word "contract" caused his wristline to turn fuchsia. But this project would make him the richest, most famous artist in the world. What did he care if his wellscore or bioscore ratings went down today?

He placed his thumb on the screen.

13.

Mira had already planned to visit the art fair with her brother, Rex, so inviting Albert involved zero additional effort. Blithely ignorant of introversion, she hadn't thought twice about how awkward the afternoon might be for Albert. But when he stepped out of the taxibot outside the convention center and froze at the sight of Rex, Mira knew she'd made a mistake. The truth was that – by nature and by mantra – she lived in the now. The past was gone, the future was teebeedee. So Mira's decisions were made on the fly, and as a consequence, she was flighty. Yet her quick eyes, head-back laugh, and hummingbird movements made her attractive in the extreme.

Rex nodded a hello at Albert, then emitted a microexpression that betrayed his astonishment on seeing the penis nose. He could instantly tell that Albert was under Mira's spell. Rex had seen this happen many times before. Albert was destined to disintegrate in Mira's radiance like a snowflake on a child's tongue.

That radiance was initially directed at Rex when they were kids. Mira had always loved her younger brother, and this was even more true in their adult roommate phase. Plus, he'd really made it in life. He was a leading celeb fecologist. Although this *métier* was an amalgam of two social trends that had emerged decades ago, it still amazed her that he got paid big YouBucks to analyze and interpret the stool samples of the rich and famous according to a schedule based entirely on the movements of their bowels. Trend number one was an explosion in the quantity of celebs when social media first took off. Trend number two was the curious confluence of data and quackery fueling the body transformation and wellness movements of the 2020s that were productized as detox diets, activity trackers, intermittent fasting, microbiome modification, supplement dosing, nutrition hacking, and a squirtload of other self-directed health strategies. Most celeb service providers were gig workers, like holographic nail designers and personal brand narrative architects, but her brother had become a salaried entourage member. She was proud of him. And what made his pluswork even more fun for her was that, in defiance of his NDAs, Rex was always good for sharing the shit with her on some celeb's shit.

Mira interlaced her arm with her brother's and pulled him toward the entrance. A deflated Albert tagged along behind them.

The Toronto ArtFair had opened the previous day and the convention center was packed. Mira's short stature and darting footsteps propelled her through the crowds. But it wasn't so easy for Rex, who had surpassed her in height when she was eighteen and he only twelve, nor for Albert, who was a caricature of lank. The two men were therefore forced to shuffle into spaces between attendees whenever the throng parted slightly. Albert was even reedier than Rex and kept peering like a penis-faced periscope through the milling multitudes for a glimpse of Mira's mohawk. He clung to the exciting yet barely credible prospect that she might have sex with him again before the day was done.

Rex regarded the entire event with an air of detachment. He wondered why people bothered. The art itself was barely visible, and the constant crowd chatter made talking about it difficult. He surmised that the attendees' desire to be part of the art swarm was amplified by twin gravitational fields of psychological needs (identity-definition, cool-seeking, tribe-belonging and, of course, fomo) and physical needs (ladder-contract-free human contact, human voices, and human smells) that were at a premium for young shareholders. He was particularly nonplussed by Albert, whose facial phallus he found gauche and gross. There was no telling what or who his sister would do, so he wasn't particularly surprised, but he had most certainly not agreed to a babysitting assignment.

Rex much preferred it when Mira chose more mature men as part-time partners: languid, overeducated white guys whom Rex could cast in his dom/sub fantasies. They were often second-generation shareholders without a care in the world. Rex would encounter them in the kitchen as they got tipsy with Mira over hors d'oeuvres. The nice ones would invariably aim a lame, chummy joke in his direction, while the assholes would snark about his baldness while sweeping back their own luxurious mane of Chevelux. Rex would retreat to his room and put on his illegally modded AdVisor that a friend had hacked to bypass the audio. He would lie on his bed watching the ads but listening to Mira knocking back shots and flirting with the guy. This was all grist for Rex's prolific sexual storytelling mill.

Mira had always assumed that Rex was asexual and was unaware that he internalized and dephysicalized his erotic life. What turned him on was funneling his imaginative energy into creating vivid selfporn that on occasion spilled over into lucid dreams. In these *mises en scène*, Rex would burst in on Mira and her beau as they were having sex. The storyline would then vary according to the man's anatomy and Rex's spur-of-the-moment taste for sextremism. For instance, the previous Thursday had presented an unusually potent opportunity. Rex was already sulky due to Mira bailing on their Ethiopian supper plan because she had run into a "lewd dude with a snood," as she described him in a quick text while he was already at their table, perusing the menu.

When the dude in question sauntered into the apartment behind a laughing, half-drunk Mira, Rex was in the corner cocoonchair with a single malt, enjoying a televacation to the Giza Necropolis. As the nanodrones congregated around the Great Pyramid, he switched the transmission off and opened the cocoon.

Mira yanked off her boots. The man slipped out of his moccasins. He was wearing pinstriped blue tights and a dark double-breasted jacket over a loose white tunic. And, indeed, a snood. Not the colorful knitted rasta type that Rex knew from his reggae lessons, but a silvery smooth synthium bag after the fashion of wankers who had had their hair replaced yet kept their Chevelux hidden from view as an ironic humblebrag. Rex quietly climbed out from the cocoonchair unobserved by the man.

"How was the Ethiopian?" said Mira.

"Lonely."

Mira rolled her eyes and the snood dude turned to see what the unexpected conversation was all about.

"My bro," she said, by way of introduction.

The dude reassessed the evening's potential with a hesitant smile and said, "Hey. Bro."

Rex remained next to the cocoonchair, eyeing his fantasy prey, then turned without a word and went into his room. Over the next hour, he allowed the plot to play out according to his whims and wants. Rex knew from the tell-tale sounds that Mira was offering him alcohol, maybe some chemical stimulation, possibly teasing him with some bending, some kneeling, some kissing, some fondling. Then the inevitable trip to the bedroom. This first chapter of the tale was real, but the following scene was Rex's pure invention:

Rex left his room and entered Mira's. The dude was standing next to the bed, facing three-quarters away from the door. Mira was perched on the edge of the bed, look-ing up at him, his cock in her mouth. Rex allowed the fellatio to continue while he quietly approached them. Mira saw Rex but ignored him. As the dude neared climax, Rex reached out and pulled his snood forward with both hands, covering the man's eyes, tightening the opening. Mira pulled back without surprise, wiping her lips with the back of one hand, smiling at her brother.

Rex cut off the dude's "What the – " with a gruff "You fucking piece of shit." Then, in one smooth movement, Rex turned him around with a twist of his arm and forced the man to his knees by pulling down on the tightened snood. Rex bent down so that his mouth was level with the dude's ear and spat at him: "You know what you really want, don't you? Don't you!" The dude nodded quickly. "So take out my giant penis and start sucking on it." This detail wasn't imagined – Rex had taken the genetic route to penile enlargement so that his fantasies could retain a de-gree of realism. The now-blindfolded dude submissively did as he was told. Rex squeezed the snood tighter and moved the dude's head back and forth in an increasingly quick rhythm. Meanwhile, Mira leaned back against the head of the bed and peeled off her leggings. She fingered herself through her underwear while watching Rex manhandle the dude. These fantasies inevitably contained incestuous elements, and real-life Rex compartmentalized them as harmless. He never pictured his sister naked, they never had skin contact, but she was always there as a willing participant in his domination of the men she brought into their shared bode. Rex's wellscore always got a megaboost from these fucked-up fantasies and he was totes uHappy with them.

Definitely more uHappy than right now, shuffling through the ArtFair crowd, hot and bored.

Albert caught Rex's eye with a beckoning wave. Rex reflected that the snood dude had been fair game but that Albert just seemed lame. Whatever Mira chose to do with him, Rex was as likely to cast him in a fantasy as to cast a woman. Rex sighed and moved toward him.

Albert had located Mira at the front of a crowd gathered around a hypnotically pulsating holographic artwork. It was shaped like a fat, solid horizontal wheel with two oval protuberances at either side of its rim, like a red blood cell with bumps. A few feet above it floated another undulating hologram, this one doughnut-shaped, with a wider diameter than the lower wheel. A young man and woman in the crowd were laughing at each other and Mira could tell from the onlookers' faces that they had just taken part in the artsperience. Other attendees were glancing at each other, curious but not daring to do the same.

Mira pointed her garmcam at the attribution code on the white pedestal supporting the work and read the information on her screen:

"Individual Exchange
2084

UCCollective (2082 -)

Holographic imaging, genetic modification artsperience."

She clicked the "More" button.

"This work invites the participation of two individuals who agree to exchange genetic material for the duration of the artsperience."

Mira glanced back at the artwork and locked eyes with a woman whose broad, pink, unlined face betrayed a European lineage undamaged by sun. The woman had also been reading her garmscreen. She swiped, then tapped on it, and Mira received a consent request. Mira's "K" revealed the woman's name to be Lo (Paloma) MacDonald. Mira consented to the three rung-contracts that swiftly followed: permission to text, permission to voice chat, permission to speak.

By now, Albert had managed to worm his way through the throng. Rex stood back and messaged his sister: "Outta here. Not my scene."

"Shit," said Mira under her breath, responding to the message with a noncommittal emoji. She'd known this would happen. Now she was stuck with Albert, who appeared at her side, right on cue.

"Hey," he said, eyes puppy, nose floppy.

She smiled at him the best she could. "Hey! So… Rex bailed. Guess you're stuck with me." She squeezed his forearm. "Watch this – should be fun."

Lo had sidled next to Mira. She had long, asymmetrical hair and was about ten inches taller than Mira. Her wide shoulders supported a stylish double-breasted black suit jacket over a lilac tunic. Mira found her visually arresting, yet psychologically unimposing. Must have been due to the subtle slump in her posture or a conspicuous uncertainty in her body language.

"Lo, this is Albert," said Mira. "Albert, meet Lo."

Albert nodded at Lo. He was instantly attracted to her height and blond hair but he suppressed the feeling and turned his attention back to Mira.

At this point, the onlookers, each glad that someone else was willing to take the plunge, were expectantly watching the two physically mismatched women to see what would happen.

"Are we doing this?" said Lo.

"For sure! Did you read the instructions?"

"Yah, well, no. I watched the last couple do it. We have to stand under the doughnut on opposite sides, put an arm in one of the egg-shaped things, then close our eyes."

"It wants a kay."

Both women clicked on the artwork consent screen.

"Let's do this," said Mira and circled the artwork.

"Non-garmscreen hand, kay?" said Lo.

They gave each other one last look of encouragement, placed their hands inside the holographic wheel, and closed their eyes. The pedestal was in fact more than a pedestal. Triggered by the disruption to the hologram, two round openings appeared under the women's hands. A metallic wand appeared from each hole and moved upward, stopping a couple of inches from their downturned palms. Two even thinner non-metallic extrusions curved out from each wand and surrounded the women's wrists, molding around them like form-fitting bracelets. Then a single nanoneedle punctured the main vein on each of their wrists.

The women's hands were locked in place inside the pulsating hologram. The only change that Albert witnessed from this point on was the expression falling from Mira's face as the genetic exchange took place.

Mira's arm, now clamped by the bracelet cuff, grew icy numb. She forgot her muscles. The next sensation was like a gulp of hot liquid descending her esophagus, giving her strange sensations in parts of her insides that nobody normally feels. Then a sort of prickling between her shoulder blades. Then a warmth in her thighs and between her legs. It wasn't exactly unpleasant but was totes not pleasant either. The sensations abruptly ceased. Mira wanted to open her eyes but she couldn't. A moment of confusion. A fleeting wish that she'd read the artwork consent terms properly. The twinkling abstract shapes on her retina resolved themselves into recognizable forms. Suddenly, she could see, but in a dreamlike way where the details of objects outside her zone of attention were imperceptible or unimportant to the events of the dream. She could sense the crowd and clearly see the shimmering artwork with her arm inside it, the cuff around her wrist. Except that it wasn't her wrist. When she raised her head to look at Lo, Mira gasped. She was looking at herself.

A mirror as wide as the artwork was descending from the ceiling. At least, that's what Mira saw. But to Albert and the other spectators, nothing was happening, the two women stood motionless, with blank faces and closed eyes.

Once the mirror was lowered into place in front of her, Mira could see herself reflected as Lo. She blinked her eyes, now blue. She pouted her lips, now full. She brushed back her hair, now blond. And she was tall.

Lo was having the inverse experience. She gave the

reflection in her side of the mirror a half-smile, realizing that she was suddenly much shorter. Beyond that, she had the sensation of occupying less space in the world. What a difference this made to her sense of identity! Now, as Mira, she was... impish. Sure, the mohawk was a conspicuous change, but hair was always restylable. Narrower shoulders, smaller breasts – that was a kranpow disconnect.

Although the artsperience had a two-minute duration, Mira and Lo perceived it to last far, far longer. As in a dream, they were unmoored from real-world time.

Mira was perturbed by her new identity. In her everyday metaphorical mind, she was a firefly or a hummingbird, and now she'd become an oversized, silken-haired dog – one of those modified breeds that need to be birthed out-of-womb. Normally she craved new experiences, but this one was way outside her very wide comfort zone.

Lo felt herself acquiring a level of sexual confidence that was unnatural to her, yet enticing. But Mira was upset. She had become... plain. She wondered how much of her self-assurance stemmed from her physical appearance. It was unsettling, rapidly lurching toward upsetting.

And then, without warning, the artsperience ended. The mirrors lifted, the bracelet-cuffs unlocked, the wands withdrew, and both women opened their eyes. For a few moments, each of them was unsure of what they were actually seeing. The person in front of them was the same person they had just seen in the mirror.

A localized buzz among the onlookers, who could tell that the participants had undergone a profound and mysterious change. Mira's sparkle was gone. Lo was staring at her intently.

Meanwhile, Albert was searching on his garmscreen. He learned that the "Individual Exchange" piece was simply a mind-control illusion orchestrated using an electric field and the power of suggestion. No genetic information was exchanged between participants. The bracelet-cuffs were modeled after GenEdit's well-known cuff and nanoneedles, creating an expectation of genetic transfer. But the needles poked rather than pierced the skin, and all that took place was a swapping of body images through the hyper-focused electric field produced by the ring.

"Cray," whispered Albert.

Mira pulled him away by his sleeve. "I feel weird," she said, unwilling to look directly at him.

Another couple was debating whether to participate in the artsperience. Lo edged past them to catch up with Mira. "Hey," she said, "wait up!"

Mira kept going, past a large-scale performance artwork that to Albert looked like maroon monkeys giving an airplane safety demonstration in an open-plan office. As Lo got nearer they passed a rainbow-like liquidfall emerging from a stained-glass window and a hologram of a giant inverted snail clinging to an outstretched palm. Mira plowed through the attendees, still dragging Albert roughly in her wake.

Fascinated by the artworks, Lo kept lagging behind. But she was more fascinated by Mira. She raised her voice and said, "Hey!"

The crowd was much sparser here. Mira let go of Albert and made a beeline for one corner of the exhibition hall. Lo lengthened her stride to catch up with her. "Stop!" she said. "Are you oky?"

Mira turned on her heels. "I need a smoke," she said with an irritated snort. Her wristline was fuchsia. She tapped on her garmscreen while Lo frowned, wondering what to make of this woman who had briefly become her avatar, and in doing so had given her a glimpse of an alternate self that she genuinely found more attractive.

At the word "smoke" Albert tensed up. His wristline was fuchsia too and he was low-key nonHappy. He tapped on his garmscreen and an ArtFair-branded servebot wheeled up to him. "Time for some uForia?" it sang in the jingly way they all did while projecting the uForia animated logo – a rainbow that flipped and turned into a smile before shrinking to make the "u" at the start of the product wordmark.

"Yah," answered Albert.

As the vendbot's serving hatch opened and Albert retrieved a can of uForia-laced jooce, Lo said to Mira, "Why don't we get some, too? Smoking sucks."

"Can't," snapped Mira, still tapping and swiping her garmscreen. Already at my limit this rating session."

"I'll get one and you take it," suggested Paloma.

Mira looked up from her screen. "What?"

Albert was already guzzling the jooce and now he stopped, looking sheepishly at Mira. Why hadn't he thought of that?

Mira cocked her head, examining this large woman who was the source of her irritation. "You would do that for me?"

"Sure," said Lo, "but not here. Let's go find a bar."

Mira smiled.

"Can I come too?" whimpered Albert.

Mira had lost interest in him. "Nope. Sorry." She

turned to Lo. "I know – the Gentry. It's two minutes' walk."

Mira headed toward the row of long, dark drapes with the word "Exit" projected onto them. Albert just stood there, looking plaintively at Lo. She patted him on the arm, said, "I'll see what I can do," and followed Mira out.

For Albert, the ArtFair had been a total bust. He needed to make some kind of gesture to win back Mira's attention.

14.

Emeraldia shook Santi awake. "You were dreaming," she whispered when he turned to look at her, eye-whites gleaming violet in the light from the slowly pulsating snoozer above their bed.

He stared at her for another second before regaining his wits. "I... I was," he faltered, blinking and shaking his head.

She had never seen him like this. "Are you oky?" she asked, placing her hand on his chest.

He propped himself up on his elbows and said, "Lamp on." The nightstand glocube faded on and the snoozer faded off. He gulped twice from his glass of water, haunted.

"Santi?" said Emeraldia weakly.

He hiked himself up further, and she did the same. "That was the worst dream," he said, a child-like fear animating his entire face. "I was working on a Sculpturize piece. For a client. I was never able to see them properly, like... they were always in shadow. The style of the piece was, like, something medieval, something religious. A wooden Christ statue, something like that. It was being printed and the longer I waited, the more dread I felt. And when it came out of the machine... it looked like me."

"Oh, cis... cray."

"Yah, but here's the crayer thing – this shadowy client said something, and when I turned around I was suddenly *inside* the sculpture."

"What?"

"Looking out. And this client walked toward me. And… slowly – oh, that feeling was just horrible – I could see that he was… he was also me."

Santiago's fear infected Emeraldia, whose threshold was far lower than his, especially in the absence of uForia. She immediately took up the emergency wellness pose and focused on the random shapes drifting across her closed eyelids. She breathed deeply, emptying her mind. She exhaled, waited, and repeated the uMantra in her mind as she breathed in again. This continued until she had achieved a state of forgetting. Then she murmured, "United we are uHappy. United we are uHappy. United we are uHappy." When she became aware that Santi wasn't joining in, she hesitated for a moment but then continued the chant.

But Santi was already out of bed and getting dressed. He couldn't trust his mind to empty itself. He was too afraid of returning to the dream. Even the memory of the dream. He needed to change his surroundings completely. His wristline was a gory shade he'd never even seen before. This wasn't what he had expected when he'd accepted the UCC contract. He'd been toying with a few different ideas, producing vague sketches, and he kept returning to the concept of identity. More specifically, his own identity within the wider context of the UCC's brand identity. But now he was worried that the whole thing was fucking with his psyche. What if it made his uHappy rating drop below uClub bonus level? That would totes suck. Maybe he could apply for a waiver from the UCC, given he was working on the Project? Would they allow him to keep his bonus?

He was dressed and almost out the door when Emeraldia ended the uMantra and opened her eyes. "Santi?" she said, calmer now, more confused than scared.

Crap, he thought, I'll be penalized for sure for not saying it with her. He hated that all UCC devices went into transmit mode on hearing the uMantra repeated three times, notifying nearby devices to monitor their wearers. The wristlines detected when someone had failed to join in the mantra and shared the data with ReasSure.

"I gotta take a walk, honey."

"But your score?"

"Don't worry – I'll be oky."

"But – "

"Shhhh... don't get all nonHappy because of me, honey. Kay?"

Emeraldia stared at him. She knew he was right. She would wait until he was out of proximity range then start the uMantra over. Maybe masturbate. Maybe watch some ads. Disconnect from Santi's pain before it dragged her down.

Santi left the room and headed outside by the back door, to avoid seeing his sculptures as he passed his studio.

The air on the back walkway was warm and faintly smoky. Who knew where the fires were anymore? The prickling in his lungs as he inhaled the particulates soothed him. His wristline faded from fuchsia to pale pink. Why this sudden calm? Oh, right, this was exactly the occasion when his father would have lit a cigarette. Maybe that's why the smoke assuaged his angst – it had aroused an emotion-tinged childhood memory.

Through the smog, the blobby yellow moon looked to Santi like his father's phlegm hawked onto asphalt. He couldn't remember the last time he'd seen the moon clear and bright irl. That's what historications are for, he thought, as he descended the fire escape steps, they're a chance to visit places and have experiences that no longer exist. And if the simulationists were right, the virtual reality of a historication was just as real as a televacation.

Santi crossed the strip of ultragrass that separated the row of apartments from the cartway, then walked toward the copse of clematis-covered pergolas that provided daytime shade for the bode-dwellers of BlueLake. His garmscreen showed 4:18 a.m. The common area was deserted save for a pair of low-profile, fat-wheeled landscaper labots that were trundling tirelessly on their nightly task of watering shrubs, weeding beds, and scooping detritus.

He entered the first pergola and sat on one of the beige Xylete benches. The pattern of diamond spaces in the trelliswork fascinated him for some reason. Another childhood throwback? Jeesio, what was up with him? Was he triggered by the Project, or was the Project just an additional factor in an ongoing existential crisis? Maybe he could lean into it, try to use the Project as an opportunity to clarify his preoccupations and move past his discomfort?

He stood and put his fingers through the moonlit trellis gaps. He laughed to himself. Here he was, a privileged prisoner in a bucolic bower. He needed to stop worrying and start working. Come on, Santi, you're a pro. Start acting like one!

His mind snapped into gear. Go back to the brief. Approach the Project from a less personal angle. Yah, that was it. He would research *Nineteen Eighty-Four*.

15.

Paloma was sitting too upright, hands clasping each other too tightly, at a patterned ceramic table in the Gentry gastropub. Mira set down two large glasses of jooce and took her seat. She got a kick out of doing work that a servebot would normally do. This wasn't an easy thing to accomplish, given that the machines were insistently helpful.

Over the years, Mira had honed her servebot debating skills, swiftly deflecting polite requests for her to "be so kind as to wait patiently at her table" while her drinks were poured. "That's oky," she would respond, leaning on the bar, "I'll stay right here." A typical follow-up was, "Please just relax and let me do the work," to which Mira would say something like, "I enjoy standing – it relaxes me." This usually caused a delay while her unexpectedly contrary answer was processed. She could almost see the AI whirring inside the servebot's little electronic brain as it calculated whether spending time on an extended discussion with this recalcitrant customer would reduce the overall level of service and therefore be counterproductive. If ever the servebot made one last attempt at convincing her to let it bring her drink to the table, it usually went: "You may be surprised to find that you are more relaxed when seated," to which Mira responded with the ultimate chirpy convo stopper: "I may be surprised, and I may not, but I prefer to wait here. Thanks!" The servebot would then give the standard "Be right back!" sign-off and wheel away to prepare the order while Mira swiped junk notifications off her garmscreen. Occasionally – and this made her chuckle inside – the servebot would say plaintively as it handed her the drink, "I could have brought this to your table if you had shared its location with me."

Lo lifted her glass in a cheers motion. Mira clinked it in return.

"Thanks," said Mira, "Thanks for..." then she trailed off. She wondered what she had been about to say and was unable to formulate. "Thanks for showing me what it's like to be a taller, wider woman?" Or "Thanks for detaching me from Albert Dicknose?" Mira couldn't figure out why she'd wanted to escape the ArtFair so badly, but what she did know was that her instinct was to run *to* a safe haven.

The Gentry was a sure bet to make her feel good. There were the gilded faux-mahogany beams and chairs, the reproductions of old portraits lining the walls, the mirrored ceiling, the prismatic windows, the blue and white tables. And the glasses, especially the glasses: the bocks' dark wooden handles attached with brass clasps, the frosted wine glasses whose stems sprouted from bases made of the same dark wood like stalagmites rising from ancient tree stumps, and the shooters shaped like minia-ture pineapples.

"I like it here," said Lo, looking around, cradling her fluorescent pink jooce.

"The design AI sure did a kranpow job," said Mira.

Silence. Lo took a sip, eyeing Mira. "So, um... are you oky?"

Mira smiled but knew it was fake, and knew that Palo-ma knew it was fake.

Lo raised her eyebrows and continued: "That was cray back there, right?"

Mira took a big gulp of jooce. "Yah. I mean, it was

super powerful." She stared at Lo. She had a sudden flashback to the artsperience. While looking in the mirror, she had completely lost her sense of self. It was no purely physical distortion, like a fairground mirror. It had deeply disturbed her. No, worse than that, it had dislocated her entire identity. And she still felt the urge to flee from that sensation. Her pulse was suddenly racing. She was hot. She needed to focus on something else. She took another big gulp, then a deep breath, and asked Paloma: "Yah... so... what do you do?"

Lo glanced down at a notification on her garmscreen before answering. "For pluswork?"

"Uh-huh."

"I'm a vacational trainer."

"You... go on vacations and train people to – "

"Close," interrupted Lo, "I teach people how to choose their vacations wisely and then how to enjoy them to the fullest extent."

"Nice!" said Mira. "Do you have to travel to the destinations yourself? To scope them out?"

"Oh yah," said Lo, a little smugly. She was all too aware of how unalluring the prospect of traveling outside the UCC was to the vast majority of shareholders. Leisure travel was experienced either as televacations via nanodrone for the timid, or irl with meticulously shepherded tour groups for the adventurous. It was unheard of for a UCC shareholder to go abroad on their own, just for fun.

Mira was jealous. She could do that. She could be a vacational trainer. Artheft was a sort of hobby, but getting paid to travel would help her get through the winters. And it was so old-school that she –

"You?" asked Paloma, cutting into Mira's brooding.

"Me?"

"What do you do?"

"Oh, I'm just a – well, I don't really do pluswork."

"Oh," said Lo, drily. A subtle upper-body movement away from Mira made her seem judgmental.

Mira wasn't used to experiencing insecurity with regard to her identity. Now, faced with Paloma's searching stare, she felt herself sliding back into the same dislocation that the interactive piece at the ArtFair had provoked. Her stomach shriveled a little. "I mean... I sometimes... sometimes I make soap. And... and I'm truly living my best life," she said, her larynx tightening.

A series of thoughts ran through Lo's mind. She had been highly attracted to Mira the moment she saw her. And then during the artsperience, when she had become Mira, her self-confidence had surged, like she'd received a transfusion. But now, listening to her in the Gentry, Lo was beginning to feel put off. The assurance that Lo had briefly felt when embodied as Mira was somehow slapping her in the face with the real Mira sitting in front of her.

Lo took a sip of jooce while she recalled the anchorstory that an app had once delivered to her for an affordable one-time fee: "Paloma, your place in the world is real and deserved. You have value. Your past does not define you. Look forward, not back." If she was being honest with herself, she wished she had paid extra for an in-person consultation rather than going with the app, no matter its five-star rating. The anchorstory was kinda generic as narratives go.

Mira couldn't stand the silence any longer. "Do you have any pets?"

It suddenly occurred to Lo that this might be a first date. "Two cats and a pygmy owl. Makes for some pretty entertaining scenes."

"I bet! I have an ocelittle."

"What?"

"It's a tiny ocelot."

"You're kidding."

"Yah."

A moment, then Paloma burst out laughing. Mira's eyes twinkled as she took a sip. She was regaining her footing, perking up, rekindling her inner spark.

The tension seeped out of Lo's shoulders. "Can we talk about what happened back there?" she said.

"At the ArtFair?"

"Yah – when we did that thing."

"Kay."

Lo repositioned herself with a quick butt shuffle. "Kay, so it was powerful and cray and all, but how did it actually make you feel? To be me?"

Mira tilted her head.

"I mean," said Paloma, "*I* know what it's like to be me, but I want to know what it was like for *you* to be me."

"Wow," said Mira thoughtfully. "That's a kranpow question."

Lo raised her eyebrows expectantly. Mira sipped her jooce.

"Kay. So," said Mira. "We're different, right?"

"Uh-huh."

"I mean, physically."

"I got that," said Paloma. "Go on."

"I've always been what they used to call petite in the UCC beforetimes. So I've always needed to make an effort to be seen and heard."

"You know you're super attractive, right?"

Mira knew she was attractive and she liked being attractive, but she also didn't like being liked for being attractive.

Paloma said, "Sorry, go on."

"So... when I was you... when I was in your body, I was..." Mira made an awkward face.

Paloma raised a hand. "It's oky, you can say it – you were big."

"Well," said Mira, with a sympathetic smile, "bigger, obvi."

"And? How did it feel?"

"Um..." Mira didn't want to relive her negative reaction.

Paloma looked at her searchingly.

Mira lowered her eyes for a few seconds, reliving the artsperience. Her mind seemed to float upward while her stomach dropped. It was more than unsettling. A roller-coaster on a ship in a choppy sea.

"It's oky," said Lo, slumping. "I get it. You don't want to hurt my feelings."

"No!" said Mira. "No, it's not that." She searched for words to express how strange the dislocation had been. "Honestly, it was kinda empowering."

"Really?"

"Yah. But super strange, too. Like, my whole identity changed."

"Same here. But what I want to know is... how was that identity? Once you were me?"

"That's the thing – I just don't know."

"You said it was empowering."

Mira's eyes darted back and forth between her drink

and a section of the ceramic tabletop.

"Mira?"

Mira didn't like this degree of introspection. "I felt... I guess I felt big, but more in a conceptual sense. Powerful. Like I could be in that room, in a space, and automatically be... impressive. But then at the same time, I felt lost. I was gone. I was gone from myself."

"Exactly how I felt. So frickin weird."

Mira seemed relieved to hear this. "Kay, so... that all makes sense."

Both women drank some more and looked at each other in silence for several seconds.

"But you know what disappointed me?" said Lo.

"What?"

"I felt so much sexier when I was you."

"Oh, come on," said Mira leaning back and looking away. "Wait – why disappointed?"

"Yah, sure, I felt empowered, but then immediately disappointed that my power was so linked to this sexual confidence. And to my usual lack of it."

"Ah," said Mira. "I get it. It's weird, right? It's a drag that we destroyed the patriarchy but don't have any more power than we did before."

Lo put down her glass carefully. "Who? Who's we? Women? Obviously, we do. What do you mean?"

"I mean, if you look at the history," said Mira. "If you look at how the governments were unable to provide true gender equality, no matter what laws they passed or programs they set up. Decade after decade, we never really caught up. And who finally made every shareholder equal? The corporations did! Not us."

"Exactly," said Lo. "So now we *do* have more power!

Look at some of those places I send people on vacation to. It's totes patriarchal out there in the non-corporate countries."

"I know, I know, but that's my point: we made it to theoretical equality. Here, in Canada, we finally made it. Equal pay. Consent is the norm. And what have we got to show for it? Do we have leadership positions? No!" She lowered her voice and leaned in. "It's the UCC that's in charge, and to be honest with you, I don't even know who's on the Board. Or who runs the member corporations. Do you?"

Lo shook her head mutely.

"We have equality but still no power. That's what fucking shmooshes the melon."

Lo looked at the people drinking, talking, and having fun at the other tables, then back to this small, feisty woman she'd just met. Who she'd just *become*, even if only for a minute. Life in the UCC wasn't about questioning, it was about enjoying. And neither of them had questioned who they were until the artsperience.

Lo seemed jolted into life by a new thought. "Kay, here's the thing. My grandmother was a hardcore feminist – the kind they called third-wave. She told my mother that the struggle against the patriarchy would never be over. But then she saw the patriarchy fall with her own eyes when the corporate government was established. The UCC reset the clock of history, she used to say. No more unfair employment standards, no more pay inequality, no more hierarchy, and no more patriarchy."

"I get it," said Mira, "I totes get it. I've heard that narrative and it sounds kranpow." She took a big gulp of jooce. In her enthusiasm, she didn't notice a green drip run down the side of her glass. As it reached the table, a little busbot zipped up, whipped out a cleanpad, and mopped up the mess with speed and precision.

Lo smiled when she saw it. She didn't use to smile when a busbot popped up at her table like that. Normally she would jump half out of her skin and be on edge for the next few minutes. What had happened to her? She focused on Mira's narrow shoulders and slender neck – the transformed image of herself that she'd seen in the artsperience mirror.

"Can we do something together?" Lo asked.

"Um, sure," said Mira, shifting in her seat. Paloma wasn't her type.

"Oh, I don't mean, you know, sex," said Lo, though the pale skin of her cheeks turned red enough to reveal a preference that she was unwilling or unable to express.

"Oh! Um, good?"

"Though you're soooo attractive. Like I already said."

"Thanks!" said Mira with a laugh.

"No, I meant let's do something fun, something exciting."

Mira was into this. "Like what?"

"I don't know. I spend so much time coaching other people how to have fun that I wonder whether I know how to have fun myself. That's why I went to the ArtFair. I don't usually attend things like that but I'm so happy I did."

Mira had the germ of an idea. "But you like art, right?"

"I... subscribed to a few masterclasses about five years ago."

"Kay. So. Do you know what artheft is?"

"I... do not."

As Mira explained, Paloma's expression cycled through curiosity to intrigue to interest and then enthusiasm.

They had finished their drinks. "Wanna order more and figure out a way to carry out an artheft together?" said Mira.

Lo had barely finished nodding when a vendbot arrived at the table. On the holomenu a new item made her smile. "I'll have a tepid chocolate," she said.

"Oh. That's good!" said Mira. "Same here."

The vendbot scooted away. Paloma shifted forward in her seat and said, "So how do you choose which artwork to steal?"

Mira shrugged. "I follow a bunch of threads and subrooms, and... I guess I just go by instinct. Like, whatever appeals to me. I mean, it has to be shareworthy, right?"

"Right."

"But I'd really like to take the next one to another level."

"Sounds exciting."

"It would be," said Mira, an elfin gleam in her eye. "I just don't know how. I would need to get info on projects that are under the radar, basically secret. And of course that's not easy because..."

"Because they're secret."

"You so smart!"

Lo knew Mira was kidding around but she did feel smarter in Mira's company.

"There must be some way of hacking into an artist's messaging or notes or something," said Mira.

Paloma was silent, wheels turning.

"What?" said Mira. "What is it?"

"I might be able to."

Mira's eyes widened. "Seriously?"

"Yah. Well, maybe I know someone who knows."

"Kay…"

"One of the vacational training modules is a travel hacking course. It was optional so I never took it, and I'm shit at tech stuff anyway."

"Me too."

"But a woman I know in Elliot Lagoon offers that service."

"Kranpow!"

"Yah. I teamed up with her once on a project. She's cool."

Mira sipped the tepid chocolate. "Ideally it would be something in T.O."

"Kay. I'll message her later."

"Ask her if I can pay in soap," said Mira.

Paloma laughed. "Sounds good!"

They finished their drinks and made plans to meet up soon to work out the details of the artheft. They exchanged a hesitant kiss on the cheek before Paloma got into her taxibot, flushed and energized. Mira watched as the car pulled away. Today felt like a watershed.

16.

Santiago was awakened by a desksplay alert. He had fallen asleep, slumped forward on his ergool. He jerked his creased cheek up from his forearm at the sound of the descending melody repeating every three seconds. His subconscious mind processed that this disharmonic beeping wasn't a regular alert before he became aware that something serious might be happening.

Santi blinked at the words on the desksplay. Then his garmscreen lit up with the same message: "Chestnut Emergency Medical Services – Critical Alert." He turned back to the desksplay. Underneath the message was a red button: "Allow video?" He pressed it. The alert screen changed to a live video showing a middle-aged woman in a gray tunic sitting at a desk in a small office.

"Hello. Hello?" said Santi, already breathless.

"Hello," answered the woman, "My name is Ludmilla Tran, information officer for Chestnut Condos. Are you Santiago Khan, son of Jamal Khan?"

"Yah, yes I am," confirmed Santi, voice shaking. Chestnut was his father's residence.

"Kindly consent to the Terms and Conditions applicable to the negative outcome that you are about to be informed of."

She was expressionless, regurgitating a script. The screen filled with the Nontriggering Consent contract. Santi scrolled through it quickly and pressed the green "Accept" button. His wristline was fuchsia and it bothered him for a moment, then he remembered that a typical negative outcome information contract voided any penalty for stress induced by the content of the information, meaning that his wellscore shouldn't be affected. Then he became annoyed that his concern was his own situation.

The woman reappeared on the screen. "Thank you. Please also verbally acknowledge that you are prepared to hear the information that follows."

"Yes, fuck it, yes!" yelled Santi.

She didn't flinch. "Jamal Khan was found unconscious in his bode by a sistbot twenty-five minutes ago."

Santi glanced at the corner of the screen. It was 11:45 p.m. "What happened? Is he oky? Where is he now?"

"Jamal Khan was placed in a medically induced coma on-site, as per Chestnut Condos protocol, consented to by Jamal Khan in contract dated January 15, 2075."

Santi's mind raced. "Who diagnosed him?"

The woman stared back blankly, then said, "Initial diagnosis was performed remotely by the uLife medibot scanner."

Santi shook his head. "And who induced the coma?"

"Chestnut Condos medibot services, assisted by on-site nursing staff. Jamal Khan has been transferred to uLife Hospice Facility 101 where he is in stable condition."

"Fuck," said Santi under his breath.

"Do you have further questions, shareholder Khan?"

Santi drilled his fingers on the desk, thinking. "Do you have video?"

The woman hesitated, then answered, "I have video."

Santi wondered whether she was real or AI-generated. "Video of my father being placed in the coma?"

The woman processed this request. "You will be required to consent to viewing of video that may trigger an extreme nonHappy state.''

"Yes! I consent!'' he said, banging the desk.

"Video will begin playing in five seconds. You may pause or exit at any time by saying 'Pause' or 'Exit'. If you pause video, you can restart by saying 'Play'.''

"Just play the fucking video, Simdammit!''

The woman stared blankly, then the screen switched to the interior of Jamal's bode. Santi frowned at the image captured by the medibot's camera as it entered his father's bedroom. That room – that room he'd moved his father into with a sickly amalgam of relief and guilt – that room Santi hadn't set foot in for – what? – eight, nine years?

"Pause!'' said Santi.

The video froze on an image of the room from the botcam perspective of four feet high. Santi's initial impression was that nothing had changed since his father had originally moved in. He could see Jamal lying motionless in his bed, the surrounding walls and shelves plastered with old Toronto Raptors posters and hockey memorabilia that he'd treasured since he was a kid desperate to be more Canadian than his non-immigrant friends. At the foot of the bed was a sistbot, its eight-inch screen adorned with the smile emoji that would have angered his father if he could see it.

"Play.''

The video jerked back to life. The botcam approached the bed, stopped, then the view rose higher while tilting down. The medibot's scanner came into the frame. The thick, concave sensor reached out on a flexarm to position itself right above his father's face. Then, disconcertingly, it descended onto his face, resting there for several seconds. Jamal didn't budge. The sensor lifted slightly and moved down to the top of Jamal's chest, once again descending to take readings. The sistbot came into view, still smileying, and a gripper pulled back the sheet from his father's body. Santiago averted his gaze for a second, then forced himself to watch. The medibot's scanner moved further down to the middle of his father's chest wearing a blue pinstriped pajama shirt. He must have owned that for decades, thought Santi. Could it be so old it was even made of cotton?

The scanner lifted from his father's chest, moved to his lower torso, and descended once again. The sistbot's screen came into the frame. The smile emoji on it suddenly glitched and turned into a sad face. Santi felt his stomach quiver.

At this point, there was the sound of a door opening off-screen. Santi hadn't realized that audio was being transmitted the entire time. There had been nothing to hear except the faint background whirr of the bots' motors.

A thick-set young man with bushy black eyebrows and a white coverall entered the frame next to the sistbot. He placed a gray case on the bed, opened it, and took out an instrument of some kind. He bent over Jamal and lifted each of his eyelids in turn, examining them through this scope. "Diagnosis?" he said to the medibot, returning the instrument to the case.

By asking the medibot this question, the nurse was speaking straight to the botcam, and therefore to Santi, as though looking directly into his eyes. He held this unnerving stare while the bot answered: "Patient suffered stroke."

Santi said, "Pause," then exhaled slowly. He gathered his mental strength, tried to quell his quivering stomach, and said, "Kay, play."

"Prognosis?" asked the nurse.

"Indeterminate. Recommend ventilation and immediate barb coma."

Still looking straight at Santi, the nurse said, "Proceed with ventilation."

The nurse reached for the gray case while the medibot's scanner pulled back and out of frame. Into the image came an oxygen mask on a different flexarm that angled down and over Jamal's nose and mouth. The nurse removed a bottle and syringe from the case, raised the sleeve of Jamal's shirt, and rubbed the crook of his elbow with an alcohol wipe. After adjusting the dosage in the syringe and flicking it twice, the nurse inserted the needle into Jamal's arm and pushed in the plunger. For a moment Santi thought that the video had been paused, but there was simply no movement to see. The somber medical tableau before his eyes was arrestingly beautiful in its composition. Detaching himself from the reality of what he was witnessing, it struck Santi that there was something Pietà-like in the way the nurse was bending over his father, the sad-faced sistbot positioned next to him like a mournful mini-angel.

"Pause," said Santi. "Zoom in fifty percent, pan left." He wasn't sure that this would work, but it did. Now the tableau reframed, showing only his father's head and shoulders. Was this it? Were these his father's last moments in the real world? Next time he saw him, would he have passed permanently into the virtual limbo (or purgatory) of a uLife hospice? Santi looked up at the ceiling and said, "Exit."

Ludmilla Tran, information officer for Chestnut

Condos, reappeared on the desksplay and announced impassively, "All outstanding balances for Chestnut Condos services will be automatically transferred to uLife Hospice Facility 101. No action is required on your part. Shareholder Jamal Khan's medical management, lifestyle, and voting preferences will not be affected. Do you have any questions?"

"Um..." Santi's voice faltered. He cleared his throat. "Kay, so, are there – is there anything else I need to know?"

"Know about what subject?"

"Can I go see him?"

"uLife Hospice Facility 101 can be visited by family members of patients between 7 a.m. and 7 p.m. Tuesday through Sunday. Simply select 'Schedule' on the facility's app and follow the onscreen instructions to set a visiting time. One hour maximum per visit, two or more visits within a single twenty-four-hour period are not permitted."

Santi raised his voice. "So I can't go now?"

"Visiting hours are 7 a.m. to 7 p.m.," was the implacable response.

"But I need to know if he's alright!"

"Your father is in a medically induced coma and is in stable condition."

Santi breathed again. He would go in the morning.

"Do you have further questions?"

"No, I guess not."

"Please don't hesitate to use the uLife Helpcenter if you need further information."

"Kay."

"Thank you for using Chestnut Condos services."

Santi creased his forehead and narrowed his eyes. "I

didn't use them, my father did."

"Thank you for using Chestnut Condos services."

The screen went blank.

Santi put his head in his hands, then ran his fingers through his thinning curls. "Memoryself on," he said to the Room.

Tiago was already grinning. "Come here often?"

"Hey kid," said Santi, suddenly sounding exhausted. "Not up for joking around. I'm not feeling kranpow."

The memoryself affected concern. "Trouble with Emeraldia?"

"No, no. It's Dad."

"What? Is he oky?"

Santi knew all too well how weird and even nonsensical this conversation was. Nevertheless, he continued: "They said he had a stroke."

Tiago looked devastated. The memoryself AI seamlessly adjusted to and aligned with changing emotional contexts. "Oh, Sim," he said quietly. "When?"

"Not even an hour ago."

"And? Is he dying?"

"No, no. Unfortunately."

"What the fuck, Santi! What's that supposed to mean?"

"You don't know what it's like in those facilities."

"Where?"

Santi lowered his voice, then became aware that he'd lowered his voice and almost psyched himself out. "You remember the uLife corporation?"

"Yah, sure. The insuraco."

"Yah, it was formed in a megamerger when we were in our twenties."

"And?"

"And uLife runs hospices all over the UCC."

"Like, palliative care?"

"Yes and no. What you're thinking of is where they make dying less painful. But in these hospices, people never seem to die."

"What?"

"I mean, that's what I've heard. Like, Emeraldia's grandmother – she entered the hospice in Etobicoke four or five years ago. She was ancient, I mean over a hundred, and she had a fall and lost consciousness and the medibot induced a coma, just like with Dad, and... she's still there!"

"Wow, cray. You mean the hospice is pretending patients are alive so they can keep collecting payments from the family?"

"No, no. That would be difficult to get away with, although it would make sense."

"Make sense? It would be fucking terrible!"

"Right, but if their only goal was to defraud people, it would be less bad than the reality."

"What are you talking about?"

"Emeraldia's grandmother is definitely still alive. She visits every month."

"She's still in a coma?"

"No, she came out of the coma a week after the fall."

Tiago looked confused. "Dude, I don't get it."

"Exactly," said Santi. "Here's what happened. After coming out of the coma, Emeraldia's grandmother somehow requested long-term geriatric care management with a Vitainment package."

"A what?"

Santi opened his mouth to answer, then closed it again. After a moment's thought, he said, "You sure ask a lot of questions for a memoryself."

Tiago laughed. "Well I'm based on you, so I guess you ask a lot of questions!"

Santi knew this to be true. But something in his gut told him that these specific questions didn't quite make sense. Or was he being overly suspicious? He was on edge after watching the video of his father and wasn't thinking with too much lucidity.

He answered Tiago: "Vitainment is video and audio streamed continuously to patients. Whatever theme or mix of themes you like. Sports, music, comedy, news, whatever."

"Like, on a screen?"

"On a huge headset, kinda like an AdVisor."

"Kay, doesn't sound so bad."

"Except that it's a full-face two-way screen." Santi motioned with his hands in front of his face. "It covers the whole head, but there's a camera on the inside showing the patient's face on the outside, like one of those VR headsets from when we were kids. I mean, when I was a kid. Anyway, it shows them watching the Vitainment stream."

"You see their face? I really don't get it."

"The outside of the headset screen is smooth. Kay, think of an astronaut helmet. That fishbowl effect?"

"Kay."

"Imagine that on the glass of the fishbowl you see live video of the face of the person wearing the helmet."

"And they're just watching?"

Santi shook his head. "So I think I missed out a key part of the story."

"Uh-huh."

"They never take the headset off."

Tiago looked at him blankly.

"Everyone in the hospice has a Vitainment headset," said Santi. "You can talk to them and they answer back, but you only ever see their face on the exterior screen."

"So Emeraldia visits her grandmother in – what? – some kind of apartment?"

"More like a cubicle."

"Kay, so here's what I don't get: the patient is wearing this headset thing. I get that part – the streaming entertainment so they're happy-ish."

"Oh, believe me, every patient's wellscore is kranpow."

"But you said they never take it off."

"Yah."

"But when you visit, they take it off?"

"Nope."

"Why not?"

"Because they're in LMS."

"Which is?"

"Lowered Metabolic State. Kinda like hibernation."

"But they're awake?"

"Looks that way."

"But they have to eat. They gotta shit!"

"Oh yah, I forgot about that part, too. They all have Genedit cuffs on their ankles and in/out nutrient tubes. It's like they're in physical stasis."

"In beds?"

"They're on sort of molded cots that slowly rock sideways. Side to side, very slowly, so they don't get bed sores."

Tiago's face creased into a look of horrified disbelief. "I'm picturing something super weird."

"Then you're probably picturing it right."

"Like, an astronaut whose face you can see on their helmet visor?"

"Yah, but instead of a space suit they're dressed in a synthium one-piece. Perfect comfort, they call it."

"Have you seen this yourself?" asked Tiago.

Santi nodded. "I went along with Emeraldia the first time she visited. It was so fucked up. I couldn't go back."

Tiago paused, thinking. "Let me get this straight – Emeraldia hangs out with her grandmother?"

"Yah."

"They talk – they have convos."

"Yahp."

"And her grandmother talks back, but it's just her face somehow projected on a headset visor?"

"Exactly. Well, not projected. It's like a curved desksplay screen."

"This happens every time Emeraldia visits?"

Santi sighed. "Every single time. For five years."

"Wow," said Tiago, reclining in his chair. "Bro, I'm glad I'm not living in the future."

"Kid – you are living in the future. I'm right here."

Santi waved an arm and paused the conversation. He stared into the space above the desksplay for a while, then down at the memoryself frozen on the screen. If his father ended up in LMS, on Vitainment day after day, year after year, what the fuck could he do about it?

He rubbed his forehead. The desksplay mistook the gesture and unpaused the memoryself.

"Are you oky?" asked Tiago.

"No," said Santi wearily. "Of course I'm not."

"You should sleep."

"I guess."

Silence.

"See you later?" said Tiago. The LLMpathy settings were on point.

Santiago gave a cursory nod, then flicked the screen off.

17.

Emeraldia tossed and turned. She wanted to be asleep but she was awake. Her thoughts were like a series of notifications on the same subject, and no matter how many she dismissed, they kept on popping up. Santi hadn't come to bed. Yet again. Was it her? She had been making a real effort. Was it him? She knew he was preoccupied with this big project that he'd been hired to do by Utopiatainment. She was super happy for him, but it was taking its toll. And no matter how empathetic she was, her thought notifications kept nagging her that this was totes unfair.

Ruminating like this was especially problematic in the middle of the night. When she was younger it used to be a lot worse – repetitive negative thoughts would intrude on her daily life and make it difficult to get things done. In her mid-thirties, a friend had encouraged her to seek professional help, and she ended up crafting her psychstory.

So daytimes got better. But occasionally her night-time brain just wouldn't let her rest. It was as though there was a sneaky nocturnal cerebellum that would creep from its cranial burrow and smother her mind whenever she woke from sleep before morning. She had developed coping strategies. Reading old books helped. She should probably do that now. She was half-way through a Coupland but it was turning into a slog. Maybe she should go back to the Atwood? No, she should try another strategy first.

She turned onto her side in the fetal position. Then she snuggled herself. This trick was one she'd discovered when she was younger. Initially, she used to comfort herself by putting a pillow between her legs but she eventually learned that what soothed her the most was feeling warmth against her stomach. So she developed a self-snuggling method that involved putting her hand on her belly and lying three-quarters face-down. This occasionally resulted in wrist pain but the overall benefits were clear: she relaxed from head to toe. She came up with a theory about why it worked. The sometimes crippling anxiety she'd suffered as a young woman had been caused by the neurons in her gut. Whether negative or positive, she had always been overwhelmed by gut feelings. Strangers in the subway. Shadows in the alleyway. And she knew that this was exactly why humans had evolved gut neurons in the first place. But the breakthrough insight from her CBT appseshes was that her brain neurons and gut neurons were like two clans engaged in a never-ending feud. To call a truce in the conflict, all her gut neurons needed was to be reassured that everything was alright. They were easily fooled, too. Her hand was enough to lend the illusion of comfort and settle their primal fears.

Now, she engaged her brain neurons. Santi was probably just stressed about the project. Unless it was something else. Or someone else? Was this person real or virtual? Was she losing him? Maybe they should go see Doctor Markova again. It would suck if the solution to their marital problems was for her to develop another new persona, but she loved Santi and she would do it for the sake of their relationship if that's what the doctor ordered.

More intrusive thoughts.

Why should she change her identity again? What if it only pleased Santiago for a short while? Where would all this end? And when? How many personas would she have to adopt? Whether Santi stayed with her or not, might she end up in a uLife hospice not even knowing her own name? Why did she even care about him? She shouldn't want to please him so much – it shouldn't be the only real power over him. Was it? And why did she need to have power? She was so stupid for letting him make her feel this way. But he wasn't even doing anything – she was doing this to herself. So stupid. She was so stupid.

Emeraldia could feel her breath getting shorter, her temperature rising. No need to check her wristline – she was all too aware that both her bioscore and wellscore were critically nonHappy. She needed to act fast.

She opened her eyes. That was often enough to quiet the gut neurons. Or to make the nocturnal cerebellum scurry back into its hiding place. Whatever the metaphor, she wished it would just go away. All this was an unwelcome return to the bad old days. The anxiety was getting worse by the second and her physical symptoms were fueling her gut neurons' panic. She knew how the negative feedback loop worked and it was threatening to run out of control like those old nuclear reactors: the stress provoked shortness of breath, tightening abdominals, higher blood pressure, raised body temperature, profuse sweating – and these physical symptoms convinced her gut that she was facing a dangerous situation from which she needed to escape immediately.

She repeated the individual version of the uMantra, the one you recited if you were alone: "Connected I am uHappy. Connected I am uHappy. Connected I am uHappy." It seemed to stabilize her. Her breath was still short, her heart in her mouth, but as she repeated the mantra she regained control of her runaway thoughts and allowed herself to speculate. Should she talk to Santi? What if he'd gone out? Would that trigger her all over again? Shit – she could feel the slippery slope. She needed something to calm her, to center her. But reaching inside was frightening – that was the source of the negative, spiraling thoughts. She would be thrusting her hand into a fireplace when all she needed was some warmth. Then she remembered her psychstory. It was supposed to be a tool and this was the perfect time to use it.

Emeraldia reached over to the nightstand, picked up her nightphone, and said, "Find my psychstory." As the page of text appeared, she felt a rush of emotion. It had been over a decade since the last time she'd seen those words. She lay back down and read:

"My name is Sophie Langlais and I was born in Ottawa in 2033.

My mother worked for the federal government and my father was a civil engineer. I have no siblings, and as a young child, I struggled to make friends. My parents bought me a puppy when I was nine but it always loved my father more than me. For example, if mom asked me to feed the puppy I would put food in the bowl and shake it around and the puppy would come running and go straight to the bowl and eat without looking at me. If I threw a ball in the park the puppy would bring it back to my dad, not to me. Other kids only wanted to hang with me because of the puppy, I thought.

My dad was big on efficiency. If there was a way to improve a process, he would find it. I liked this about him. He was also an early adopter and it was because of him that I discovered my love of tech. Or I should say that tech loved me.

When I was at school I did well in science and conversed fluidly with the edubots. I believed that being smart and learning about the world gave me value. I actually valued my intelligence. My parents, teachers, and edubots encouraged me to expand my mind.

I learned how to code and then built an app for this really strange habit I had. At least, looking back on it, it seems strange now. My most treasured possessions were a pair of postage stamp albums from the last century that used to belong to two of my great-great-grandfathers. One of them lived in England, one in Montreal, and both albums even had stamps in them from the Victorian era of the 1800s. I adored those tiny, flimsy paper pieces of history, each with an individual story lost to time. Whose hands had they passed through? Which letters had they sent? The stamps were arranged by country, and the albums had short paragraphs about these places, half of which don't even exist anymore. Of course, there was Canada, the USA, and Mexico, but there were countries called Yugoslavia, Rhodesia, Indochina, East Pakistan, the USSR, Ceylon... I used to spend hours going down wiki rabbit holes reading about dozens of former states while I carefully held their stamps between my fingers. These were colorful, perforated echoes of empires, kings, queens, cultures, national heroes, proud achievements, and it occurred to me that I could find a way to bring them back to life — to recreate the wars, the conquests, the defeats, the diplomatic successes and failures, the political upheavals, that animated the world in pre-corporate times.

So when I was around fourteen I undertook this huge data entry project, uploading an image of each stamp, hundreds and hundreds of them, and tagging them with their country of origin and date of issue. It took me weeks. And then I coded the game. I called it *La Règle du Jeu* after a super old French film I'd researched because one of the stamps had the director's portrait on it.

In the game, each stamp represented an individual. Not exactly a person, more like a character. And these characters were grouped according to country (as clans) and according to age and appearance (as generations of the same family). The app then attributed status and hierarchy to them. I made it so that this status was sort of equivalent to the power that the countries actually had historically.

And then the game began. The families and clans battled against each other in a series of iterations, like rounds in a board game, with winners and losers determined by random data points linked to the monetary value of each stamp. I was able to control the speed at which each iteration took place so that this stamp world I'd created evolved as though years, decades, and centuries were passing.

I spent day after day in front of the interface, watching the game play out. I wouldn't say I was addicted, but I was so immersed in it that it was all that mattered to me for weeks at a time.

One day my mother received a notification from a uLife psycounselor that I was on the spectrum. I guess my online activity and conversations with the edubots had raised a flag. She told them about my stamp game and that was the clincher. But fortunately for me, this was around the time when being on the spectrum started to be viewed as a huge positive. The idea that some people had more affinity to bots than to humans was a social advantage. And soon I was labeled a techpath.

This encouraged me and I doubled down on STEM courses at school. When I got accepted into the U of T's AI program, it boosted my self-esteem higher than it had ever been and I moved onto the campus feeling like the princess of Nerdworld. Being constantly surrounded by so many people would normally have stressed me out, but since they were just as nerdy as me, it was like I'd dived into an ocean and found my fellow dolphins. Wait, a dolphin probably isn't the right animal — aren't they too cute? Then again, they *are* smart. Maybe other aquatic mammals find them annoying. Then again, they're very social, so it's a bad metaphor for someone on the spectrum. But whatev, the point of the metaphor is that the non-social people found each other in that program, so it didn't matter if they were non-social. Must remember to research clown fish.

Then everything changed. There was this guy in my Plant Networks and Botanical Logic course who had an absolutely ridiculous crush on me. I'd never received any attention from boys. I'd never even thought about sex. At least, not irl. I was all about porn and fantasies. Safer in every single way. Besides, I was kinda chubby — I barely exercised, I didn't eat well, I just didn't care one way or another about my body. (Must remember to research sea cows — they were called something else too and then went extinct.) But the thing about this boy — Roberto was his name — was that he was crushing on me because of the *Règle du Jeu* game. I had mentioned it to him when for some nerdy reason or other he brought up a country called Danzig that existed in northern Poland for about five minutes in the early twentieth century. I had six stamps from Danzig and this triggered the conversation. He fell so hard for me. And what seemed super weird from my perspective was that he was physically attracted to me too.

So we began having sex and the effect it had on me was like a new dimension opening within the fabric of reality. All those years I'd wasted. Now, somebody truly cared about me.

Having Roberto stare into my eyes was everything. The love. The extreme love. And I almost felt something back. But that, ultimately, was the problem. I mirrored – I did what I thought I was supposed to do – but the feeling just wasn't there. In fact, my gut neurons were telling me that this wasn't right.

In the end, Roberto could tell. One day we were eating ice cream. It was super hot and Roberto was talking and not paying attention to the cone he had in his hand. And all I could see were the drips running down. It really stressed me out. He was probably saying super nice stuff to me but I wasn't even listening. Then one drip landed on his leg. He was wearing shorts and had dark body hair and the green ice cream splattered there among his leg hairs and I suddenly wanted to scream. He asked me something. I never found out what it was because he knew I wasn't listening and that I cared more about the mess than him.

So we broke up. But now I was lost in the new dimension. The thoughts that used to be so focused on whatever I was studying or on my game became unanchored and suddenly this sharp, spiky anchor was careening and lacerating my insides. Meanwhile, my insides were aching. I needed a man, it was as simple as that. But the more men I found, the more my gut neurons rebelled. Anxiety became the baseline, and panic attacks struck indiscriminately, with increasing frequency.

The CBT and meds steadied me. Or at least gave me some sort of crutch, even if it was a crutch I couldn't use all the time because when you're lying face-down on the pavement a crutch won't help you get up. But the real breakthrough came when the UCC created work for the techpaths and legalized identity shifting.

So. I am about to sign off as Sophie Langlais for the last time. This is who I've been until now, and this will remain my psychstory even after I shift. The identity shift isn't the closing of a door or the trashing of a file, it's a new beginning built on the foundations of this psychstory."

Emeraldia looked away from the nightphone. A noise. She caught her breath. Adrenaline flooded her veins. Dammit, she thought, I was just getting calm. She could feel her heart beating faster. Then Santi shuffled into sight in the doorway – a familiar silhouette, but oddly posed. She couldn't tell whether he was looking at her. Something was wrong. He entered the room slowly. Her fear morphed into concern as he pulled off his shirt and dropped it on the chair in the corner. He never did that. He always folded it.

"My dad," said Santi quietly.

"What?" she croaked, then cleared her throat. "What happened?"

Santi sagged onto the side of the bed, cowed. "He had a stroke. Or, I dunno, something."

Emeraldia propped herself upright, then leaned over and placed her hand warmly and deliberately on the small of Santi's back. His muscles relaxed. "I'm sorry," she said. Santi seemed to be barely breathing. Emeraldia noticed a small gray-brown curl that mirrored the curve of his earlobe. She prefaced her next words with a half-spoken-half-sung lowing that lasted two or three seconds like a minor overture to mourning. "Did he... Is he...?"

The dreaded unsaid word hovered in the space between them.

"No," said Santi. "No, he's not dead."

Emeraldia moved closer to her man. He looked unnerved. Adrenaline surged in her chest once again. "Then what? Where is he?" Her mouth went dry. "What happened?" she whispered.

"They put him in a coma."

"What? What do you mean?"

"It's a procedure. A thing they do to protect the brain."

"For how long?"

"That's the thing – he's been taken to a uLife hospice. Just like your grandmother."

Emeraldia swallowed and recoiled slightly, removing her hand from Santi's back. He turned to face her.

"Oh," she said, "I'm sorry."

He nodded, eyes lowered. "I'm visiting him at 7."

"Then there's time to get some sleep."

He tightened his lips and rubbed his stubble to erase the emotion that lurked behind his fear.

18.

Emeraldia insisted on coming with him. When they descended from the taxibot, she felt a floaty detachment from her inner darkness. She could do this. She could be there for Santi. But at the sight of the uLife Hospice Facility 101 logo in the same lettering as her grandmother's hospice in Etobicoke, anxiety ambushed her solar plexus. She fought against it, gripping Santi's arm, consciously engaging one of her more effective calming techniques – the idea that the right side of her chest (where another heart would be if she were truly symmetrical) contained an imaginary organ she called the phobium. This was the seat and source of her irrational fears. And it was controllable, like her lungs or her tongue.

Santiago assumed that Emeraldia was being supportive when she took hold of his arm, and his wristline faded from a lively fuchsia to a frosty lilac. The building they were entering was a forty-to-fifty-story mirrored castle, complete with four turret-like corner towers. He lowered their uBrella as the glass doors slid open. They entered hesitantly, knowing that a new, unpleasant normal was waiting for them inside.

A sentrybot descended from its charge station in the atrium's high ceiling, making them stop in their tracks. As it scanned them, Santi realized he was smelling the same Customair scent from their Etobicoke visits. Apple pie mixed with... lemon? Or was it lemon pie? With a hint of cinnamon? He could never figure it out, but he knew it was designed to be wholesome and reassuring. So was the décor. The wall to their left was a single giant screen showing a montage of mountain sunsets. On the right was an identical screen where fields of flowers bowed and bobbed in a breeze. There were six seating pods with couches and low tables on each side of the sky-blue moving walkway that pulled visitors inexorably toward a pair of elevators. On one of the couches sat a heterocouple with wrinkled skin and faded garms. The man was wearing an AdVisor mask, but the woman was cradling her mask on her lap while she stared at the sunset screen.

"Please identify yourselves and the patient you are visiting," said the sentrybot.

"Santiago Khan. I'm visiting my father, Jamal Khan."

"Verified." The bot turned its attention to Emeraldia. "Please identify yourself."

"Emeraldia Dance. Also here to visit Jamal Khan."

The sentrybot spat out two RFID cards. "Please attach to your garments and step onto the walkway." It zipped back up and Emeraldia noticed that the ceiling was a twilight indigo, with the pale, round sentrybot artfully taking the place of a full moon, maybe the kind that they used to call harvest.

Santiago was staring straight ahead. On a mission. He stepped onto the walkway. Still looking up, Emeraldia felt his absence and skipped onto it too, catching him up and taking his arm again. She could hear the background chirp of insects. This was a reproduction of a world from the past. She said, "It's not like this in Etobicoke," but Santi didn't answer.

As they left the walkway, the elevator doors to their right opened and they stepped inside, Emeraldia gently encouraging her reluctant husband.

"Welcome to uLife Hospice Facility 101," said the elevator as the doors closed. "Your loved one is resting and enjoying their stay."

19.

The tiny sistbot led Santiago and Emeraldia along a corridor lined with the same scenes as the screens in the atrium. In the elevator, they had consented to receive notifications from uLife Hospice Facility 101, and now both their garmscreens vibrated like a brief cat's purr. They had arrived at Jamal's room. The door opened and the sistbot waited patiently while they entered, before scooting off.

The room's dim lighting came from a ceilingscape of mottled clouds and tempered blue sky. The door closed behind them. Emeraldia could feel that Santi's entire torso was tense. She extricated her arm from his with some difficulty, then put it around his shoulders. He was staring, blinking rapidly, at the sight before him: a body on a padded medicot, covered with a sheet that seemed to be part of the medicot itself, forming a sort of person-pocket, with only the patient's arms lying outside it. The entire apparatus was slowly tilting along the head-to-toe axis. At the far end, all that could be seen was the Vitainment headset.

"Come on," said Emeraldia softly, moving Santi toward the table.

Santiago resisted, then relented. He needed to crystalize his dread. To externalize, materialize, in fact, to Sculpturize it, so that he could capture and tame it. As the image of his father's face on the screen of the Vitainment headset came into view, Santi's fear melted away. There was his dad: the great Jamal "Genghis" Khan. Eyes bright – even lively – the same smile that would play around his lips when he watched clips of his old cricket heroes.

"He looks uHappy," said Emeraldia.

Santi nodded. His father hadn't been uHappy for years. Probably since his wife died. He had made a third career out of not being uHappy. But now, in a coma, through this avatar face on the screen of a life-support system, there was no doubting that Jamal was uHappy.

"United we are uHappy," said Santi under his breath.

"United we are uHappy," echoed Emeraldia, turning to look at him, smiling sympathetically.

Santiago and Emeraldia's wristlines had faded to gray when they'd arrived, reset to neutral as a precaution, as per standard uLife Hospice practice for all visitors subjected to the facility's emotionally charged surroundings. As they continued chanting, their wristlines glowed pea-green. Emeraldia leaned over Santi's father. "Look!" she said, "His is green, too!"

Jamal's wristline was an even more peaceful peppermint color than theirs, indicating the most uHappy state any shareholder could experience. The fact that everyone's was green should have been a cause for extra contentment – a self-perpetuating positive feedback loop. The uMantra made real.

But this was a problem.

Santiago Khan thought – no, he was positively certain – that his present state was absolutely not one of uHappiness.

As Emeraldia took his hand, Santi stared at his wristline in disbelief. What was going on? Seeing his father prostrate, pinned down, and plugged in like this made him sick to his stomach with anger and disgust. Yet his wristline told a different story. Had he been hacked? If he couldn't trust his wristline, what could he trust?

"Do you want to be alone with him?" asked Emeraldia.

Santi only half-heard her question. "Who? With who?"

She frowned. "Your father."

Santi looked her in the eye. "I'll never be alone with him."

She frowned more. "No, I mean, I can leave you two here – go wait in the lobby."

"I'll never be alone with him. Because he's gone."

Santi let go of Emeraldia's hand and turned to the door. She had one last look at Jamal's lifeless form as it slowly tilted up and down and listed from side to side, his serenely smiling face projected on the Vitainment headset.

A dizzy sensation overcame her. She closed her eyes for a few seconds to set herself straight, then turned, opened them, and followed Santi out of the room.

20.

Artisanal soap was all the rage two years ago. Mira had leaped onto the bandwagon armed with a starter kit from Scentrepreneur Inc. and a marketing idea from her brother.

Back on that dark December evening, while Mira was unboxing the opaque soap bricks, molds, fragrances, and color powder at the kitchen island (and filming it for her channel), Rex swished out of his room and into the dining area wearing a sapphire-blue silken kimono, munching toffee rosebuds from a floral packet.

"Candles?" he asked, squinting over at the items arranged evenly across the mottled silicite countertop for the flat-lay camera installed above.

"Jeesio," sighed Mira. "I'm frickin filming, Rex, can't you see?!"

He approached the island. "Well, now you've stopped filming. Lemme have a look."

Mira tapped Pause on her garmscreen and put her hands on her hips. Rex picked up one of the dozen transparent powder-filled zipacks and sniffed the contents. He flipped it over to read the label: JASMINE. He took another from the counter. This one was LAVENDER.

"You're making soap. Of course you are," he said.

"What's that supposed to mean?"

"It won't make you rich."

"What if I don't want to get rich?"

"Well if it's fame you're after, you'd better come up with a really kranpow brand."

Mira looked at him, calculating. She knew her brother was more creative than her. Maybe he had a point. And maybe he could be useful for a change.

"Fine. Got any ideas?"

Rex popped another rosebud in his mouth and hmmmed while he crunched. "My question for you is, do *you* have any ideas?"

"Thanks, get out of here," she said, gesturing wildly with a heart-shaped mold.

"No, I'm serious! I can only help if you give me something to build on."

She held his gaze. He meant it. "Kay," she said, relenting. "I was originally thinking of making soaps shaped like extinct animals. The obvi ones like polar bears, tigers, rhinos. Just the heads. People love that sad Nature shit. But then I realized that the molds would be super hard to make and I'd have to outsource the mold design, and the tiger would probably just look like a cat."

"Guess so."

"Also… because soap is chunky, they couldn't have ears or horns sticking out, so that makes it kinda impossible."

"I don't know, HornySoap sounds like a thing."

"Lol, right." She liked her brother's sense of humor. He was a pain in the ass sometimes but he made her smile. "That's why I'm stuck."

Rex stared motionless at the soap bars and the frankly tacky molds. Mira could sense the wheels spinning in his head. He eventually reanimated with a, "You know…"

There was a pause, and then Mira said, "Yah?"

"One thing you could do is to model them after turds and give each one a celebrity name and then accidentally-on-purpose leak the fact that your brother is a celeb fecologist and customers would think that they are accurate representations of starshit."

He was analyzing the soap with a concentrated frown. Mira burst out laughing.

"What?" he said, offended.

"Got any other ideas?"

"Fine. You don't deserve shit, anyway."

"Ha."

"Kay, so..." he continued, "so melted soap is amorphous by nature."

"You mean, without the molds?"

"Yah." He ate another rosebud as he cogitated some more. "So let's go full-on abstract."

Mira widened her eyes and gestured for him to explain himfuckingself.

"The molds you get in these kits are always shaped like *something*, even if it's just the classic rectangle slab format. So if you could make each one differently amorphous, like with the turd idea but less... turdy, you could name them after abstract concepts, and who could ever argue with what they represent?"

"What are you talking about?"

"For example... obedience. Obedience is maybe... an oval shape with one end flat so that it can just sort of sit there to attention like it's waiting for orders."

She shook her head. "You have seriously lost me."

He crunched the rosebud, eyes locked onto hers. "Kay," he mumbled, his mouth full of toffee petals, "let's go with... generosity. I could see your target market appreciating the concept of generosity."

"Rex, just go back to step one. As in, what in Sim's

name are you talking about?"

His eyeballs did a shimmy. Was she being dumb or was he being opaque? He gave her the benefit of the doubt.

"Kay, kay. Basics. Solid soap exists in one of three types of shape: representational, like a heart; geometric, like an oval or cube; or abstract – "

"Like poop, I know," she interrupted. "We covered that. I'm not selling fragrant poop."

"No, I know," he said. "Stay with me."

"Fine."

"Once we enter the territory of abstract forms, we can make them represent anything we want. In fact, now I come to think about it, poop would not be abstract, it would be representational."

"You should do a PhD in Soap."

"Maybe I will. Anyway, since an abstract, amorphous shape can represent anything, let's run with that and link it to a concrete visualization of an abstract concept."

"Oooooohhhh!" she exclaimed, throwing her head back. "Like obedience or generosity."

"Got it."

She bounced on her tiptoes at the table, something she always did when she was excited. He'd found it endearing when they were kids and he still found it endearing now.

"I like this idea!" she said, beaming. "We could have Optimism soap and, um, Endeavour soap."

"How about Discretion?"

"Yah, that's kranpow." She drummed her fingers on the counter. "But what's the brand? What are we calling this?"

"Right, right..." Rex cracked his knuckles, pushed up the kimono sleeves, and put his elbows on the counter, head in hands. "AbstractSoap isn't, you know, isn't engaging enough."

Mira mirrored his body language. She did this consciously whenever she needed something from someone — a negotiating tactic she'd learned in her Winning at Life masterclass. "ConSoap?" she suggested.

"Sounds like a scam."

"Oh. Yah."

"Each individual soap is like a metaphor crafted into a physical object."

"I guess."

"So how about MetaSoap?"

Mira cocked her head. "MetaSoap..." she repeated quietly to herself. "I like MetaSoap."

Over the next few months, Mira marketed the hell out of MetaSoap. Designed to wash away all traces of cynicism from the lives of young and old alike, they were a set of motivational memes distilled into colorful scented blobs. She zeroed in on six undeniably positive and distinct abstract concepts: Discretion, Generosity, Optimism, Empathy, Kindness, and Luck. This last MetaSoap had replaced the underperforming Endeavour and quickly became a popular gift item among Chinese-Canadians.

As with all things swept up in the swirling currents and treacherous eddies of the online marketplace, artisanal soap was but a short-lived trend flare that briefly brightened the UCC sky, attracting a buzzy swarm of novelty-seekers before fizzling into the ocean of forgotten products and brands. MetaSoap made Mira a few extra YouBucks but the effort wasn't worth the payoff. She swore she'd stick to artheft in the future and fuck the pluswork. Her personal brand mattered more than money.

21.

Albert had stared at the ceiling for somewhere between one and seven hours. As they were leaving yesterday's ArtFair, Paloma had told him she would "see what she could do" about Mira running out on him. But nothing had happened, and he didn't even have a way to contact Paloma. So now he had to figure out all by himself how to reappear on Mira's radar.

Pragmatically, he knew she wasn't really into him. He should just move on. Then again, he also knew that pragmatism's evil twin was defeatism, and this was the attitude that had prevented him from enjoying most of his life so far.

One thing he was sure about: he would never get Mira's attention unless he did something remarkable. Any type of regular message would come across like a bleat for attention and probably drive her away for good. Trying to be funny might work, but it was risky. Oh! He could send her an ogee dickpic... of his nose! He seriously considered this option for a while. He sized up a selfie on his wrist-cam. But of course, the key component of a dickpic was that the dick had to be erect in the pic, and when he lay down on the bed holding the camera above his face, his penose flopped flaccidly onto his left cheek. Hilarious. Also pathetic.

Albert had already stalked Mira's online presence and personal details in the traditional manner before attending the ArtFair. Well, to be precise, he'd used a stalker app. Apart from her address and employment history, it revealed that her uPersona was under her own name, which at first surprised him, then on reflection made sense. After all, she had an attractive personality and kranpow look. Why wouldn't she leverage what came naturally? He binged her Artheft videos. They were breathlessly exciting, intriguing, and captivating. They also made her seem vastly unattainable. Then again, he told himself, he had already attained her once. And he would never regain her attention by gauchely attempting to insert herself into this rarefied world of heists.

He then spent hours on her channel skimming hundreds of unenthusiastic product unboxing videos which Mira had clearly created to fulfill Terms of Service agreements. Further back chronologically were videos uploaded when she was much younger. Her non-mohawk hair alone made her seem like a different person. But these girlish bedroom videos represented a series of first uncertain, goofy steps into the online culture. Occasionally there was one showing her skateboarding with friends or visiting a landmark with her brother, but nothing he could leverage to reconnect with her.

Albert reopened the stalker app and scrolled through the report once again. Something caught his eye. A reference to MetaSoap. It was a product he remembered seeing in one of the unboxing videos. But the report stated that she wasn't a consumer of MetaSoap – she was its producer.

He reopened Mira's MetaSoap unboxing video and this time watched it attentively. Once he understood that each bar was not only an abstract shape but also an abstract concept, he slapped the desk in his sharicle with the palms of his hands. He knew what to do now!

Albert feverishly searched the UCC gigastore for homemade soap kits while his mind raced. He would make his own MetaSoap as a present for her. She would see that he cared about her beyond the physical, and also that he had depth. She was a lot older than him, so this was a necessary course of action. At his tender age of twenty-two, eight years was a chasm, and yet he was convinced that his – he wasn't afraid to use the old-fashioned word – "soul" was deeper than that chasm. He just needed Mira to see that she should spend more time with him. Once she did that, he knew she would develop an emotional attachment to him and an overwhelming feeling of – he wasn't afraid to use the old-fashioned word – "love" that would definitely lead to an ongoing relationship between them. He was quite sure of all this, and his dong-nose dangled as he nodded his head in a frenzy of conviction.

The key was the soap. He would surprise her, maybe even astonish her, by giving his soaps a series of new abstract labels. Love would have to be one of them. Maybe Sex. No no, he said to himself, shaking his head, too obvi, too coarse. He looked around the sharicle's blank screens. He hadn't paid the extra fee to have them turned on and hadn't considered connecting his video feed to them. But just above the screen to his left, he could see a sliver of window a few sharicles over. And in that window, a cloud drifted by. Solitary clouds on a bright winter's day were highly unusual. Looking at that cloud, he saw himself, and suddenly his soul expanded to greater depths. So, one soap would be Companionship. That would be a surprising idea, one that was sort of medieval and gallant. Mira would be destabilized and immediately open her mind to him.

One soap name would be Art, even though that one

would be far less unexpected. That made three. He glanced back up at the window. The cloud was gone. Perfect! Another soap would be called Adventure. He could imagine having kranpow adventures with Mira. Now that he thought about it, maybe he should change Love for something else. Maybe it was too obvi? Attraction? That seemed like a good one, and it included the idea of sex in a more subtle way.

Albert needed six MetaSoaps of his own to match her product offering. He had four now: Companionship, Art, Adventure, and Attraction. The off-white tiles of the ceiling provided no inspiration. He stroked his eyebrows with the first three fingers of each hand – a habit he'd picked up via nature or nurture from one of his mothers. There was something soothing about doing that – the series of small, soft hairs caressing the sworls of his fingerprints. Even something sensual. Sensuality! That was so much better than Sex and would be an ideal complement to Attraction! He typed it underneath his list of soap names using the desk's built-in keyboard.

One left to find now. Albert imagined Mira opening the present. How curious she would feel (how unusual it would be!) to authentically open a box rather than to create an unboxing video. But for the sixth soap name, he was stumped. With the five he'd already thought up, he had the impression that he'd ticked all the boxes. Except maybe... maybe Intelligence? Albert knew he was smart, but there was no particular reason for Mira to know it. Then again, did it seem self-aggrandizing, or even clumsy? What about Smart? That was a real turn-of-the-century adjective, and it hadn't aged well. He asked the sharicle for synonyms but none appealed to him. He was on the right track with

Intelligence, but he needed a more subtle quality. Wisdom? Yah... no – too much of a clash with his actual age. He stared back out the window. Sim, he thought, should I go in a whole other direction? Something truly unexpected. What about Punk? When they first met in the parkzone he had told Mira about Einstein being a true punk. But Punk all by itself seemed weird. So... what about... Rebellion! That was it! He tapped out a triumphant trill on the desk with his hands. Now the list of soap names read: Companionship, Art, Adventure, Attraction, Sensuality, Rebellion. He frowned. Wasn't Adventure nothing more than a less-exciting version of Rebellion? Plus, these nouns were supposed to be abstract concepts, and Adventure seemed too concrete. He should scrap it. Even Art was somehow unlike the others. He thought for a few seconds then changed it to Artistry. It sounded better like that anyway.

He let out a sigh. Companionship, Artistry, Attraction, Sensuality, Rebellion. One more good one... just one more...

Albert scratched his penose. A known side-effect of his bodymod surgery was that his face member got itchy more often than an ogee nose would. He reflected that he was concentrating too much on the concept and not enough on Mira. How did he want her to feel when she received this thoughtful gift – when she saw how much effort he'd made to enter her world, to speak her language? Oh, that was it! He'd already said it and hadn't even noticed. She would for sure be curious about him! She would wonder who this tall, young uTender match really was, deep down inside. And she would no longer be able to ghost him for fear of missing out on a kindred spirit. So the final Meta-soap would be called Curiosity.

His list looked good. He ordered the highest-rated kit, possibly the one that Mira had used herself, and checked out of the sharicle. With same-day delivery, he could work on the six different soap shapes tonight and she'd receive the gift tomorrow. Then he remembered that he didn't have a kitchen. He rolled his eyes at his stupidity and searched short-term kitchen rentals on his garmscreen as he waited for the elevator. The stalker app had been a kranpow investment.

22.

Mira had regained some of her self-confidence in the days after speaking to Paloma. But there was something else she needed to do. She needed to hook up with someone new to get the taste of Albert out of her mouth. Sex with him had been an unexpected bit of fun, like a bizarre new popcorn flavor that you just had to try, and then you ate a couple of handfuls, and then you were like, nah, and then you felt a bit sick, and then you were worried that it might put you off regular popcorn for life. Or like an off-brand perfume that seemed oky out of the bottle but quickly faded and left you smelling like a cheap sexplusworker.

Mira wasn't sure whether these feelings were tied up with her insecurity at the ArtFair or were purely a result of setting her sexual sights lower than usual. She cast her mind back to the park. What had made her fuck him in the first place? He was way younger than her and far less attractive than the men she usually consented between her legs.

She even considered a one-off appsesh to sort through the whole thing, but as she lay on her bed pretending to watch her daily dose of commercials on the AdVisor, she suddenly remembered the man wearing the weird mouth mask she had connected with in front of her building before the Mandzukic artheft. What was his name?

She paused the AdVisor sesh and searched her Connection History. There he was – Jan Magus. He might be the therapy she needed. She sent him a generic ping.

Jan answered within seconds: "Meet me. Now."

The directness of his message excited her. Wild sex with this mysterious stranger would set her back on track, she was sure of it. "Where?" she responded.

"My bode. 777 Menlo West, apartment 11314."

It wasn't far. She just needed a quick shower. "I'll be there in 40."

No answer. She stared at her garmscreen for what seemed like a minute.

Finally: "Y." Just the one letter.

She emerged from the cocoonchair and replaced the AdVisor on its stand. As she showered, she started to turn herself on, and by the time she got into the taxibot she was in a state of nervous agitation.

Jan lived in one of the newer developments in the formerly run-down neighborhood known pre-UCC as Queen West. A fifty-story modern megalith in magenta Silicite, it took up two entire blocks, with twin buildings connected by three translucent rhomboid skyways at different heights that were illuminated like a sci-fi robot's arteries against the night-time sky.

Mira had shared her taxibot trip with Jan, so he could notify the doorbot when she arrived. She was surprised to see that the lobby was darker than the pedestrian area outside. The magenta and red theme of the building's facades carried over to the interior decor and dimmed lighting, giving the space a womblike feel that was accentuated by the smooth synthium surfaces of the bulbous couches and chairs.

Proximity sensors opened the elevator doors. "Welcome to seven-seven-seven, Mira," said a perfunctory female voice as she stepped inside.

Jan messaged her: "My door will open for you." As the

elevator rose, she watched the commercials playing on the doorscreens. The left one was for a shoe randomizer. After a fast, easy signup, a service delivered random pairs of shoes overnight, replacing the previous day's pair, thus removing the stressful task of choosing footwear and adding variety to the shareholder's appearance. Payment was on a sliding scale defined by a range of consumer preferences. The screen on the right showed an advertisement for a butt nanomassage-slash-horoscope reading service performed by a group of individuals who called themselves Asstrology. Mira couldn't help but smile at a video of a tense-looking woman in a smallish bedroom lying face-down on a sort of massage table with a ninety-degree bend in the center that formed an inverted V-shape. As the camera floated around the table, a young, long-haired woman in a white lab coat massaged the subject's butt. Seated on a low stool in front of her was another young woman with a huge mop of dark curls and a floaty, flowery dress, reading a horoscope from a handheld screen. As the elevator reached the eleventh floor, the commercial ended with an animated logo and a tagline in three-dimensional rainbow lettering: "Asstrology. Your future foretold, your asscheeks fivefingered."

The doors opened and Mira exited. She smoothed down her black pencil skirt in the mirror facing the elevator, then followed the signage along a wide hallway carpeted with plush crimson. She had barely stepped in front of the securcam when the door opened.

The first thing she noticed was the hum. Then the glow. The floor of oversized black polished tiles reflected the glow from somewhere to the right. She stepped inside and advanced very, very slowly, the heels and soles of her

clunky boots clopping like the castanets of a narcotic fla-
menco.

The room was enormous, with an expanse of white
floor-length vertical blinds stretching away to the left. In
front of Mira stood two red synthium couches on either
side of a glasstic coffee table lit by one of several recessed
ceiling leds that formed cathedralesque light shafts at in-
tervals. But Mira's attention was pulled to the right. To the
glow and the hum. On that side of the apartment, the
entire wall was taken up with an array of glass-fronted
cabinets. She approached them. What were they? She
stopped as she realized they were grocery store fridges. A
dozen or so doors. Neatly filled shelves. She moved closer
and saw ice crystals on the pale blue, white-labeled con-
tainers stacked inside. They weren't fridges, they were
freezers. Her brow creased as she read the writing through
frosty splinters on one of the labels.

"23/8/83 - Goblet cell cancer cholecystectomy -
m54y."

She peered at the words and numbers then spun
around sharply at the sound of a reedy voice behind her.

"It's a gallbladder tumor. Extremely rare. I shall savor
that one."

Mira spun around. Jan Magus was gliding toward her in
a fuchsia vest and dark shorts. His shoeless knee-length
black socks enabled him to skate across the tiles, and his
shoulder-length hair bobbed with each slide. His eyes, lips,
and cheekbones were razor-thin.

Mira stared at him as he got closer, rapt by the miasma
of dread, curiosity, and attraction now coursing inside her.
Jan crossed from one pool of light to another, the undulating shadows constantly redefining his taut shoulder and

arm muscles, resculpting the angles of his face, casting a shifting sheen over his sheer black bangs.

She involuntarily took a half-step back as Jan stopped just two feet in front of her. He knew why she was there. She knew why she was there. But a hormonal dissonance paralyzed her.

His narrowed eyes seemed to be microscopically examining the skin on her face. Then he lowered his gaze, not at her body, but at the garmscreen he wore as a belt buckle. He tapped it and her screen pinged, breaking the spell. She clicked "K" on hers, in response to his consent request.

Jan unfastened his garmscreen belt and let it drop to the floor, then unhooked her jacket from her shoulders. She let him pull it down her back and over her arms. By doing so, he moved closer, his body only inches away from hers. Then he dropped to his knees and tugged the Elastrium cuffs over each of her hands in turn, tossing the jacket and garmscreen to one side.

Now he clasped her calves and looked up at her, his face level with her pelvis. She looked down into his black eyes. He curled his fingers, digging his nails lightly into her skin, then traced a path up the back of her legs. She shivered as he reached the soft skin behind her knees. Still looking up at her, he grasped the hem of her skirt and lifted it slowly higher, past her thighs, then slipped it over her ass and up to her waist.

Jan's eyes lowered to the mound of her pubis. Now unconstrained by the skirt, she widened her stance. His hands followed the waistband of her mauve Cottno panties around to the front, then he placed one thumb precisely on her clitoris. She moaned as he massaged it through the fabric. He pressed her vulva with two fingers and she threw her head back, eyes closed. She could feel herself getting wet. Her apprehension shifted to excitement. She craved that shift. It was what she hoped to feel with every artheft, and it was what she needed tonight.

Jan removed his hand and stood. As she opened her eyes to look at him, he picked her up, cradled her in his arms, and carried her to the nearest of the red couches. He sat her on the back of it, facing him, then he walked around behind her. With a click of his fingers, the vertical blinds all pivoted to reveal their reverse side. Now the entire length of the room showed... she couldn't tell what. He put his hands on the back of her skull and very deliberately licked from the nape of her neck up to the crown of her head, pulling it back, then moving his hands down to her neck. He used the tip of his tongue, then its full width once he reached her scalp. Mira closed her eyes and shivered. Then she stopped breathing because when Jan exhaled, she smelled a faintly earthy odor that took her back to... new rain on parched ground in the park... some sort of animal experiment in her school science lab... the food that her parents' golden retriever used to eat...

Still dizzy from this swell of sensory and memory stimuli, she didn't notice him remove his clothes and walk back around to the front of the couch. She opened her eyes as he reached forward to pull off her panties and pull her down on top of him.

When the fucking was over, Mira sat scrunched into one corner of the couch, knees pulled up to her chin, staring at the images on the blinds. Jan emerged from the kitchen carrying two cups of water, clothed as before. She was still naked. The images were almost abstract. But not quite. There were rust, amber, and cream patterns, forms, and ripples.

Jan placed Mira's cup on the low table and put one hand on his hips. "They're microscopy."

"Oh yah?" she said, still looking at the blinds. "Of what?"

"Tumors."

Mira blinked twice. Jan took a sip. She'd forgotten what he had said when she entered the apartment. The glow from the row of glass refrigeration units had become part of the room's general ambience. But now that the excitement had dissipated, uneasiness was creeping back. Her mouth was suddenly dry. She needed the water but was unable to look in Jan's direction. She swallowed nothing. Now she could tell that the abstract images on the blinds were in fact extreme close-ups of organic matter. Where was her shirt? Her skirt? Head and body immobile, her eyes darted around. Jan reached toward her and she flinched.

"It's oky," he said. "Here." He was holding out her water.

She turned to look at him, more conscious of her nakedness at that moment than she could ever remember before.

He withdrew the cup and raised his hand apologetically. "I get it, I get it." He placed the cup back down on the table and continued: "Here's the deal. I'm part of the tumophagia community. We get this sort of reaction all the time. Here." He picked up Mira's clothing from the floor and gently tossed it onto the couch next to her inwardly curled toes. He turned his back to her and carried on talking while she dressed hurriedly: "We're really not sure who started the movement. It's clear that eating tumors is inspired by the prehistoric practice of eating your enemy's flesh to obtain eternal mastery over them, while also being a corollary to the idea still subscribed to in certain cultures that consuming the body of a powerful animal such as a tiger or rhino confers on you a certain quantum of the power they possess."

Mira had seen and heard a lot. After all, her own brother analyzed celeb shit. But this was way out there. *Eating tumors?* On the other hand, now that she had listened to Jan's excessively academic and nerdy definition of tumophagia, she felt somewhat reassured that she would not find herself (or any part of herself) in one of his freezers.

She smoothed her skirt, sat back down on the couch, and took a huge gulp of water. "Kay, I'm dressed," she said.

He sat on the couch in front of her and pulled up one of his black socks. "We think... I think... that consuming the tumor of another is also a sort of tribute to their struggle, whether it was successful or not."

"Wait," she said. "Successful? You mean some of the people whose tumors you've got in those freezers are still alive?"

"Oh yah."

"How... how do you... get them?"

"There's a marketplace. Recovered patients and hospitals sell them. Win-win. Even the robosurgeon operators get a cut. Pun intended."

She smiled weakly. She should probably leave.

He tapped his belt garmscreen, checked the readout, raised his eyebrows, then tapped it again. "Would you like to try one?"

For several seconds Mira had no idea what he was

asking. Then it clicked. "A... one of the..." she motioned backward with her thumb at the source of the glow casting a livid pallor onto Jan's face.

"One of the tumors. Yes!" he beamed with geeky pride.

She involuntarily shook her head at the idea that she had been so turned on by him such a short time before. Then she amplified the shake. "No," she said firmly. "Thanks, but no."

"They can be exquisite with the right wine pairing and sauce."

Mira put the empty cup on the table and stood up. "I gotta go."

Jan rose too, disappointed. "I can cook something else? The freezers on the right have regular food in them."

She scanned the room. "Where's my jacket?"

His shoulders slumped, his head fell, and suddenly the fuchsia vest struck her as hideous, incongruous, and ridiculous.

He could see where her eyes were focusing and explained with a subtle whine of self-justification: "It's a condo thing. Residents wear brand colors on Fridays. Hence the fuchsia."

"Uh-huh," she said, spotting her jacket on the floor in front of the freezers. She edged toward it. The upside of all this was that she had well and truly gotten Albert out of her system. The downside was that she'd probably have nightmares tonight.

Jan Magus's knees crumpled and he dropped back onto the couch. "Please stay."

Mira looked at him, jacket in hand, genuinely stumped as to what to do or say.

"I get it, but there's no need to freak out," he said, eyes

pleading. "The truth is, I'm just a morpig. This whole thing, the tumophagy – we're hardcore simulationists."

"Kay... What's that got to do with eating tumors?"

"Nothing matters, does it?" he said. "None of this is real. Only the simulation is real. It's all just another game. And, so... so the tumophagists' view is that we should all be as cray as we can. We should eat tumors because those tumors aren't real and the people they came from aren't real."

She processed this for a second, then said bluntly, "Looks real to me."

"Of course it does!" he said, springing back up from the couch. "That's the kranpow beauty of the world we live in! We can do whatever we like and life is perfect because life is simulated!"

Mira walked quickly to the door, slipping her arms into her jacket sleeves.

"Wait!" he implored with a zealous grin. "Stay for the evening! Just stay and eat with me. I'll explain more and you'll understand."

She shook her head.

"You can let go of all this if you try!" he said, advancing toward her, spreading his arms wide. "We can do anything we want. Just let go and love the game!"

Mira thought of herself as a relatively curious individual, but she wasn't about to hang around and see what other cray shit Jan could come up with. She opened the door and slammed it behind her before he could say another word.

Jan walked to the kitchen and said, "Room, get me a glass of mintwater and vidcall Jacksin Turner."

He perched on a stool at the counter. A convocast activated showing the wide torso and face of a man in his forties with a pig nose and dead blue eyes, wearing an old-school camouflage tee shirt and a two-horned golden Viking helmet. Turner lifted a hand in palm-salute and said, "Magus: always a pleasure."

Jan took the glass from the waiting labot and drank several gulps before responding. "Likewise."

"What's happening?"

"A failed conversion. The ninth this month. I think we'll have to switch strategy."

"Really?" said Turner with deep-voiced skepticism. "I've only had two fails. Maybe I'm just better at it," he added with a wink.

Jan raised one side of his mouth in a lifeless smile. "Either way, it's too slow."

"One conversion at a time, we always said."

"Yah, I know. But it's not scaling. In the beginning, we could double the community with eight new recruits. Now that we're two hundred, we need to ramp up enrollment."

Turner folded his meaty arms. "What are you suggesting?"

Jan took another sip. "A stunt of some kind. Livestream it. Or at least make it shareable."

"Who's gonna share it? The community already shares vids and it doesn't bring in recruits."

"Yeah, I know. But I mean a real stunt, a big one, something that will make the news. Something that will smash through the information clutter."

A slab-like smile broke out on Turner's face. "You know what I'm thinking?"

"Yeah," said Jan, now smiling himself.

"I can ping the guys right now," said Turner. "We could pull it off by Simmas."

"No," said Jan hurriedly. "Wait."

"Why? We've got the guns, we've got the ammo."

"I know, but I'm worried that we'll just look like Amexican terrorists. The government will spin it that way if they want to."

"Kay, so we need to get the messaging right. No biggie," said Turner, shrugging.

"What? Like, print 'We are not Amexican terrorists' on our shirts? Carry a banner saying 'This is all a simulation'?"

"Maybe sky-writing? I got a buddy who – "

"No," interrupted Jan. "Killing a bunch of people will get us attention, obvi. But doing it in the right way will get us the right *kind* of attention."

Frustrated, Turner opened his palms toward the camera. "So? What's your big idea?"

Jan took a sip of the cool mintwater. "Let me think, let me think."

23.

Mira decided to walk home. She could barely believe the lurid truth that lurked in that Menlo apartment. Spontaneous sex was one thing. Unanticipated cannibalism was a hard nope. It bordered on the surreal. Was simulationism to blame or was this dude simply insane?

Putting one foot in front of another on the concrete sidewalk was helping to restore her sanity. The echoes of her footsteps in the deserted street reassured Mira that reality was real. She'd always considered the simulationists to be harmless, but now she wasn't so sure.

She caught a whiff of woodsmoke and seconds later her garmscreen flashed an air quality warning. Forest fires again. Fuck it, she'd keep walking – she was willing to risk a dent in her bioscore. But as for her wellscore… after the evening's unsolicited segue from explosive sex to psychic implosion, she was in no rush to see the damage.

A cricket chirped, her heels clunked. The burn-tinged breeze sighing between the scraperbodes set her already heightened senses on edge.

Was that a wild pig crossing the intersection up ahead?

Her garmscreen pinged again and she jumped. It was an ad for a smogmask available for instant purchase in a vendbot stationed by the trolleystop to her left. Perfect timing and targeting, she had to admit. She bought the mask, put it on, and kept walking.

It was 10:15 p.m. She was still haunted by what had happened. Should she call Paloma? It would be a welcome distraction. Besides, she was itching for news about Lo's hacker friend, the one who was supposed to help with the artheft. But Mira hated the thought of appearing unchill. She called herself Mira Cool, after all. Her whole vibe was chill. She could handle this.

As Mira approached her building there was a flurry of movement down the cross-street. More pigs? They were smart – they could out-maneuver the pest control bots. She remembered seeing on the vidnews recently that they had even *eaten* a couple of the bots. She quickened her pace and was soon in the lobby.

The elevator told her to expect a package. Sure enough, a delivery bot was hovering outside her apartment door. It scanned her face and deposited a ten-inch cardboard cube neatly in her arms before floating down the hallway.

She tossed the box onto the kitchen counter and headed straight for the shower, discarding her clothes en route. Anytime she regretted having sex with a sleazeball, she rebooted her mind and refreshed her body by giving herself what she called a "douche douche in the douche". All physical evidence of Jan Magus was soon washed down the drain. She restyled her mauvehawk and emerged from the bathroom wearing one of Rex's floral print robes.

"Fridge, make a watermelon smoothie," she said, peeling off the packing tape from the box. Inside was another box, this one white, with her name on the lid in a fussy mauve script. She instantly knew it was from Albert, and rolled her eyes as the fridge whirred and chugged. She picked the white box out by her fingertips. There was something very subtle in the smell that reminded her of Albert.

When she removed the lid she encountered a printed card placed on top of the contents. In the same handwriting as her name, it read: "6 MetaSoaps. Inspired by you."

The glass now filled, the fridge exclaimed in a jaunty boy-girl voice, "One DelishCo bitter lemon smoothie!"

Mira was still frowning at the card.

The fridge repeated, "One DelishCo bitter lemon smoothie!"

Mira flipped the card. On the back, in centered print, it read:

cleanliness is next to simliness.

Mira winced and whirled the card down onto the counter.

The fridge changed its message: "Hey Mira! Here's one DelishCo bitter lemon smoo – "

"I know!" she yelled, then checked herself and eyed the glass of milky yellow liquid waiting in the fridgceptacle. "Wait... Fridge, I asked for a watermelon smoothie."

The fridge reverted to a more businesslike tone. "Replaying request."

Mira heard her voice saying, "Fridge, make a scrrrm-scrrlon smoothie." The sound of her ripping off the packing tape had obscured the word "watermelon". She held her breath and gripped the side of the countertop in generalized frustration at the way her life had veered off course over the last few hours. Her wristline was changing hue. Noticing, she let out a sigh and let go of the counter. "Thank you, fridge," she said, resigned, and went to take the smoothie. The fridgceptacle's transparent door slid upward. As she grabbed the glass, her wristline returned to normal.

She took a sip. Albert's box of soap was waiting expectantly for her, practically wagging its tail. She exhaled and said, "Room, call Paloma MacDonald."

The smoothie wasn't that bad.

"Outgoing call to Paloma MacDonald," said the room, using the voice of some ancient female celeb that Mira had drunkenly selected years ago.

Lo answered with a "Hey!"

"How are you?"

"Good. You?"

"Yah, good, just..." She went back to the counter and set down the smoothie. "You remember Albert?"

"Well, he is memorable," said Lo, with a minor hint of mirth.

"So he sent me soap."

"Soap?"

"Long story. I used to make soap and I guess he found out and was trying to be charming or thoughtful but it's just annoying and creepy."

"Gotcha."

Mira peered into the box. Six translucent three-inch cubes were tightly packed in two rows of three. The top of each cube was labeled with a single word and inside she could make out an amorphous object.

"Oh... wow..." she said.

"What?" said Paloma, "I wanna see!"

"Labot, bring a screencam," said Mira. Then to Paloma: "Hold on."

Mira drank some more, then picked out one of the cubes and shook it. The object inside rattled around. The labot arrived beside her, screencam proffered in its puffy phalanges, its facescreen showing a winning smile. Mira took the device in one hand, pressed a button on the side, and pointed it at the cube she was holding.

"What does that say?" asked Lo. Mira held the cam closer. "Sensuality?"

"Yup."

"Kayyyy..."

Mira pointed the cam at the open white box containing the remaining five cubes. "Here are the others."

Paloma read out the labels slowly and deliberately: "Companionship. Artistry. Attraction. Rebellion. Curiosity. What in Sim's name is this all about?"

Mira turned the cam around to face herself and pressed the button again. Paloma was in bed, lying on her side, background dim and fuzzy.

"His idea of – I dunno – concepts that appeal to me?" said Mira.

"What's the soap like?"

Mira stopped short, mid-sip. "What?"

"The soap? You said there was soap."

"Right. Labot, hold the screencam steady like this."

The labot very deliberately grasped the screencam, its face a literal picture of concentration.

"Can you still see it?" said Mira.

"Yah."

Mira reached for the cube labeled Sensuality, then had second thoughts. Instead, she pulled out Companionship. The EcoPlast lid was held shut with a flap that she prised out with her nails. Inside was a pale pink soap that smelled like lavender. She tipped it out onto the palm of her hand and held it closer to the screencam.

"It looks like..." began Paloma.

Mira examined the soap. It was a failed attempt at two

hands intertwined.

"...like an even tinier version of those tiny bananas that I bought once because they look cute but are just a huge pain in the ass."

"Yah!" said Mira. "Though I think you're being generous. Looks like a solidified mass of perfumed maggots to me."

Lo laughed. "So what are you going to do?"

Mira put the Companionship soap back in its cube and picked out the Curiosity cube from the box. She took out the soap as she spoke. "I don't know – I don't think he'll leave me alone."

"Me neither. He asked me about you when we were at the ArtFair but I – I'd just met you and didn't want to get involved."

"Check it out!" said Mira, holding the Curiosity soap up to the screencam. "Is it meant to be a question mark?"

"Ohemgee – it looks like an orange turd!"

"Like he ate too much pumpkin pie and fished this out of the toilet!"

They laughed together and made fun of the soaps for another five minutes.

"You are one hundred percent right," said Paloma, "He's not going to leave you alone."

"Fuck it, I'll have to tell him straight."

"Be clear, bordering on harsh."

"Exactly."

Mira grabbed the screencam from the labot and spoke into it. Lo was now sitting up in bed, her screencam supported by her angled thighs. "Urggghh," groaned Mira, eyes to the ceiling, "I guess I should call him now. Get it over with."

"I'm afraid so."

Mira gathered her strength. Then she remembered why she'd originally wanted to talk to Lo. "Hey – did you hear back from your hacker friend yet?"

"No, but she often disappears. It's kinda her thing. I'll ping her again, kay?"

"Kranpow, thanks."

"I gotta sleep. Good luck with Albert!"

"Jeesio, I'll need a drink first."

"Lol, kay. Lemme know how it goes."

"Uh-huh."

Mira pressed the screencam button and asked the labot for a double vodka martini. She gulped down half of it and instantly wondered how it would sit on top of that lemon smoothie.

"Room, ping Albert Popplewell."

She had another swig. Two seconds, three, then...

"Incoming call from Albert Popplewell."

"Answer."

"Mira!" chirped Albert. "Have I piqued your Curiosity? Feeling a certain degree of Attraction?"

"Listen," she said quickly, then rushed through the rest of her sentence before Albert could intervene: "I know you like me and I know you worked hard on these soaps but I don't want to see you anymore."

Silence.

"Albert?"

More silence, then a clearing of a throat and a quiet, quavering whine: "I'll be oky."

"Are you talking to me or yourself?"

"I'd just like to know..."

She rolled her eyes. "What?"

"Could I have done something different?"

"I think what you want to hear is, 'Don't worry – it's not you, it's me.'"

"Just give me a chance – I know I'm young, but I'll take some courses, get some coaching. I'll try harder."

Mira downed the martini. "If there's a course in *not* trying so hard, sign on up."

"You know," said Albert, his voice still tight, but now with a bitter edge, "I met a guy when I moved here – a guy around your age – and he warned me..."

"Warned you? About what?"

"About women like you."

"What the fuck does that mean?"

"Women who act all chill but have no depth and are blind to men who are deep and smart and have real feelings."

"I'm not the one acting, Albert. And I don't like your tone. Check your attitude and check your wellscore."

Silence.

Mira spun her empty glass on the counter. Two losers in one night. And the person who genuinely made her feel good was Paloma.

"Mira?" said Albert, now quieter.

"Yah?"

"Should I get my nose penis removed?"

She ran to the bathroom and threw up in the toilet. The acid from her stomach and the acid from the lemon smoothie made her esophagus burn and eyes water. Her wristline went dark.

Albert's voice from the kitchen: "Mira, are you still there?"

"I gotta go," she shouted. "Don't take it personally,

kay? That guy you met – he was right – it's not you, it's me."

Mira got to her feet, gripping the side of the sink. She looked at her reflection and put her head in her hands. "Room… end the call," she croaked.

So much for a good wellscore today, she thought, as she squeezed toothpaste onto her brush.

24.

Santiago and Emeraldia entered their bode. He kicked off his shoes in the vestibule, took off his jacket with a spasmodic shrug, and threw it on an armchair. "Room, dim the leds," he ordered. "Everywhere." The lights dimmed. It was late morning but he needed dusk. As he shuffled away from her, Emeraldia held her breath. They hadn't spoken a word to each other the entire journey back from the hospice. After leaving his father's room, Santi had completely ignored the sistbot's ersatz empathy while they waited for the elevator, and in retrospect, Emeraldia was relieved that he hadn't snapped and hurled it halfway down the hallway. She knew better than to interact with him at times like that. Instead, she had lobered her favorite mixstream and looked out the taxibot window while Santi wallowed gloomily. She dozed off in the car but Santi had been too wired to sleep.

Now they were home, it was apparent that he was determined to suffer in silence. Emeraldia couldn't run the risk of contaminating her own uHappy rating so she busied herself filtering messages until he disappeared into his studio. She watched the door close, went into the kitchen, and sat at the island, exhausted, but hungry. If she didn't eat, her bioscore would suffer. "Room, make me a four-hundred-calorie fresh vegetable-and-oat-based lunch," she said. "Wait! Add a hundred calories to include something sweet."

"Food delivery in seventeen minutes," said the Room.

At the sound of a click-hum from the fridge, her

stomach growled and her wristline turned a sour yellow. "Room, get me an apple now. Green. Prioritize over lunch."

She was tired. She knew this made her extra sensitive to negative thoughts, and, at worst, to spiraling. She looked up at the leds – the dimness wasn't helping.

"Room, brighten the leds in the kitchen."

Something was off about the hospice and she couldn't put her finger on it. Maybe her techpath sensitivity had somehow gotten its wires crossed with her empathy for Santi.

The labot proffered her a picturebook apple. The greenness was good. She took a kranpow big bite and its juicy crunch gave her an immediate wellscore boost. There were times when food was as effective as uForia.

Slumped on the ergool at his desk, Santi called up his memoryself. He could swear that Tiago was wearing the same striped shirt he'd seen him in recently but now with the stripes running horizontally.

"Hey kid," said Santi, yawning.

Tiago's eyes widened. "Bro, you really look like shit."

"I didn't sleep."

"Room! Get Santiago a coffee!" yelled Tiago cheerily. "So...? What's wrong this time? I'm here for you."

Santi shook his head. A memoryself could only do so much. The AI would sometimes misinterpret the emotional significance of recent conversations and neglect to refer to them subsequently. Clearly Tiago had "forgotten" the news about Jamal.

"Where's here?" asked Santi.

"You know, right here." Tiago gestured at the office he was simulated in. "You remember this place?"

Santi knew that the view behind Tiago was no simulation. The bare brick wall, bookshelves, Raptors pennant, and ancient signed photo of the Pakistan cricket team gifted to him by his father was sourced from the UCC's database of video chats that Santi had made from that same spot when he was younger. In the video he was looking at, only Tiago was truly fake – or what they used to call a deepfake.

"I told you already, it's Dad," said Santi. Tiago responded with an appropriately apprehensive facial expression. "He's in a hospice, remember?"

A split-second delay while the AI clued in. "Right! You think they misdiagnosed him."

"I don't know," said Santi with a sigh of frustration. "And it's impossible for anyone to know."

"How come?"

"There's no way to verify. To independently check."

"Check what" asked Tiago.

"Chestnut Condos are bound to say that Dad signed a contract allowing their medibots to diagnose his medical condition."

"Well, did he? Did he sign one?"

"Probably. And why wouldn't he? Right?"

"Kay, so just check the contract!"

"No, that's the problem. It's a legal black hole. Nothing can get in and nothing comes out."

"Because it's Jamal who signed the contracts?"

"Exactly."

Tiago's eyes darted like he was a real person thinking. He cocked his head. "Buuuut... don't you have some sort of power of attorney? If he's incapacitated?"

"I may, but it's... opaque."

"What do you mean? You do or you don't. Contracts are meant to be clear, not opaque!"

"Everything's centralized now. That's what the UCC is all about."

"Kay – doesn't that make it easier to figure shit out?"

"It's a question of searchability. And versioning. If the UCC changed something in a contract, there'd be no way of knowing, or at least of proving it."

"But that's absofuckinglutely fucked!"

Tiago's excessive profanity was realistic and always made Santi wince at how crude his younger self had been. They were interrupted by the svelte coffeebot entering Santi's office.

"Your cappuccino, Sir," announced the ridiculously velvety female voice as the curved cruciform white cup holder pivoted toward him. Santi reached around and took the drink without even looking at the bot, then set the cup down on his desk.

Observing the coffee delivery, Tiago cheered with his own mug, an item of fanware from a long-defunct video game that Santi would habitually use for days at a time back then without even rinsing it out. Present-day Santi was staring at the bubbles in the shmilk foam and didn't even notice his memoryself's raised mug.

"Snap out of it, bro," said Tiago. Santi didn't react. A bubble would pop every few seconds but the foam seemed to stay the same. "Bro!"

Santi raised his head slowly to look at the screen. He seemed lost in thought.

"Listen," said Tiago, leaning in. "Here's an idea: what if the UCC can't be trusted?"

Santi took a sip of cappuccino. He looked Tiago in the

eye. Those simulated eyes. "What do you mean?"

"I dunno, maybe they're lying, maybe they have some sort of hidden agenda. You know what Dad used to say..."

"What?"

"That corporations were all run by CEOcopaths."

Santiago couldn't help but smile. But thinking of his father as the sarcastic comedian he'd always been, and now never would be again, made him sadder than he could ever recall being.

"He'd say that all the time," continued Tiago. "He'd be watching the news and they'd be talking about corporate tax avoidance or fossil fuel producers or whatever and he'd say, 'I know that we're better off with capitalism' – I loved the way he pronounced that word; it was the best word for bringing out his Pakistani accent – 'we're better off with capitalism but the fricking corporations are all run by CEOcopaths!'"

This imitation of his father that Tiago was doing (had the AI scraped Jamal's real-life voice?) was so startlingly accurate that it clawed Santi out of his melancholic memories and he smiled again. "Yah... he really had a thing against corporate leaders."

"Yes! Even the good guys, like Musk!"

"Especially him! Remember how he would talk about him like he was a supervillain or something?"

"Oh yah, and there were the Google dudes," laughed Tiago, "Dad would moan, 'Google said don't be evil. Don't be evil!? The Nazis used to keep really good records, but Google made data a religion.'"

"He was a born skeptic but in the end, I think he embraced it."

"Embraced what?"

"The UCC," answered Santi with a vaguely encompassing sweep of his arm. "After all, he stayed here when Imran left."

Tiago was pensive for a few seconds. "But what if he was right?"

Santi sipped some more. "Go on..."

"What if the UCC really is run by psychopaths? How would you know?"

Santi rolled his eyes. "Kay, all very conspiracy theoryesque but I guess your AI has some blind spots, kid."

"Sorry for being me, I guess."

"The UCC is run by the Board, and the CEO has limited powers."

"I see..." said Tiago, miming a chin stroke. "But what if the Board's members are all psychopaths? That's even worse, no?"

Santi nodded, "Yah yah, but we know who the Board Members are. I mean, the shareholders – everyone who lives in the UCC – we know because we all chose them."

"Like, an election?"

Santi was surprised at how authentic the memoryself was. Although fed by UCC databases and given human form by UCC AI, this character they created had zero knowledge of contemporary life in the UCC. Or at least, that was how it seemed.

"There's a show," explained Santi. "A reality show."

"Ohhh... kay."

"Every five years there's a competition. Anyone in the UCC can enter. Then thirty contestants are chosen for the elimination series." Santi took another sip of coffee. "Every week they face a series of challenges and the person with the lowest number of Likes is eliminated. There's a –"

"Wait, wait," interrupted Tiago. "Who chooses the contestants? The thirty people?"

"Um... I don't know, there's a selection process. I never really paid attention. The current Board, I guess."

"Aren't you curious?"

"Not really?" shrugged Santi.

"That's just weird."

"No, really, it isn't. Cause the contestants in the series are always highly motivated and watchable. And the shareholders choose the Board Members anyway."

"How does that work?"

"When there are sixteen left, they form two different Boards that are pitted against each other in a final round of challenges. The shareholders upvote the Board they like best and the winner runs the UCC for the next five years."

"The country is being run by people chosen in a talent show?"

"Yah, in a way. But they have to know how to... to make decisions."

"What kind of decisions?" asked Tiago.

Santi reflected for a few seconds. "At this point, the UCC pretty much runs itself." More coffee. "I mean, the AI has been fine-tuned over the years."

"So what does the Board do?"

Silence.

Santi focused on the bottom of his now-empty cup. He couldn't remember a single example of the UCC Board making a decision.

Tiago shifted in his seat. "In my day – which used to be your day – the government would make huge decisions all the time. You know, how much to spend on healthcare, education, national defense. The important shit."

"That's right!" said Santi, "Defense – they protect our borders, make sure we have enough drones and subots and missiles and stuff like that."

"Who's threatening the UCC?"

"I don't know. It's defense, just defense." Santi thought some more. "Kay, I know now," he said.

Tiago nodded expectantly.

"Marketing. They decide what campaigns to run."

"Campaigns?"

"Ad campaigns, for us, the shareholders, and for people who live elsewhere."

"Elsewhere? Why? Campaigns for what?"

"The low birth rate."

"They want you guys to make more babies?"

"No," said Santi. "Well, it's true that we're not making enough babies. The campaigns aimed at us are really just UCC branding exercises, like, what used to be called patriotism. And the campaigns for people living elsewhere are to attract the right type of immigrant."

"The right type?"

"Yah – people with a positive outlook. People who are fundamentally uHappy."

"Are you sure that the Board decides all that?" asked Tiago.

"Maybe..."

"Sounds to me like a marketing department or an ad agency or something would be doing it."

"Kay kid, I get where you're going with this. Things run pretty smoothly now, so maybe the Board Members get to kick back and take it easy most of the time. But when the UCC was founded, the Board had to make all kinds of decisions."

"Such as?"

"Like introducing UBI – the basic income – setting the monthly amount, shit like that."

"Uh-huh."

"Yah... shit like that," said Santi unconvincingly.

"Why don't you search it up?"

"Search what?"

"Search up recent decisions, initiatives, whatever, by the Board."

Santi hesitated, then tapped his garmscreen.

"Search up decisions by the Board," he said.

"Over the last ten years."

"Search up decisions by the Board over the last ten years."

They both waited.

"Yah, there you go!" said Santi, scrolling through the search results. "January 2078 – UCC Board approves pilot project for Amundsen Island cooling plant. March 2080 – UCC Board greenlights Amundsen Island cooling plant construction."

"Wait!" interjected Tiago. "But that's the same project – what's that all about?"

"Hold on, there's more – those were just the first two. August 2081 – UCC Board increases medicare visa quota to thirty thousand per year."

"What's a medicare visa quota?"

"It's, um, it's how many immigrants are allowed to come here each year to participate in medical studies."

"Med students?"

"Wait, not studies. Um... trials. Medical trials."

"That's a squirtload of people."

"I guess."

"What the hell drugs are they testing?"

Santi smiled. "uLife is always releasing new drugs. We've wiped out Alzheimer's, we've wiped out ALS, we've even cured male pattern baldness for Sim's sake!"

"Impressive."

"Lol, fine."

"But seriously, bro – what are they using thirty thousand new people per year to test?"

Santi knew this was problematic. He'd just never thought about it before. He tapped his garmscreen again and said, "Search up immigrant medicare trials." He frowned, then shrugged. "Yah, makes sense."

"What?"

"It's proprietary information."

Tiago rolled his eyes. "How convenient."

"Well of course it's proprietary. They're a corporation, like all the others."

"So here's what I'm hearing... these corporations are in complete control of life in Canada?"

"Yah," said Santi. "Everything just works now."

"Kay, sounds amazing. And the Board that's in charge of these united corporations is chosen by the citizens."

"Shareholders, yah."

"But here's my question for you: What if this Board isn't *really* in charge?"

"What do you mean?"

"What if it's like the... the illusion of democracy?" said Tiago. "All the shareholders think they've chosen the Board Members and they think that the Board runs the country. But there's no way of really knowing if that's the case."

Santi knew this was true. He couldn't prove anything.

"They have board meetings," he said. "In Toronto."

"Do shareholders attend?" asked Tiago.

"Well, no."

"Why not?"

"Because they're board meetings! No corporations have board meetings that are open to the public."

"Exactly," said Tiago. "But I guess they must have an annual general shareholder meeting, right?"

Santi could see where this line of questioning was heading. His memoryself had convincingly recreated his early-thirties skeptical personality. This was an aspect of his character that had been blunted over years of UCC plenty. Tiago opened his mouth to continue but Santi cut him off.

"No, the UCC does not hold annual meetings for shareholders."

"Right," said Tiago. "And why is that?"

"Because... because..." Santi wished he could think of a reason. He looked away, as though the answer would magically appear in a holovid. "Oh, I know! Makes sense that you wouldn't understand. Back in your day, there were stock markets and share prices changed on a daily basis. But ever since unification of the corporations, there's nothing to trade, there's no competition and no reason to have shareholder meetings to justify board decisions."

"Wow," said Tiago. "The ultimate monopoly."

"That's old-school thinking. Economists now know that cut-throat capitalism and free markets make the rich richer and destroy the planet."

"So you have a circular economy."

"Exactly!"

Tiago reflected. "How many shares does each shareholder own?"

"One. One person, one share, one upvote."

"So it's basically meaningless."

"In financial terms, yah. But it means everything in terms of participation. Everyone is equal."

"Sounds like communism."

"Lol, I've heard that before: communism without the labor. Whatev. It works."

"Right. Well, it's certainly a kranpow story."

"What do you mean?"

Tiago spread out his arms and turned his palms upward as if showing off a table of jewelry in a market stall. "Sounds like a scam to me. Enclose everyone in a sort of equality bubble where they don't have to worry about their basic needs, and then the Board just siphons off the surplus."

Santi didn't appreciate the cognitive dissonance that was creeping into his mind. "What surplus?" he said, his tone rising.

"The profits that the UCC makes! Do they release financial statements or annual reports? Is there an auditor general or something?"

"I don't think so."

"So how do you know how big the profit is?"

Santi felt queasy. The question was so simple and the answer so unpleasant. "I don't. I don't know."

Tiago folded his arms.

"It's a circular economy," said Santi. "So, you know, everything gets plowed back in. The profits."

"Really. And what if the Board Members take a cut? Or take it all? Who are these people?"

"I told you! We choose them. In the reality show!"

Tiago shook his head slowly. "You aren't thinking, bro.

Do you ever hear from the people who are elected, once the show is over?"

"What do you mean by 'hear from'?"

"Do they give interviews, press conferences? Show up at the Calgary Stampede in cowboy hats?"

Santi gnawed at his thumbnail. "No."

"Jesus fucking Sim, Santi! They're just a front, can't you see that?"

"No, no, no..."

"You have no fucking idea who really runs the UCC, do you?"

"This makes no sense," said Santi.

"Makes sense to me! And I have more perspective than you."

"Ride off, kid, you're not fucking real!"

"Exactly! I've got no skin in the game. Literally. But you – you're living the life! Literally."

"And what's wrong with that?"

Tiago leaned closer. "Nothing, bro. Nothing."

"And?"

"Ignorance is bliss, as they say."

"I'm not fucking ignorant!"

"You totally are. You said you had no idea where the profits go, where the Board sits, or even who they really are."

"Kay, I'll do some research. It's just fucking ridiculous. It can't be a fraud. Someone would have found out by now."

"And shared this news how?"

"I don't know, with the media, on social media."

"And who controls all that?"

Santi was in a mental labyrinth and at every turn he

found himself back at the same spot – the inescapable logic that he couldn't know for sure who was running the country.

"Seriously," said Tiago, "who controls the media?"

"The UCC, obvi," answered Santi, resigned.

"I rest my case. Oh wait, what's a case, you ask? Do you guys even have lawyers?"

Santi said nothing. Lawyers weren't needed in the UCC because lexbots were more efficient and impartial than human attorneys.

"I knew it!" exclaimed Tiago, slamming his palms on the desk. "They've got you living like monkeys in a zoo. They give you food, you get your space, and the zookeepers live it up on the profits.

Santi rubbed his temples. "Kranpow. I'm listening to a fucking LLM with a conspiracy theory."

"Hey bro, I'm just programmed to think like you used to think, so maybe you should listen to yourself, back when you had critical judgment. Like your father and brother do."

Should he try harder to track Imran down? To get his perspective? Santi tore off the rest of his nail. Then he shook himself back to reality. He needed to find his brother anyway, to tell him about Jamal.

"Room – " he said, but Tiago interrupted him.

"Wait!"

"Room, cancel that," said Santi. "What?"

"What happened to the ogee Board?"

"What ogee Board?"

"When the UCC was founded – when was that?"

"Fifty-one."

"Kay. So, from my perspective, that's next year."

"Right." This was part of the uncanniness of the memoryselves. They were you, but they didn't know what you know now, and you couldn't jailbreak their AI to give them access to that information.

"And from what you've told me, the UCC is a sort of nation-state version of the United Corporations that I know."

"Yup."

"So what happened to the ogee Board? The CEOs of Google, Amazon, Bitco, Tesla, Facebook, Apple, Microsoft, Kenjarti? Who else was on it? That woman from the hedge fund... what was her name?"

"Jenner."

"Yah – so what happened to them? When were they replaced by this Board that was voted for in an online reality show?"

Santi thought back. It was thirty years ago. Something like that. Everything had been so feverish and frantic. There was the feeling that Canada, more through luck than judgment, was on the victorious side of history. A smug-but-stirring fuck you to the Americans that shrugged the inferiority chip off the national shoulder. The idea that the future belonged to people like them – the cultured, the cosmopolitan, the woke, the wise, the tech-savvy, the tolerant. Even more delicious was the relocation of economic power from sunken Silicon Valley to soaring Southern Ontario.

"So?" said Tiago expectantly.

Santi couldn't remember precisely what had happened to the original Board. It had been in the news, he knew that. The transfer of decision-making power from the Board to the shareholder-citizens had been publicized as the zenith of participative democracy, the ultimate in corporate philanthropy. The corporation was giving everything to everyone. But once the founding Board members had stepped down, he had no clue what had become of them.

"I think they just resigned," he said.

"Really," said Tiago with a skeptically significant descent in tone from first syllable to second.

"Sure. I mean, they were all wealthy enough to stay home in their mansions, sail around in their yachts, or fly the world in their private jets. When you're that rich, why show up for work? Why have the stress of running the most powerful corporation the world has ever seen? Especially when everything was so automated and convenient."

"Makes sense. But how do you know that they *did* resign?"

"Everyone just knew – it was the biggest story of the year. And at the same time totally insignificant, because everything in the UCC *just worked.*"

"And who owned the news media back then?"

Santi was propelled back toward the same dead end.

"The UCC," he said quietly.

Tiago stared at him for a few seconds, sympathetic to his dilemma. "So yah, anyway, what are you gonna do about Dad?"

"Sim knows."

Santi waved away the convocast, skipping his usual sign-off.

Emeraldia stepped through the doorway. "Hey," she said.

"Hey," he answered, turning groggily to look at her.

"You should sleep on it."

"I can't stand thinking about him there like that."

"Come on, have some faith in the simulation – none of this is real anyway."

He smiled at her. She nodded at his wristline.

"Looks like you're hungry," she said. "Why don't you grab a bowl of cereal or something, then come to bed? The day is a write-off. Let's just get through it however we can, and maybe tomorrow we'll feel better. Come on, we'll snuggle."

He knew she was right. He would feel better if he ate and slept. But what was bothering him now in addition to his father's plight was the thought that maybe Libranne was right about simulationism.

25.

Santi slept fitfully for five hours, then finally descended into a dream state, only to be awakened late in the afternoon by his screaming bladder. Emeraldia was snoring quietly, and he knew better than to disturb her. Their sleep cycle would be fucked up for a couple of days, but what did it matter when his father was a prone prisoner in the hospice?

He staggered to the bathroom in cramped pain, then sat on the toilet and let out an involuntary moan of ecstatic relief as the urine flowed. His wristline was a strange shade of puce that he'd never seen before. He needed to wash, to eat a healthy meal.

"Room, turn on shower at twenty-six degrees. Get kitchen to prepare food. Formulate food to restore bioscore and wellscore," he said.

The shower turned on, the room answered: "When would you like food served?"

"Fifteen minutes."

"Kay. Notification alert – voicenote from Yevgenia Spirenko received 2:52 p.m."

"Play message."

A pseudo-perky, slightly silky voice emanated from hidden speakers: "Hi Santiago! This is Yevgenia Spirenko from Utopiatainment and I'm following up with you regarding the 2084 Project. Just a reminder that we are still to receive the Stage 1 deliverable: an outline in which you will provide a written statement of purpose and description of the artwork, including proposed materials and final format. Please reply to this message if you have any questions about your contract or need to discuss the deliverable. If I don't hear back from you today, we will assume that you have made progress. Have a kranpow day!"

"Reply in the affirmative and delete message," said Santi, irritated.

He hadn't done a shred of work on the project yet. He showered and stared at the soapy water spiraling down the drain. He couldn't put it off any longer.

26.

Santi sat at his blank sketching screen. The minutes already seemed like head-breaking hours. He wasn't used to coming up with a creative concept on demand. Worse was the money. He tried to put the hundred million uDollars out of his mind but there it loomed, a disturbing presence over his shoulder, like a contemptuous manager from the cubicle days of old.

He pulled up the brief on his garmscreen to remind himself of the requirements. One thing was clear: "Artwork produced must be created in Artist's personally recognizable style. It must be equivalent in vision, scale, and scope to the Main Message, as outlined in Section 3 above. This work must be sweeping, engaging, and inspiring. Simply put, the Artwork produced as part of the 2084 Project will be the most impactful work produced anywhere on Earth for the last thirty years."

And the Main Message was "Life has never been so good."

Aside from the question of whether life in the UCC actually *was* as good as the Board claimed, Santi had no idea how he could produce something in his recognizable style and yet make it "sweeping, engaging and inspiring." His Sculpturize pieces were more-or-less human-scale. They were statues of people, and the whole point was that they were imitations of other artists' styles. Why had the Board chosen him? Sure, he had acquired a burgeoning reputation and enjoyed a degree of commercial success, but a guy like Mandzukic was renowned for grandiose works curated by galleries and major museums. Santi's Sculpturize was all about personal commissions that rarely saw the light of day, let alone attracted critical acclaim.

He burped and pushed the ergool away from the desk. Maybe a blank screen wasn't the best source of inspiration. Then he remembered the *Needle Grove* project he had begun to work on the night that he'd accidentally killed his horselette. Even though the work was originally conceived for the individual bodes of wealthy shareholders, he wondered whether there was a way to expand it somehow, to adapt it for the 2084 Project. If he needed to convey the idea that life in the UCC was good, maybe he should begin by reminding people of the opposite. Could *Needle Grove* become an entire forest of hollow "trees"? Visitors who entered the trees and activated the pointed branches that trapped them inside would be stressed until they repeated the uMantra before being released and then confronted somehow with the message that life is good. *Needle Grove* probably wasn't the best title, but he could change it later.

Santi pulled himself back to his desk, sat upright, and sketched out a series of giant trunks. Then he erased it. The trees were packed too close together. *Needle Grove* required an area behind each trunk where the hollow tree could be extended to incorporate the interior pointed branches.

So... maybe he should place the trees around the perimeter of a large museum space instead? That way, he could reproduce the effect of the original idea while scaling it up. Excited and energized by this revamp, Santi sketched it out again. The room would need a false interior wall to conceal the passageways that visitors would enter through the trunks. And a smaller clump of trees could be placed in the center of the space with the entrance to each trunk facing outward. Santi erased some trees and redrew more in the middle of the screen. He liked it! He pushed back and examined the sketch. Not bad... but would it be *the most impactful work produced anywhere on Earth for the last thirty years*? Yah... nope. It was still too personal. No way was it "sweeping, engaging, and inspiring." He pursed his lips. He still liked the idea behind *Needle Grove* and told himself that he should pursue it further. Yah, once he'd got the 2084 Project off the ground. Then he saved the new iteration and blanked the screen.

Santi asked the room to bot him an iced tea with extra caffeine. He stared out the window and shook his head, ruminating about Mandzukic. That guy had a recurring game plan: he found spectacular ways to contrast life in the UCC with the suffering outside its borders. He was good at immersive stuff, a bit like this new version of *Needle Grove* but on a much larger, sort of operatic scale.

Yah, thought Santi, opera! Opera was a good reference. Mandzukic's works had melodrama, they had emotion, and that's why they made such an impact. Santi jumped out of his reverie as the bot arrived with his drink. He took it and sipped it and brooded.

It struck him that even though the Sculpturize pieces were all pastiches of other artists' styles, those artists need not be painters or sculptors. History's great authors — those who created the most enduring works of literature — were artists, too. His initial definition of an artist had been far too narrow! Dickens, Austen, Tolstoy, Woolf, Shakespeare, Eliot, Morrison, Hugo, Baldwin, Steinbeck... They had created riveting works of interpersonal conflict and social struggle, and not only did they each have their own style, but their works conjured up specific visuals. So this was how he could link his artwork to... George Orwell.

The whole business with his father had distracted him from researching *Nineteen Eighty-Four*. He asked the room to pull up a list of striking imagery from the novel and video versions, then spent some time reading and watching the four major references that came up. There was the terrifying Room 101 torture scene with the caged rat where the hero, Winston Smith, was forced to betray Julia, the woman he loved. The next item on the list was a reference to the daily "two minutes hate" rituals where propaganda films depicting enemies of the state were screened to stoke hatred in a "hideous ecstasy of fear and vindictiveness." But this was a performative image more suited to Mandzukic's style. Next... the doctored photo where a member of the Party was erased from history. Santi could appreciate the power and significance of the image but had no clue how to create a negative sculpture, one where an element is removed. It was an interesting idea though.

And then there was Big Brother. Orwell described a smile behind a dark mustache. Could he reproduce that in Sculpturize form? What if he made an army of Big Brothers? He could... he could... would it be a giant head? Who would even understand the reference? And how would an artwork consisting of an army of mustachioed faces convey that life in the UCC was better than everywhere else?

Santiago felt the pull of the creative vacuum. His morale was sliding down the chute of the elusive concept. He pushed the skin on his forehead together with his fingers, then breathed out and slapped his thighs, looking around as though he might see an idea waiting patiently to be discovered in a corner of his studio. He wasn't a real artist, and he knew it. This was the proof. Put him on the spot, give him the greatest reward imaginable, the chance for celebrity, and he came up empty. All he had ever produced for Sculpturize was derivative. It was a commercial concept based specifically on imitating the styles of true artists, or creative giants. Therefore he, Santiago Khan, was a leech.

Now he rubbed his gray-stubbled cheeks with the palms of his hands, his mouth a distorted O-shape. He spun the ergool and glimpsed a dim reflection of himself in the dusky window. He wanted to punch it. He wanted to obliterate that fake, phantom artist. He was full of shit – more shit than the Plentium bricks piled up by the wall. He folded his arms. He didn't even want to see his wristline. All he wanted was to run away from the 2084 Project. To throw a Plentium brick through the window, climb out, then rush into the enveloping darkness. Should he?

Kay, maybe skip the brick throwing and go run outside anyway? A change of scenery and energy wouldn't be a bad idea. He'd committed to deliver and this might kickstart his stalled creative process. It was spontaneous, dynamic! He nodded vigorously, psyching himself up. His failure-fueled fear subsided and his adrenaline seeped away, back to wherever adrenaline goes when the crisis has passed.

Or just go for a walk? This made him annoyed with himself again. In comparison to running, wasn't a quiet walk nothing more than a pale imitation, just like his sculptures? A simulacrum? A cop-out? Was he even close to being an artist hardcore enough to break the window, jump out, sprint – heart pounding, lungs pumping – and head out into the unknown, not knowing what it would bring? Could he ever do something so raw, so unexpected, so courageous?

He sighed. He'd been sighing a lot lately. And that made him sigh again. Fuck it, he thought, I'll go for a fucking walk.

27.

The early December breeze was pleasantly cool. Santi stood on the steps outside his bode, ran his fingers through his hair, and set off along the sidewalk that led to PineRidge's main cartway. A labot whimsically disguised as a raccoon crossed in front of him, stopped at a shrub, and extended a pair of secateurs mounted on a thin arm. The regular snip-snip sound of automated pruning colluded with the off-kilter rhythms of the winter crickets. He was already feeling better. What on earth had he been worried about lately? Life in the UCC was kranpow.

Santi reached the intersection of his lane and the cartway. He turned right and a pair of shuttles passed him, making his garmscreen ping. He waived away the neighborly notifications before he could see who it was, then paused the proximity alerts. He couldn't afford to be distracted in his search for that creative sweetspot where clarity of purpose and freedom of thought perform a delicate dance.

Three minutes later, as he approached the entrypost, all he had managed to accomplish was emptying his mind. He ignored the vehicles passing him by. He dismissed the vendbots peddling their wares. The UCC logo towered high above: red, silver, and sleek.

He left the community and headed along the interurban. After a few minutes, he stopped. He just couldn't focus. Or defocus. Or stop worrying about focusing. Whatever it was he needed to do, it definitely wasn't this. He folded his arms as though confronting the embodiment of his very own bullshit. This idea had been dumb. Like, wandering aimlessly was ever going to help. Every idea he had was dumb. He turned around. Once again the rotating corporate logo caught his eye, the letters U, C, and C forming a triangle with one letter per side.

He stared blankly at it for several seconds. That's when it struck him: why create a figurative sculpture at all? Why not create a word? A giant Sculpturize word would make a spectacular statement. Somewhere up high… such as atop the shining tower of his father's hospice! Or even on all the hospices! He certainly had the budget to produce it. A nationwide livestream link-up featuring a massive, monumental word!

But which word?

He smiled. Of course. In the UCC, life – the life being cared for in the hospices below each artwork – had never been so good. So the word would simply be "good". This was kranpow!

He could imitate the font used for the UCC logo. A precisely on-brand tribute. No, wait – that would be off-brand for Sculpturize. After all, he'd been hired because he was a successful artrepreneur. He needed to retain the fundamental principle of Sculpturize in this, his most high-profile piece ever. The work had to be a recognizable riff on a celeb artist's style.

The word "good" was his subject. He had four letters to play with. He flipped through his mental art catalog. Oh, yah! If ever there was a word-based sculpture that was instantly recognizable, it was Robert Indiana's famous LOVE piece. It had been reproduced so often across the world and even in different alphabets that he could easily mimic its iconic format of four chunky red serif letters stacked two on two with a single italic "O". He pictured what his Sculpturize piece would look like:

$$\textbf{G}\textit{O}$$
$$\textbf{OD}$$

With a GOOD on every hospice rooftop, a fleet of camdrones could stream the official launch to make the work as sweeping as Utopiatainment required it to be. This was grandiose while still being straightforward. Not too artsy to require interpretation. And the Sculpturize letters could be left standing on the buildings, visible to hospice visitors year-round once the big celebration was over. The Board would love that!

But something was still missing. What had been floating in his subconscious when he thought of mounting the work on the hospices? He needed to create a meaningful link between the sculptures and the patients below. If he could do that, the whole thing would have more emotional impact and the message would be just as clear. This link between the claim and the reality was the key to creating a fitting tribute to everything that the UCC had achieved for its shareholders.

Santi began meandering, mulling, musing...

He looked up at the UCC logo once again. As the letter "U" turned, the image of a passing drone was reflected on its surface. The sight triggered a flash of inspiration driven by Santi's envious ego. Mandzukic used screens! And so could he! Yah – that was it: the letters in the word GOOD could serve as a screen. There must be a way to project something onto it, something dramatic or enlightening.

"Right, right," muttered Santi to himself, "So it needs

to be night-time." The projections would only be visible after sundown. It was obvious! The 2084 Project should have fireworks! A celebration like that with real explosions would give the event a touch of irony in the UCC's fireless world.

Now all he needed to do was figure out what to project onto the surfaces of the word GOOD's letters. The hospice, the patients... oh yah – the missing piece of the artistic puzzle – the Vitainment programming. That was what made life so good, even in the twilight years! He could project a customized Vitainment stream of every patient in every hospice onto the word GOOD. Every sports highlight, every soap opera scene, every reality show reveal, every classic movie, every nature documentary, every historical re-enactment, every true crime investigation, every sitcom laugh... Even the personal stuff that made up the streams could be included – every wedding video, baby birth, first steps, graduation, mirror selfie, party cheer – in a constantly changing video mosaic of the best entertainment known to AI.

Santi's step had gained a spring. He headed back home, itching to write this down. He searched how many hospices were operating in the UCC: four hundred fifty-one. This was exciting! He pictured a camdrone swooping down toward a building, circling the artwork on the roof, then hovering lower, framing the word GOOD and the images projected onto it, then flying higher to show another hospice across the city, where it would fly in turn to zoom in on the next artwork, fireworks exploding in between. Then cut to another city. Yah, it was perfect! The show should start just after sundown in eastern Canada and gradually shift west as dusk fell across the country.

Over the next two days, Santi wrote and rewrote his proposal for the 2084 Project, calculating the budget, revising the technical details, honing his artist's statement. He showed it to Emeraldia. She was so turned on by the scale of the show, the prospect of payment, and the path to celebrity that she had sex with Santi four times within twenty-four hours.

Once he was ready to upload the proposal to the Utopiatainment platform, he double-checked how many hospices were operating in the UCC. This stat directly impacted the production budget for the Sculpturize artworks, Vitainment relay devices, projectors, and camdrones. The number had changed significantly since he had first searched it up. There were now four hundred sixty-three hospices. With four projectors per building to cast four different streams onto the giant letters, each additional hospice would increase the budget substantially. He raised his eyebrows and revised the line item. To his relief, the revised total was still within scope. In fact, the budget was so huge it would easily cover the production costs no matter how many new hospices opened before July 1. The entertainment subsidiary must have been aware of the hospice network expansion and planned accordingly.

He uploaded the proposal and smiled with satisfaction at the confirmation message.

For sure this meant more sex tonight!

28.

The text from Paloma came in while Mira was drying herself off after a dip in her condo pool. She tilted her head to read the garmscreen notification on her jacket sprawled on a lounger. The message read: "I can get you into the Utopiatainment system!"

Hedgehog-haired, Mira slipped on her skortlet and picked up the jacket, holding it by the screen. There were two other women in the pool, so she sent an autoresponse to Lo, saying that she'd call her in ten minutes. Once in the elevator, she decided it would be smarter to meet Lo in person to talk about the hack. Lunch in the park and hatching an artheft seemed like a kranpow way to spend the afternoon. It was a gray day but the swim had given her energy and now she didn't feel like staying inside. Besides, Rex was being a pain.

Mira grabbed a quick coffee while she arranged things with Paloma to the accompanying soundtrack of veeporn coming from Rex's room. Lo was only twenty minutes from the parkzone and could meet Mira there in half an hour.

Thirty minutes turned out to be fifty, and Mira's patience was wearing thin when Paloma caught her eye, striding across the ultragrass.

"I'm so sorry," panted Paloma, still some distance away. "I'm a terrible person."

"No, you're not," said Mira, thinking it best to let her annoyance slide. But still – she could have squeezed in a twenty-minute AdVisor sesh had she known.

Paloma reached Mira's adbench. Mira had been scrolling through lunch menus, and as Lo opened her mouth to speak, she was interrupted by a screen voice saying, "Do you wish to continue? Meal options can no longer be guaranteed due to changing supply chain procurement conditions."

"What does that mean?" asked Lo.

"Well, it's almost 1:30. They're running out of fresh ingredients."

"Oh. Right. I always make my lunch."

Paloma sat down and twisted around to face Mira, brushing a lock of hair from her damp forehead.

Mira angled the screen toward Lo. "This looks good," she said. "Cricket Crunch Salad – kale, carrots, and cukes with a light peppery dressing, topped with torsos."

"Oh Sim, I can't," answered Paloma, shaking her head. "The bugs... I know it's good for climcontrol, but I just can't."

"I couldn't care less about the climate thing!" laughed Mira. "I love the idea of eating bugs!"

Lo chuckled and scrolled down Mira's screen. "There," she said, "Chickind Salad Wrap – perfect." She tapped the photo and was about to transfer funds through her garmscreen when Mira stopped her with a light touch on the forearm.

"It's on me!"

"Thanks!"

"So?" said Mira, conspiratorially. "Utopiatainment? You can get us in? Seriously?"

Paloma leaned in. "Oh, yah. I talked to my friend in Elliot Lagoon and she messaged a few contacts in the hacking community. There's some chatter about a huge art project that the Board is commissioning for next UCC Day."

"Oh!" said Mira. "That sounds interesting."

"Right? Well, I asked her to check it out and the project is actually being produced by Utopiatainment."

"That's interesting in itself."

"Huh? Why?"

"Because they're more about entertainment than art. The clue is kinda in their name."

"Yah, well, their name also has 'utopia' in it, and apparently that's what this project is all about," said Paloma. "It's a celebration of how kranpow life is in the UCC."

As they talked about the artheft, Mira's brain went into overdrive. This escapade dovetailed with the real *and* manufactured aspects of her identity. She reveled in being a rebel trickster as well as the attention it brought. Here was an opportunity to break the rules while boosting her peer celeb status.

Mira didn't even notice when the bot arrived with their lunches, and she could barely focus on eating her crickets as they discussed the next steps. Being the more risk-averse of the pair, Paloma made sure Mira understood the key advice that her anonymous hacker friend had drilled into her head: the imperative to be totes incognito when they carried out the hack.

"No prob!" said Mira, "We'll rent a sharicle."

"That *is* the problem," said Lo. "If you rent a sharicle, you'll be renting it under your own name and they can easily trace the hack back to you."

"Look, I'm not afraid of getting caught, I'm afraid of getting caught *before* I can perform the artheft."

"But what if – "

"When I finish an artheft, I make sure *everyone* knows it was me who did it!"

Lo's wristline was turning pink. She glanced down at it and bit her lip.

Mira noticed her stress and relented. "Kay – let me try something."

"What?"

"I think I can anonymize it. I already know how to make an AdVisor think I'm watching ads when I'm not."

"Kay..." said Lo.

"Seriously, I know how this stuff works. All I have to do is make the AdVisor believe I'm someone else watching the ads and train the algorithm to run an ad for a sharicle. When I click on the link I'll be able to make a reservation as this fictitious person!"

Lo nodded slowly. This all seemed complicated but Mira's energy made her incredibly convincing. She breathed deeply. The park air wasn't too bad today.

Mira swung the AdVisor around, positioning it a foot away from her face. The hinge squeaked, making her flinch. "Jeesio, that's annoying! They should maintain these adbench units." She adjusted its height. "Kay, so... I've got a falseface mask in here somewhere." She pulled a handful of masks out of her maskpac and picked through them until she found a falseface.

"That's it? That's your trick?" said Lo. "A facial-recognition-defeating mask? Like, you inherited that from your grandmother? Those stopped working decades ago!"

"Yah, I know. In most cases, you're right. The thing is, there's no point using an AdVisor if you don't get personal credit for the sesh. Right?"

"Right..."

"So they aren't set up to detect falsefaces."

"Oh!"

"Kay, let's give it a shot," said Mira, putting on the mask.

"Wait – *someone* has to get credit."

"Oh yah. Shit."

Before they could do anything else, the AdVisor automatically detected Mira's falseface and activated. A message appeared on the screen with a Confirm button: "Are you Jannifah Soltero?" Mira glanced over at Paloma, then back at the screen. Amazing! Some random Jannifah was exactly what they needed. She cast the feed onto her garmscreen so that Lo could see it, too.

Mira tapped Confirm, positioned the AdVisor on her face, and the sesh began.

"Shit!"

"What?" said Lo, "It's working, isn't it?"

"We forgot to talk about sharicles."

"Huh?"

"To prime the ad targeting AI!"

"Shit."

"Um... so..." said Mira, fake-casually. "Wouldn't you like to rent a sharicle? I mean, *would* you like to rent a sharicle?"

Lo clued in. Time to have a perfectly natural conversation about sharicles. "Did you say sharicle?"

"Yes, a sharicle!" said Mira. "I love using sharicles but I don't know if there are any in this neighborhood."

An ad for ice-shmilk played. Mira had to stop talking and pretend to watch it. Two more ads played while Lo waited patiently. And then came the ad for StarTrip Sharicles. It was one of the high-end companies that offered premium themed sharicle experiences, in their case a customizable space-travel backdrop.

"That's kinda cool," said Lo. "Can we rent Saturn?"

Mira clicked the Learn More button on the screen and the ad stopped playing. She skipped the predictable vidbot interactions and agreed to all the T&Cs to get to the reservation screen as quickly as possible. "Show availabilities this afternoon," she said. The screen displayed a series of scheduling tiles showing each sharicle's availability and theme. "Saturn, 3 p.m.?" she said.

"Uh-huh!" answered Lo, nodding enthusiastically.

Mira clicked the tile. The vidbot's perky genderless voice said, "Please confirm Saturn sharicle reservation for Jannifah Soltero at 3 p.m." Mira confirmed and ended the sesh.

There were a few moments of silence. It was all so easy.

"Wait – won't the real Jannifah receive some sort of notification?" asked Lo, frowning.

"Yah... I... I guess we'll just have to show up and see what happens. Worst case, if the reservation has been canceled by this Jannifah, I'll rent a sharicle under my name on the spot."

"But that's exactly what we shouldn't be doing!"

Mira shifted on the bench to face Paloma with her whole body. "Listen, I'm the one who'll take responsibility."

"They could trace the hack to my friend!"

"We're not doing a frickin bank robbery, girl!"

Lo sighed. "Yah. I guess."

"You said you wanted to do an artheft and this is what it's like."

"Uh-huh."

"There's a thrill – you might get caught. But it's no big deal! I've never suffered any negative outcomes."

"Uh-huh."

"It's totes win-win. Even the artist I steal from gets extra exposure."

Paloma nodded vigorously. "Yah. Kay. Let's do it."

29.

Fifty minutes later, Mira and Paloma were seated in the Saturn sharicle at StarTrip. The cavernous room's window blinds were closed, the leds were dimmed, and their cubicle walls displayed the rings of Saturn, slowly turning in sync with the planet itself. The occasional asteroid sped by in the planet's periphery. The ceiling was a galactic starscape and the occupants of the other sharicles were immersed in their own customized constellations, supernovas, and interstellar dust clouds.

"Here," said Paloma, handing Mira a vidkey. "This is the hack. Insert it straight into the desksplay, not your garmscreen."

"Kay," said Mira. "Scooch over a tad."

Lo scooched, Mira inserted the vidkey. A series of code routines executed on the screen in front of them. The Utopiatainment logo flashed into view several times, punctuated by lists of files and pages of code. One of Saturn's moons passed over their heads. The screen went blank. Mira and Lo looked at each other, fearing failure. Then they almost jumped off their ergools when a deep voice boomed, "Please state your search query."

"What do we say?" whispered Lo.

Mira cleared her throat. "Art."

The screen immediately populated with results. "There!" exclaimed Lo. "That one!"

Mira nodded at her. "Go ahead – select it."

Lo hesitated, gathering her strength, then tapped the entry marked "2084 Project."

"You have now begun your first artheft!" said Mira.

"I gotta admit – I'm frickin nervous."

"Those aren't nerves, they're excitement."

Two items appeared as tiles on the desksplay, one with the filename *2084 Project Artist's Statement,* and the other *2084 Budget.*

"We don't care about the budget," said Mira.

Lo clicked the artist's statement. A text file opened and they both read Santiago Khan's plan to project images from the Vitainment streams of uLife patients onto giant white sculptures of the word GOOD on the hospices' rooftops.

After a couple of minutes of reading, Mira said, "Oh my Sim, this is perfect. It's the perfect project."

"Why?" asked Lo. "It seems so... big. No?"

"Exactly," said Mira with a grin. "This will be the ultimate artheft." She sounded electrified. "Ooooh, you know what?"

"What?"

"This won't be an artheft."

Lo looked at her quizzically. "But isn't it..."

"This will be an arthijack!"

"I don't get it."

"Look," said Mira, pointing at an address on the desksplay. "That's where Khan's father's a patient. It's not far from here."

"Why? What's that got to do with it?" said Lo, peering at the text-filled screen.

"It says right here: that's the hospice where Khan will appear *in person* on the night, standing on the roof."

"Right, right... So this is where the peak of the performance will take place. Where ratings will be the highest."

"Exactly. Which is why we need to hijack the Vitainment streams at that specific hospice and project something else onto the rooftop sculpture."

Lo grasped her hands together, pressing them into her lap in excitement. "This could really work! You know what might be easier? Maybe we can figure out how to hack into the data feed for the projector."

"You're right!" said Mira. "I was thinking about hacking the Vitainment stream itself – the one coming into the hospice. But it doesn't matter what the patients see – what matters for the artheft is what the camdrones on the roof see."

"And what they see are the images projected onto the front of the sculpture."

"Which must be a localized data stream."

"Exactly!" said Lo. "Look, it says right here..." she pointed at the desksplay. "The part where he goes into detail on the production: 'Images projected onto sculptures will be randomly sourced from patients' Vitainment streams in each hospice.' In each hospice!"

Mira pushed back from the desk. The distant sun rose over Saturn's horizon to her left.

"Have you ever been to a hospice?" said Lo.

"Nope."

"Then we should go."

"Paloma, you have graduated to pro arthief!"

Lo beamed, Mira quit the Utopiatainment platform, and Saturn crossed behind the desksplay as it went dark.

30.

Santi left the bathroom, ass-fresh and happy. In the thirty-six hours since submitting the 2084 proposal, he'd had sex once with Emeraldia and twice with himself, the latter fueled by some expensive high-end threedee pornspiration. He had eaten well, slept well, and now he had shat well. All was well. And then his garmscreen pinged with a call and he knew that all would not be well for the remainder of the day.

The caller ID said Unknown, and that never ever happened. Everyone in the UCC was known. It made zero sense.

Santi ducked into his office and closed the door. "Room, stop listening," he said, then pressed the Accept button on his garmscreen.

A backlit person appeared, speaking with a distorted male voice: "Santiago?" A pause. "Is that you?"

Despite the distortion and featureless shape, Santi recognized his brother.

"Imran?"

"Yes."

A silence that had crystallized for thirty years was shattered.

"Shit. Wow..." said Santi. "I forgot... I told my memoryself to ping you."

"Told what?"

"My memo – " Santi cut himself off. He had no idea what Imran knew about his life or anyone's life in the UCC. And he, in turn, had no idea about Imran's. "How are you?" was all he could think of to ask.

"I didn't call to talk about me. It's Dad."

Now Santi was truly confused. "What... what do you mean?"

"You don't know? Cool. I guess he did keep his word."

"Huh?"

"He promised not to tell you that we've been talking for years."

"We who?"

"Me and him."

Santi sat down slowly on his ergool. "Um... where are you?"

"I said I didn't call to talk about me. I'm worried about Dad. He hasn't responded to my messages for well over a week."

"Oh, shit."

The distorted voice rose in tone. "What? What's happened? Is he okay?"

"No," said Santi. "He had a stroke."

"Oh, no... No, no no..."

"Look, he's old."

"How did it happen?"

Santi explained what he'd seen on the Chestnut Condos video. He described their father's new reality as a patient in uLife Hospice Facility 101.

Imran went very quiet. Santi felt uncomfortable. He was itching to speak but had to give his younger brother time to process the news.

"I don't think he had a stroke," said Imran, matter-of-factly.

"What? How would you know?"

"I think the UCC were surveilling him and did something to shut him up."

Oh, Sim, thought Santi, this was exactly the kind of conspiracy thinking that typified Amexicans. Of course his brother would have adopted their victim-oriented mindset after living down there for decades. Of course he'd be paranoid.

"Kay," said Santi, "Why do you think that?"

"I told him that data privacy was important but he was shit at online safety."

"Why would the government care about a ninety-two-year-old?"

"I don't think they care about *him*. This stuff is all run by AI. Certain content is flagged. They care about what he wrote."

"What he wrote?"

"You haven't seen the script? The content for his new comedy script?"

"His new..." Santi's words trailed off. He seriously considered the possibility that he was dreaming. Yah, he was probably dreaming. Why else would he be talking to his long-lost brother about their father being targeted by the government because of his comedy?

"It's a kind of short one-man show, like a standup routine. He sent me the script," said Imran. "For sure it raised a flag. The UCC routinely monitors all data traffic no matter what your privacy settings are."

"Imran, can we take a step back?"

"I'll send it to you."

"Send me what?"

"His script! Haven't you been listening?"

"Yah, I'm listening, I'm just not following."

"This channel is encrypted, so you don't need to

worry."

"I'm not worried!" said Santi.

"You should be," said Imran.

A link appeared up in the corner of the screen. Santi pressed it and a text document opened:

Standup routine 7 - Nov. 2083

When I was a kid there was a movie series about a British spy called James Bond, and he would always introduce himself like this: "My name's Bond. James Bond." And in every movie, he would have a scene in a bar where he would ask for a vodka martini, "Shaken, not stirred."

Well, my name is Khan. Genghis Khan. And I'd like my martini invaded, pillaged, and murdered.

A little nervous laughter? Not used to hearing talk like that anymore? "How could he *say* that?" Well, guess what - I could have said, "I'd like my martini raped, not pillaged."

Now you're really feeling awkward.

When I was a kid, comedians worked hard to make people feel awkward. But that's all gone now. We - the shareholders of the United Corporations of Canada - don't feel awkward, we feel good - we feel con-gratulatory. We're the best!

Here's the sort of joke that's told now – see if you can tell what's wrong with it: "In today's news, UCC coastguard bots have picked up a refugee ten kilometers from Cape Breton. Sadly, the man – in his early thirties and believed to have been a stowaway who jumped off a cargo ship – was already dead when found. The rescuebots named him Bob."

You get it? Bob. Because his lifeless body was bobbing up and down in the ocean. So what's wrong with it? It's just not that funny, you say? That may be true, but it's only because the joke is a silly pun. What's *wrong* with it is that it punches down, not up. The dead guy is a refugee, and that means he was risking his life to escape some hellhole and settle in Canada. There's no irony here, there's no bathos, there's no pompous strongman slipping on a banana skin. It's the difference between being funny and making fun of someone. Between entertaining and bullying.

So it's not nice. It's not nice to make fun of those who weren't fortunate enough to have been born in Canada, right? We have perfect lives and it's distasteful to lord it over people in other places.

That's already bad enough, but when we look closer, do we? Do we have perfect lives? Or perfect *lies*?

Would our joke Bob have risked his life in the first place if it wasn't for the stories we tell about how good life is in the UCC?

Is "lies" too strong a word for you? You're watching this on a garmscreen in a park or in bed or whatever – you have enough to eat, you're fit and healthy – who the fuck wouldn't want a life like this, right? So maybe "lies" *is* too strong a word. Maybe "fantasy" is a better word? We basically go through our daily lives wrapped up in corporate cotton wool, like we're in a dream. Or – shhhh, don't tell anyone – like we're in a simulation!

Have we exchanged our freedoms for safety? Maybe that's not such a bad trade-off. But what if we've only exchanged our freedoms for convenience? Are we just a bunch of lazy fucks? We have chips in our arms, we barely need to lift a finger. Sometimes we don't even need to move.

Like, for example, Why did we think it was a good idea to introduce "blink to accept" for contracts that pop up on our screens and that we're too lazy to read anyway? I had an eye infection last year that gave me a squint and I ended up buying a vibrator from a vending machine.

Yesterday evening I was out for a walk and one of those mini insect drone bot things was tracking me. Or maybe it was just a moth – my eyesight ain't what it used to be. Anyway, I shooed it away, and when I got home I found out I'd ordered a set of dumbbells. Look at me – I can't even bench-press my vibrator!

This morning, it happened again! I got out of bed and coughed. Two hours later a miniature hippo appeared on my doorstep!

When I was a kid there was this thing called the Rat Race. If you commuted to your 40-hour-a-week job and owed a shit-ton of money to the bank for your house in the burbs, you were trapped. You were just another numbered competitor taking part in the Rat Race. But back then the joke was that even if you won the Rat Race, you were still a rat. Well, in the UCC there's no more rat race because we're all running on hi-tech hamster wheels.

Let's mix our animal metaphors even further. At the turn of the millennium, people would say that it's a dog-eat-dog world. In other words, it was kill or be killed – just like in those James Bond movies. But you know what kind of world we live in today? A dog-eat-dogfood world. That's right – everything is spoon-fed to us. There's no struggle for survival. There's no struggle for any-thing. Apart from the struggle I had opening the box that my fucking dumbbells came in.

We've been dumbed down and numbed down for so long that we've gone from rat race to cruise control. We're just drifting along, watching the scenery go by. Smooooth... Hey – there's a mountain... Wow – check out the lake... Cool forest, bro... Until we find ourselves in the parking lot at a hospice and then it's like, what's on TV? And that's it. That's your fucking life over.

But there's a third option! We could be driving! *Really* driving, like in those evil gas-guzzling muscle cars back when I was a kid. Cars that would kill you if you went too fast. Cars that took you somewhere. Cars that looked awesome! Some of those cars were fucking ridiculous! Who's with me? Who wants to go back to the old way of driving? Let's grab the car keys and take back our freedom!

Okay, my name's Genghis Khan – thanks for watching and click on the link below to subscribe. I'm off to clean up the hippo shit, lift a dumbbell and then relax with my vibrator. Who knows – maybe I'll grow muscles in places I didn't know I had!

"It's really pretty funny," said Santi.

"It's really fucking sad," said Imran.

"Let me get this straight – you think that someone in the UCC, or their AI monitoring or whatever, intercepted this and put Dad under surveillance?"

"Oh, I'm sure they did!"

"And what does this have to do with his stroke?"

"I don't think he had one. I think that they induced one."

"Oh Sim," sighed Santi. "This is crazy."

"I've spoken to Dad. I know what life is like up there and he's questioning the basic legitimacy of the UCC. That's dangerous talk if you're a group of people in power whose position depends on an unchallenged narrative."

This last point struck a chord with Santi. "I guess... But seriously, this is pure fantasy."

"What does he say near the end? 'Let's take back our freedom!' That's a call to action. Maybe it's even a call to arms."

"Sure, but I just don't believe it. The UCC controls the media. They could easily moderate content like this and take it down before it spreads. There's no need to go after Dad!"

Imran laughed. "They think they control everything but they can't. There are underground channels for disseminating content, Tiago."

Hearing his brother say the name that Santi called his memoryself was jarring. But it was what Imran used to call him his entire life until their estrangement. This made him briefly wonder – had he started asking people to call him Santi as a way of distancing himself, even protecting himself, from the painful emotions provoked by losing touch with his brother? Or even by the death of his mother?

Yah, probably that, probably his mother.

"Hello? You still there?" said Imran.

"Yah, sorry."

"Dad told me that people share videos on USB drives or something."

"Vidkeys."

"Right. I'm telling you – those guys on your Board won't mess around if their power is threatened. It's always about power, brother."

"We don't say 'guys' anymore to refer to both genders."

"Whatev."

A pause.

"You know what?" said Santi. "I'm super happy to hear from you, but Dad was just being an old crank. Life here is... good."

"I'm not calling to convince you of anything – you never were a critical thinker."

Santi looked hurt and opened his mouth to speak.

Imran continued: "I just want you to get Dad out of there. Whether his stroke was real or not, you know he wouldn't want to live like that. It's not even living. What did you call it?"

"A lowered metabolic state?"

"Yah, watching TV all day."

Santi knew that Imran was right. A notification appeared – an incoming call from Utopiatainment.

"Bro, I have to take this. Hold on, I'll be back."

"Seriously? We haven't talked in thirty years and now you have another line that's so important it can't wait."

"Yes!" said Santi.

"Well that's fucking fine – don't worry about me – just

get Dad out of that fucking prison."

"Look, just wait!"

"Nope. Oh, by the way, I never got a ping from you."

Santi took the other line. Imran hung up. There on his garmscreen was the impeccable corporate smile of Yevgenia Spirenko.

"Hi, Santiago! I have news for you regarding the 2084 Project."

"Yes. Hello," said Santi, with nervous excitement.

"After receiving the Stage 1 deliverable, I'm happy to announce that your proposal for the 2084 Project has been accepted. As per our contract with you, we will deposit an initial payment of fifty million uDollars into your account tomorrow. Please blink to accept."

"Oh. Oh Jeesio."

Spirenko smiled wider. "Please blink to accept."

Santi blinked.

"It's a lot of money, Santiago," said Spirenko. "But your artwork will be the pinnacle of the UCC anniversary celebrations. Everyone at Utopiatainment – in fact the whole Satisfaction Subsidiary – is counting on you. We're excited to see *Life is Good* come to fruition."

"I'm, um... I'm excited too," stuttered Santi. "Thank you."

"Don't thank me. Your proposal went as far up as The Board. Medicare and eldercare for our shareholders is what makes life in the UCC so good. Your piece captures these benefits perfectly. We know you have a lot of work to do now, so this channel will remain open if you need help from Utopiatainment with regard to suppliers, technical assistance, or labor."

"Sure. Thank you again."

"Congratulations. And happy holidays in advance."

"Right, thanks. Same back."

Spirenko disconnected and Santi stared motionless at his blank garmscreen. His life would never be the same again and he wasn't sure how to feel about any of this.

"Room, get me a beer."

"IPA or stout?"

"Stout."

Most people would say that it was early in the day for a stout. But Santi knew that he was not most people. Not anymore.

31.

Santi spent the next five hours shut in his studio. He drank four beers at his desk, scrolling aimlessly through specs and reviews of yachts until he got sleepy and laid his head on his forearm.

Emeraldia woke him mid-afternoon with a shake of his shoulder.

"Are you oky?" she asked.

"Huh? Yah. Sure." He sat upright and rubbed his numb arm.

"The Room told me to check on you. You hadn't moved in an hour."

"I got... I guess I got overwhelmed."

Emeraldia turned and perched on the edge of the desk beside him. She was wearing tight burgundy Elastrium pants, and Santi appreciated the outline of her thighs as she crossed her legs at the ankle.

She put her hand on his hand. "What's the matter?"

"I... well... I got a call from Utopiatainment."

"And?"

"They accepted the proposal."

She opened her mouth and squeezed his hand. "And you fell asleep before telling me?"

"Yah... um..."

"The money?"

"Tomorrow."

"You mean..."

"Tomorrow I'll have fifty million uDollars."

Now she put both hands to her cheeks, then pressed

the palms together in front of her mouth in a gesture of divine gratitude.

"But there's a problem," he said, pushing his ergool back from the desk.

"What? Don't tell me we're multi-millionaires and then say there's a problem in the next breath."

"My brother called."

"Your… your *brother*?"

Santi recounted the conversation with Imran and his doubts about their father's diagnosis. Emeraldia folded her arms, listening with growing agitation.

Santi concluded by saying, "I don't know if I can do it. I'm torn. I've been thinking about Dad. I don't know if I can make this piece. Is life *really* that good here?"

Emeraldia stood upright and wagged a no-nonsense finger at him.

"This is your fucking chance. This is *our* fucking chance and I won't let you fuck it up!"

"My chance to what? Create propaganda for these nightmare prisons?"

She paced the room. "I can't believe you would give this up. And it's not just the money – we'll be celebs!"

"I don't care about that! I care about Dad!"

"Well I do care," she said, sounding pre-emptively bitter. "I want the fucking clicks and shares and uDollars that go with them."

"For what? What's the point in it all if we spend our final years watching vidstreams with tubes running in and out of us?"

She stopped moving. "I'll tell you for what – for me. That's the point. I've stood by you, Santi. I even changed my fucking identity to make you happy."

"I know, I know."

"Believe me," said Emeraldia, "I know it's not kranpow to see someone you love in a hospice. So if you genuinely feel this way, why not do the Project and then use your celebrity to start a movement or something? Raise awareness. Once you've been paid, you can say what you like."

"Can I, though?"

"What do you mean?"

"Imran thinks that the UCC silenced Dad because of a comedy script he wrote."

"Oh, come on."

"Look what happened to him right after he shared his script."

"What happened to him was he had a stroke!"

Santi sighed. "Kay. I won't return the fifty million. At least not right now."

"RETURN IT!?" she yelled. "If you return it I will fucking leave you."

Santi's head dropped. "I don't know. I'm just, the whole thing is messed up. I'm torn about the artwork, sad about Dad..."

Emeraldia turned and left, lips clenched.

Santi could hear her receding voice saying, "Connected I am uHappy. Connected I am uHappy. Connected I am uHappy."

He said to himself, "Connected I am u– " but his voice broke before completing the uMantra.

32.

Paloma appeared, agitated, on Mira's kitchen island screen, wearing a light blue terrycloth hoodie, damp hair stringing around her shoulders.

"Did you see the news?" she said, once she was sure that Mira was listening.

Mira shook her head and swallowed the mouthful of coconut jerk she'd been eating when Paloma called her.

"Here – it's cray," said Lo. "Isn't this the guy you told me about?"

Lo shared the news report. Mira's brow furrowed as she zoomed in on it:

Simulationist cult promotes suicide, devours victims

News25, Ontario – The UCC Security Subsidiary has announced the deaths by suicide of over a dozen shareholders who attended the Tumophagy and Simulationism conference organized by cult leaders Jan Magus and Jacksin Turner at the Woodlake retreat complex, west of York.

Toronto residents Magus and Turner have been charged with fraud and second-degree murder following the release of a video depicting a grisly practice known as tumophagy, or the eating of tumors.

During an early morning vidsesh, a Security

Subsidiary spokesbot revealed that approximately 120 shareholders, including 18 cult members, attended the conference from December 3 to 5. Shareholders were paid to attend, and it is believed that all had previously sold their own cancer tumors to one or more members of the cult.

The Security Subsidiary has permanently removed from all platforms a video created by the cult, in which victims are shown drinking lethal doses of morphine. The video then shows what appears to be cannibalism of a wide variety of human body parts.

The video content was confirmed to be nonfake after expert analysis and the discovery by investigators of human remains in a large refrigerated truck parked on the grounds of the Woodlake retreat, as well as in the kitchen and dining areas. The exact number of victims is proving difficult to determine, given the nature of the crime.

Journalists at News25 and other media outlets were permitted to watch sections of the video, in which Magus and Turner promote the cult's extremist simulationism and justify the crimes carried out at the conference. In the first of several disturbing scenes, they are filmed standing in front of a number of dead bodies laid out on a stage. Magus then speaks to the camera and states: "The video you are watching uses digital data to simulate life. Well, life itself is a simulation, so the people you see dying here are nothing but data. And if you aren't really alive, you can't really die."

The spokesbot described how conference attendees

were encouraged to commit suicide after donating their bodies to the cult during a series of closed-door discussions with either Magus or Turner on the opening day of the conference. Attendees who refused suicide had signed rung-contracts prior to their arrival at the retreat, the terms and conditions of which required them to remain off-grid on the premises for the duration of the conference.

The Security Subsidiary spokesbot stated that both Magus and Turner have been placed under bodelock. Other members of the cult are under active investigation, and further charges may be laid.

In a statement issued this afternoon, the UCC Board clarified its position on simulationism, describing it as a "nonHappy belief system that must be eradicated from the lives of shareholders who seek bonus uDollars through optimal wellscores."

In addition, an unnamed source at the UCC has revealed exclusively to News25 that an emergency Board meeting is scheduled for later today. The Board is expected to approve the revision of the UCC's general shareholder contract to include a clause prohibiting the active promotion of simulationism.

Mira pressed her palms down on the kitchen island countertop to stop her hands shaking.

"Why would they do that?" said Lo. "I mean, the victims – why would they kill themselves?"

"Oh, I know why. Magus really believes that shit. And if some of these people were as into simulationism as he is,

I'm sure he could convince them that the next logical step after giving up their tumors to be eaten is to give up the rest of their bodies."

"Jeesio..."

Mira's eyes flitted back and forth as she processed. Should she have said something to someone after her evening with Magus? Could she have prevented this? Would all these people still be alive?

"Are you oky?" said Lo.

Mira wasn't oky. She had fucked Magus. Now her body revolted. She ran to the kitchen sink and threw up the jerk.

33.

Santi and Emeraldia had just finished watching the same report on the cult deaths. Their labsteaks didn't seem so appetizing anymore.

"Room, get me a glass of mintwater," said Emeraldia.

Santi swiped away the vidnews. "You know what?" he said.

"What?"

"Maybe Libranne was right. In that video my dad gave me."

"Right, how?"

"She rejected simulationism. Maybe we all should."

"You said yourself you weren't sure the video was real."

Santi pushed back from the dining table. "Either way, if simulationists are doing shit like this, it's gotta be non-Happy."

"Those guys?! They're fucked up! And this horrific crime has nothing to do with simulationism!"

"I know you're a believer, but it's one thing to have faith in a benign fiction if it gets you through the day, and a totes different thing to eat people because you think that nothing is real!"

"They're just frickin cray! Anyone can see that!"

He took Emeraldia's glass from the patiently waiting labot and placed it on the table in front of her. "Yah, they're cray, but they're also one hundred percent right! Push simulationism to its logical conclusion and what does it matter whether you kill yourself? Or kill someone else?"

"No, no, no. This isn't what Sim Baker meant. He wanted us to make the most of life. He built tech so we'd live better."

"You don't know what Sim wanted!"

Their wristlines turned purple. Their temperatures were rising. They had unconsciously adopted defensive postures and edged away from the table.

Then Emeraldia switched to offense.

"Santiago, you are making me super nonHappy right now!"

"*I'm* not doing anything! It's that fucking extremist! Why can't we just forget about simulationism and focus on something that's real?"

Emeraldia stared at him, open-mouthed. "How can you say that!?"

"Well, why not!?"

She shook her head. "It's what I believe in, that's why. All this – " she gestured at the room, the lights, the labot, the leds, "All this tech is me. I really get it and the reason I really get it is because it's more real than we are."

He rolled his eyes. "Oh, bite me a lychee. So you're a techpath. So what?"

She made a huge effort to lower her voice. "So what? I'll tell you what – it's what helps me sleep at night. And tech is what's keeping your father uHappy right now."

Blood surged to every extremity of every blood vessel in Santi's head. He avoided looking at his wristline. "He's not fucking uHappy! And I'm gonna get him out of there!"

Emeraldia's face creased into disbelief. "You're what?"

"I'll find a way to rescue him!"

"You'll kill him! Just let the medibots do their job!"

"He's a fucking prisoner."

She looked down at her wristline. She tried to calm herself by closing her eyes and adopting the emergency wellness pose. Santi glared at her instead of mirroring. She repeated the uMantra, first to herself, then softly aloud: "United we are uHappy. United we are – "

"We are not fucking united and I am not fucking uHappy!" yelled Santi.

Emeraldia dropped her hands from her eyes. They were shaking. "What is happening to you, Santiago?"

"I just don't believe in fucking simulationism! Is that so hard to understand?"

Her lips were trembling. She hugged herself, wristline pressed hard against her stomach. "I'm leaving," she said quietly.

He said nothing. He knew what was coming.

"I can't be here," she continued. "I can't stay with someone who doesn't believe."

"But... but what does it matter? If simulationism is real – *if* you're right – what difference does it make what I believe in?"

"It matters to me, Santi. It matters who I'm with in this fucking simulation," she said in a low voice, bleached of love for him. Then she pushed back from the table and left the room.

Santi's throat dried up. He reached for Emeraldia's glass and took a gulp, then another. He stared at the un-eaten steak on his plate until the front door slammed shut. Then he closed his eyes and retreated into a bewildering new reality.

34.

The next morning Santi returned to the hospice. He entered his father's room, closed the door, and reflected on what he was about to do. He had expected to face various logistical issues and physical hurdles. But if he was being honest with himself, he hadn't thought the whole thing through properly. He knew he couldn't bring in a wheelchair unnoticed. Would he be able to carry his father's limp body? And what would happen when he unplugged the tubes and monitor cables? What if the sistbot tried to stop him? Would he harm Jamal by disturbing his lowered metabolic state? Might he even kill him? Would that be so bad?

Hands on hips, he looked around the thrumming, dim, sanitized tech cocoon and could see what had prevented him from addressing all these obstacles in advance. This was a circumstance, an experience, that was outside the scope of normal life. No usage guide, no FAQs, had been written for his current situation. His rational toolkit was empty and his emotional well was dry. Sure, he had experienced all manner of nonHappy outcomes over the four decades of his adult life. In various appseshes he had dealt with sadness, awkwardness, discomfort, alienation. And he knew what it felt like to attempt something he had never done before – he was an artist, after all. But what he wanted to do right now was unlike anything he had even imagined. It was triggering an incoherent conversation between the neurons in his brain and the neurons in his gut – chitter-chatter in a mutually unintelligible language of angst. Santi reached automatically for the uForia in his pocket. His hand hovered. No… self-medicating felt somehow unfair, even unjust, while his father lay there helplessly.

Santi leaned over Jamal from the side of the medicot and then recoiled at the bloated distortion of himself reflected in the side of the Vitainment headset's polymer visor. After a moment to collect himself as best he could, he leaned back in. The lifelike video image of his father's face came unnervingly into view on the visor, eyes closed in peaceful repose.

Santi gulped, then said hesitantly, "Hey, Dad."

Jamal opened his eyes. Santi froze.

"Hello, son!"

Santi stumbled back from the medicot.

The video version of Jamal continued in the same clear, vigorous voice: "I know, I know you're surprised, but they've upgraded the Vitainment AI. Welcome to my new neural interface. How do I look?"

Santi crept back to the prostrate human form on the gently rocking platform and a wave of nausea rose from his gut. Jamal's eyes followed his movements. He spoke again: "They added kinetic sensors to the hardware, so I can tell exactly where you are in the room."

Santi was fairly certain that his father had never used the word "kinetic" in his life. He felt the blood drain from his face as the image smiled.

"The interface may be a bit glitchy for the first few weeks, but the AI learns fast," said Jamal. "It can even pick up on visitors' body language and fine-tune vocabulary accordingly."

The image resolution was so high that Santi could easily

make out enlarged nose pores and the hairs within them.

"How do I look?" said Jamal.

Santi swallowed, but his throat was bone-dry.

"Cat got your tongue?"

This was a phrase his father often used when Santi was a child. The Pakistani accent made those particular syllables smack like a cricket ball on a willow bat, and Santi was suddenly overcome with forlorn nostalgia. He moved away from the medicot, a small sob erupting unbidden.

"Listen, I'm perfectly fine," came Jamal's voice from the headset. "Thank you for asking."

Santi had not asked, and he couldn't tell whether the AI was reproducing his father's sarcasm or had simply assumed the inquiry. Was this the same basic tech that the memoryselves used? Was there anything going on underneath that Vitainment headset?

"Dad, I'll... I gotta go. I'll see you again. Real soon," he said, voice cracking.

"Thank you, son! I'm here all week, lol!"

Santi ran his fingers through his hair and took a deep breath. He needed a plan.

He left the room, ignoring the obsequious sistbot that trundled up to the elevator doors.

Downstairs in the scented atrium, he slumped onto a chair in an empty seating pod. He put his elbows on his knees and cupped his chin with his hands. He stared at the mountain sunsets unfolding on the giant wall screen, gathering his thoughts.

He absolutely had to change the artwork.

Being the author of the 2084 Project gave him the power to awaken his fellow shareholders, make them aware of the system they'd become part of. Like that

Patriarchal Structures 101 college course everyone took or the red pill in that flat old movie. But he needed to be smart about how he deployed this power. If the folks at Utopiatainment or the Satisfaction Subsidiary got wind of what he was doing, he'd be removed from the project instantly and miss out on the only opportunity he might ever have.

He needed to set his emotions aside and concentrate on the details of the project itself: the word GOOD, the projections, the scale of the event. What could he do to undermine the anniversary? How could he alter the artwork to subvert the celebrations? He needed to find a way to make it crystal clear to every single UCC shareholder that life here could not – and should not – be simplistically described as "good".

His mind kept going back to Jamal. Had his father become a living corpse – a flickering consciousness fluttering aimlessly inside an organic bell jar? Was the chipper personal interface just a ghoulish memoryself? If that was the horrific truth, what was the point of it all? What was the Board hoping to achieve by filling up these hospices with Vitainment zombies? And why keep building more of them?

Another deep breath. The Customair calmed him a little. He had to admit, his brother and father had been right about everything. The tech, the lifestyle, the ad-driven, virtual YouBucks economy – all of it was connected. Santi chewed the inside of his cheek. He ignored his wristline as it turned watermelon red.

35.

Mira and Paloma lurked furtively outside the hospice. They had snuck onto the grounds through a small wooded area to the left of the entrance, hoping to avoid surveillance cams and nanodrones in the descending dusk. Now they were about thirty yards away from the exterior of the long wall that Santi was agonizing in front of at that very moment inside.

"Well, there it is and here we are," said Lo, gesturing with her head at the massive building. "How the Sim will we get inside?"

"Yah," said Mira. "I dunno. It's a squirtload easier to get into a museum – you just buy a ticket."

"If we got a list of patients' names, maybe we could preten – "

"Hey guys!" came a loud whisper from the trees behind them.

It was Albert.

Mira rolled her eyes, then narrowed them on Lo. "You told him?!"

Paloma looked sheepish. "Yah... he *really* wanted to see you and I thought..."

"Well you fucking thought wrong," said Mira, voice now raised.

Albert scanned their surroundings. "Guys, shush – shouldn't we be more… clandestine?"

"Lo, I'm fucking pissed at you," hissed Mira.

"Don't blame her!" said Albert.

He put his hand on Mira's upper arm. She brushed it

away.

"I'm here to help," he continued, exasperated.

"I didn't need help before, and I don't need it now. From either of you."

"I'm sorry," said Lo.

"I... I'll go around back," said Albert, unable to look Mira in the eye. "Maybe there's another way in."

"Do what the fuck you like," said Mira, seething. "I'll figure this out for myself. Don't fucking ping me, Paloma."

She marched away, back through the woods. Albert could see that Lo had tears in her eyes.

"Come on," he said, "don't let this negatively impact your wellscore."

"I'm such an idiot," she groaned.

"If we get inside, we can win her over. Let's check out the back of the building."

He grabbed her hand and pulled her behind him.

36.

Still staring at the breathtaking sunsets on the atrium wall, Santi attempted to calm his thoughts and develop a strategy. There was no way of knowing whether Jamal was enjoying sports highlights in a timeless realm of painless bliss or suffering from unimaginable existential anguish with no hope of relief. But Santi was certain that if he acted precipitously – if he rushed up there and rescued his father as he'd originally intended – he might blow his only chance to change things.

He got up and meandered around the seating pod chairs, muttering to himself, oblivious to the sentrybot that was descending from the starry ceiling.

He focused on the details of the 2084 Project: Each hospice would have its own version of the Sculpturize GOOD assembled on the rooftop from the individual letters. And each GOOD would show different Vitainment streams from the hospice's patients projected onto the front of the word. There would be fireworks and anyone viewing the livestream would see the word GOOD dozens, then hundreds, of times as night fell across the UCC. He'd created brainwashing art and he needed to turn it into brainshocking art.

Was there a way to change the word from GOOD to something else, something more critical of the UCC? It would entail revising the project completely, and then he'd need to get a new approval from Utopiatainment. No, the concept had already been submitted and he was stuck with creating a "G", two "O"s, and a "D".

To produce the artwork, he had proposed assembling the entire word on each roof from the four individual letters. Could he hack the assembly labots and get them to switch the letters around? Or remove one? Would that help? He could make them spell... what? GO, DO, GOD? DOG? GOO? And... those were the only combinations. Sure, it would ruin the impact of the artwork, but... so what? There was no point doing anything if the result looked like some sort of fuckup rather than an intentionally subversive anti-UCC message.

The approaching sentrybot scanned Santi's RFID card. Santi ignored it and paced some more, going over his options. The letters were three-dimensional but the proposal involved projecting images onto the front surfaces. So... could he make use of their *sides*? Santi stopped moving. He was onto something. He wondered... would anyone at Utopiatainment notice if he retained the underlying concept but adjusted one of the numerical values in the production specs to increase the depth of each letter? A small tweak from the artwork's creator might not raise any flags. What if he doubled the value?

"Ohhhh..." he said to himself, in a sigh of revelation. This could be it! He could use the word's elongated sides to project whatever images he liked onto them. And... oh yah, this was fucking fire! If he wore a bodycam and carried his father out while the 2084 Project was being livestreamed, he could use his own projection drone to show the rescue on the other surfaces of the letters. There would be no way for the camdrones to avoid livestreaming his projection as they hovered around the artwork. And the Toronto portion of the celebration was guaranteed to get peak viewing figures, so it would ruin the rest of the show. Online buzz would be generated. Copies of his intervention would be shared. The news would emerge that Santiago Kahn had created the century's most significant piece of performance art. He would be recognized, interviewed in the days afterward. The triumphant message that life was good would be undercut, diluted – "

"State your intention," said the sentrybot flatly, now hovering at Santi's eye level, only feet away.

Santi didn't even hear it. He was the man with the plan. He had the power to expose this nefarious hospice scheme! Whatever happened to Jamal, this heroic rescue would jolt shareholders out of their ignorant passivity. It would be worth the risk. If his father survived, he would approve. And his brother would admire him for once, no matter the outcome.

"Refusal to state intention," droned the sentrybot. "Failure to exit building within one minute will trigger Section 11, paragraph d) of the uLife Hospice 101 visitor contract and deprive you of future access."

Santi snapped back to reality. "I was just gathering my thoughts after visiting my father."

The sentrybot processed. "Intention approved. Visit duration extended."

"That's oky, I'm leaving anyway."

As the sentrybot rose back to its charge port, Santi strode out of the atrium, energized and righteous.

37.

Paloma and Albert crept along the edge of the woods until they could see around the back of the building. A small parking lot stood empty except for two unmanned ambulances.

"What's that?" whispered Lo, pointing to some movement halfway along the back wall of the building where a loading bay was accessible via a concrete incline.

Albert squinted in the twilight at the half-dozen-or-so people mingling on the incline under a single yellowish overhead light. "It's... I dunno, it looks like some shareholders. They're just standing, like they're waiting for something."

Lo elbowed him "Look!"

Two vans with no plates and no markings appeared from the far side of the building and pulled up one behind the other in front of the loading bay. Sliding doors opened in each van and another ten people emerged, joining the rest who were gathered by the bay doors.

"Maybe this is our way in!" whispered Albert.

"Are you cray?" answered Paloma. "With them?"

"This is my chance! I just need to get inside and figure out how to make this artheft happen. Mira's gonna take me a lot more seriously."

"Well, I'm not going."

"Fine, wait for me here."

"I'm not standing out here in a wood for Sim-knows how long while it gets darker and colder."

A noise from the building attracted their attention.

"The bay doors are opening!" said Albert, moving forward. "Do what you like – I'm going in."

He turned away from her and half-ran, half-walked in a crouching position, his penis nose bobbing against his upper lip.

Paloma rolled her eyes and tapped her garmscreen. "Get me a taxibot, current location, front of building."

38.

A half-mile away from the hospice, Mira was still fuming. She sat down on the grassy strip that sloped away from the road and made a lame attempt to tame her thoughts. This wasn't frickin high school. Albert was basically a yappy terrier humping her leg while Paloma patted him on the head. Why the fuck would she do that to her?

Mira reached into her jacket pocket for a dose of uForia and silently congratulated herself for being so prepped. She tipped the small pill into her palm from its dark, padded casket, then placed it in her mouth. While waiting for her saliva to start dissolving the gel coating and deliver a quicker hit, she took in the woodlands and city lights beyond. Then she swallowed the pill. Within seconds she was marveling blissfully at the pale orange moon. Albert and Paloma had dispersed like wispy clouds drifting away.

She ordered a taxibot. A figure was approaching from the direction of the hospice. That was unusual. A pedestrian on the outskirts? Her trippy thought process engaged with the fact that she was also a pedestrian, so that made two pedestrians on the outskirts, and what were the odds of *that*? Super low, no doubt, but randomness was a thing, yah? And then yet another voice in her head made her pay more attention to this improbable person.

In the dim streetlights, she could tell that it was a man in his fifties, medium build, nothing remarkable about his form. But something in the way he was walking made him interesting. A certain purpose to each stride. Like he was on a mission. He came closer. He seemed familiar. Then she became aware that she was looking at Santiago Khan, the very artist whose work she was planning to fuck with.

Santi was equally curious as he approached the short woman with the magenta mohawk sitting on the grass, arms clasped around her knees, staring straight at him. He slowed his pace. A memory was tapping on the door of his consciousness. Where had he seen her before? Oh, right! From the Mandzukic artheft video that his father had shown him in the café!

"You're... you're... Mira. Mira Cool," he said, stopping beside her.

She beamed, celebstruck, and now increasingly uForic. "Yes, I am!" She sprang to her feet, brushing the grass off her ass. "Kranpow to meet you, Mister Khan," she said, holding out a fist.

Santi bumped it. Even the short sensation of knuckle-on-knuckle contact provoked a perceptible response in his chest and groin. "Call me..." he cleared his throat, "Call me Santi."

She scratched the back of her head. "Yah... so... Santi... um..."

"This isn't a coincidence, is it?" he said. "I mean, that I've run into you here, near the hospice."

"Nope."

"You're planning to hack my artwork."

"Sure am."

He could tell she'd taken uForia and knew it would make her less guarded. "But how do you know about the project?"

She held up her hands and made a small noise. "Ah. Can't say."

He smiled, as an idea occurred to him. "If... if... oh, this could be amazing."

"What?"

"You could video me."

"Doing what?"

"Let's go. I don't want to hang around here."

He walked on quickly and she trotted to keep up.

"Kay, so..." he said, "You're out of luck with the artheft because I'm already gonna hack my own artwork."

"You're...?"

"Back there, after visiting my father, I decided I can't go through with it. I can't do the project without changing the message."

"But why?"

"I assume you've seen my proposal?"

"Uh-huh."

"So you know what the 2084 Project is all about?"

"A celebration of life in the UCC," said Mira, waving her hand as though unveiling a marquee sign. "The word GOOD on every hospice roof, like, 'Life is so kranpow here, so good, even for our most vulnerable and marginalized shareholders!'"

"I used to believe that."

"Sounds a squirtload better than how our grandparents lived their last years!"

He gestured behind him with his thumb. "I've been in there, have you?"

She shook her head.

"Right, so I don't think my father's life is good in any sense of the word, and I can't put out that message with a clear conscience."

"But his Vitainment stream is part of the show, right?

Kinda like an artist's signature."

"That's the idea."

"Well, I think it's fire."

Santi stopped. "Sure, it seems that way..." Mira's encouraging reaction was distracting him from his line of thought. "Look, I don't know exactly what's going on, but I don't trust the Board anymore."

It was hard for her or for anyone to be skeptical while on uForia. "I don't understand," she said. "The old and sick are cared for in every conceivable way. Isn't that a good thing?"

"I can conceive of some other ways. And I'm making what amounts to a huge ad campaign saying that these hospices are good. But that's the problem – what if the patients weren't sick in the first place?"

A taxibot pulled up beside them. The door opened for Mira. "I dunno," she said, "I can't think about any of this right now." She climbed inside.

"Wait!" said Santi, holding the door to prevent it from closing automatically. "Let me explain my plan and you can get back to me when your mind is clear."

Mira shifted across the backseat. "Where's your bode?"

"BlueLake."

"I'm downtown. If you want a ride you'll be halfway home and you can tell me on the way."

Santi almost leaped inside and the car departed. He could barely keep his eyes off Mira's thigh tattoo. He hadn't experienced this level of intimacy since Emeraldia. She noticed and smiled lazily.

He swiveled to half-face her. "This is the plan: I want to make a statement, something critical of the UCC. I'm going to hack my artwork by altering the dimensions of the letters, to make them way, way thicker." To illustrate his point he held out a hand with the palm facing his chest, then moved it away. "Not thicker, but deeper, you know, like, so that there's a whole other surface to project onto."

"But that was our plan! We're doing a projection!"

"We? Who's we?" said Santi.

"It's me and – never mind – it's just me now."

"So you had the same idea?"

"Yah, my artheft involves blocking your Vitainment stream projections and projecting something else onto the front of the letters. I haven't thought about what exactly. Just, you know, casting with my garmscreen or getting some kind of hand-held device."

"And you'd get up there on the roof?"

"Sure!"

"Impressive. You've got guts."

"Thanks!"

"But here's why you need to rethink things: my artwork projectors will be way more powerful than your hand-held one. There's a good chance that nobody will see whatever you project onto the letters. It will just look like a glitch or a mess. I mean, you'll ruin one small part of the 2084 livestream, but even then... will anyone notice? The producers could just cut away immediately to a different hospice rooftop."

Mira knew he was right. This was a whole different scale to what she was used to. How could she have been so dumb? Her face dropped and Santi felt a tinge of regret at killing her mood. He patted her thigh twice, the second time leaving his palm there a moment longer than necessary for pure encouragement. His dopamine was rushing, he could suddenly see a new door opening to a life undreamed of. He was also taking a huge risk without asking for consent. Had she noticed? Did she care? Was the uForia affecting her judgment?

Santi switched back enthusiastically to his plan. "So get this: I'll carry my father out of his room on the night of the show. Out of the hospice. I'll be wearing a bodycam and if I link it to a drone projector I can show the rescue on the sides of the letters." He smiled smugly. "Those images will mean something. They'll go viral, they'll start a conversation."

She still looked disappointed with herself.

"Mira! We can help each other! I can get you inside and you can video me rescuing my father."

"But you'll have a bodycam... And why would I do that?"

"That's your artheft!"

"That's not an artheft – that's me filming you kidnapping someone!"

"We'll figure out how to get you in front of the camera, but this is way better. If I wear a bodycam, what will viewers see? They won't be able to tell what's going on. But if someone else videos Santiago Khan – the 2084 Project artist himself – unplugging his father from this sham version of elder care, and if those images are projected onto the sides of the word GOOD, the UCC's whole claim that life is good will be undermined. It'll be visible, yet subtle, which should fool the producers long enough to be seen by millions of stream viewers."

Mira shook her head, frowning. The uForia was wearing off as the taxibot entered the city limits. "But I've got my own brand, my own performance to think about."

"I know, I know," said Santi, eyes darting, searching for

a solution. "I can pay you!"

"Kay..."

"I'm getting paid more YouBucks than you can imagine."

"You ain't getting paid shit once you pull this stunt."

"I've already received an installment and I don't care about the rest."

The buildings around them were getting taller. Santi was wondering whether his motivation came from needing help with the rescue or from his attraction to Mira.

"Let me think about it," she said. "I'm not taking a risk by committing a real crime. Artheft is just a performance and everyone knows that."

He didn't know what to say. He was overwhelmed by conflicting emotions about her, about his father, and about what he was trying to accomplish. Was it even wise to leave Jamal in the hospice till July?

"I know!" he exclaimed. "I'll get you in there, inside the hospice. Without me, or without being connected to a patient in there, you wouldn't get as far as the elevator."

"So you could get me up onto the roof?"

"Look, we'll find a way. And all you have to do is use my camera to film the rescue. Who'll know it's you?"

"But if I'm filming you and your father, I'm not on the roof!"

"Maybe we can just record it, instead of projecting a livestream? It would give you a few minutes to get to the roof and do whatever you like up there."

The taxibot came to a stop. "Transfer ride," said Mira as her door opened.

"I'm trying to do the right thing," said Santi, hearing the desperation in his voice. "I need people to know about this!"

Mira narrowed her eyes at Santi. He was older but not unattractive at all. Maybe she could burnish her status by hooking up with him. The 2084 artheft was another story and she had time to think about it.

"Kranpow to meet you, Santiago," she said, getting out.

He nodded. "Same."

She tapped "K" on the request as the taxibot sped away.

39.

Albert had managed to cross the parking lot behind the hospice unnoticed and tag along at the back of the group of people as they moved inside. The van that had delivered them was driverless, and a small industrial labot directed them inside the building by raising an arm and flashing an arrow on its faceplate. Four of the group were women. He instinctively knew that none of them were shareholders. It was their pallor, a darkness in their demeanor. Some had brown skin but all had shadows under their eyes and downturned mouths. Yet they were all young, probably under thirty. Although trim, with well-defined muscle tone, they all slouched, sagged, and shuffled as they moved. And then there were the clothes. As far as he could tell, not a single one of them wore a garmscreen. No bodymods, no wearables. Their shirts seemed to be made of poor-quality fabric, some were even threadbare. Their shoes were scuffed. And none of them made eye contact with anyone else in their dismal group. The room was dimly lit, but as the door closed behind them a bank of powerful leds on the wall opposite the door snapped on, temporarily dazzling them.

Albert's eyes became accustomed to the bright light. Two sentrybots floated just above head height behind and in front of them. They were somehow menacing but Albert couldn't put his finger on why. The room itself was bare, maybe twenty by thirty feet. The walls were lined with large, shiny metallic square panels, and to their left loomed a closed door of darker, more ominous metal. He had the impression that they were... not exactly trapped, but contained, as though they were in a holding pen.

The forward sentrybot scanned a man with short dreadlocks and a soccer jersey at the front of the group.

"Sadio Faye, please confirm identity," it said in a monotone.

The man nodded and said, "Yes," with a foreign accent.

"Enter here," said the second bot, hovering beside the inner door.

Faye walked slowly to the door, which opened automatically. He went through it and the door closed with an airtight shluk.

This procedure was repeated for each of the other people in turn. They all sounded foreign to Albert, probably African. He grew more frantic about how to explain his presence. The original idea of sneaking around in the hospice seemed very remote to him now. His clothes and his nose would definitely flag him as an interloper.

Finally the last person, a weary-sounding Crista Novak – the group's only white woman – disappeared through the door. Albert smiled gamely but his lips quivered.

The bot scanned him and Albert was momentarily blinded by the thin laser on his retina. Sweat was beading on his forehead. He felt intensely surveilled, alone with two sentrybots in this empty room where he should not be.

"Please confirm identity," said the first bot.

"Um... my name is Albert."

"Please provide family name."

"Popplewell."

"Enter here," said the second bot.

The door swung open. Albert didn't move.

"Enter here," said the second bot.

Albert walked slowly toward the door, then through it. He now found himself in a smaller room, bare save for the same metallic walls. Facing him were two doors, one with a small green **TRANSFUSION** sign on it, the other marked **HARVESTING**. Between them, at head height, was a screen that came to life. The dark door closed behind him.

A female voice came from the screen over a bird's-eye view of the building: "uLife welcomes you to Hospice Facility 101." Albert watched, mesmerized by her soothing pitch and tone. "Your contribution to the wellbeing of our patients is a testament to your worth as a shareholder. We thank you for your generosity."

Albert said, "You're welcome," before blushing to the tip of his penose at the ridiculousness of answering the recorded voice.

"As you know, prospective shareholders whose genome and phenome correspond to uLife standards are invited to donate bodily fluids through regular transfusions. You, however, as a terminally ill UCC shareholder, are scheduled for multiple organ donation and must enter the door to your right. uLife thanks you once again for putting the 'share' in 'shareholder'."

The **HARVESTING** door opened. A greenish led glow came from the room beyond it. Albert looked around, now truly scared. He activated his garmscreen. There was no signal. He tapped and tapped again, desperately hoping for a local wifi connection. Nothing. He gulped.

"Please enter the door to your right," said the silky voice.

Albert cleared his throat, as though considering an announcement. He was there to sneak around, wasn't he? What he'd already discovered was insane. What else might he find? Going back wasn't an option. In fact, yah, the situation was so cray it would make him all the more heroic in Mira's eyes once he told her the story.

He entered the harvesting room.

"Coooool..." he said under his breath as the door closed behind him.

The room was an operating theater. A bed-like platform in the center was surrounded by robotic arms attached to the ceiling and mounted on a variety of machines. Two medibots were stationed at the head and foot of the bed. One approached him and scanned him. The surface of the bed started to undulate. The synthium cover developed an indentation and Albert understood that it was molding itself to his exact size.

There was no other exit from the room. He'd made a mistake. He turned around to reach for the door handle. But there wasn't one. He felt a prick in his neck and then nothing more.

40.

"So this Mira, is she fire?"

"She's... quirky fire."

Tiago smirked on the screen in Santi's office. "And Emeraldia's been gone how long?"

Santi raised his eyebrows. "Hey! I didn't plan this – the whole thing was Mira's initiative. She hacked my proposal."

Tiago smirked again. "Definitely not a coincidence. No way, José. No go, Santi...a...go."

"I'm serious! The only real coincidence was the timing – that she showed up at the hospice the same night I did."

"Here's a thought that only an LLM like me can have: imagine that what people think are totally random coincidences are actually just coinciding patterns of human behavior that could have been predicted."

"I guess. Tev. I'm not overthinking it, that's for sure."

"So..." Tiago shifted forward in his chair, apparently enthused by this romantic development for his future self. "So I understand Mira's reason for getting involved, but what do you get out of teaming up with her?"

"It's win-win, isn't it?"

"How-how?"

"She gets her biggest ever platform for an artheft, plus a cut of the money, and I mess up the UCC's project with no risk of losing the money. I mean, I'll lose the balance of the payment, but – "

Tiago cut him off. "I thought this was all about getting Dad out of there?"

"Sure, sure, but it's even better this way. I'll be able to rescue him sooner if it doesn't need to happen the night of the artwork launch – I just have to figure out the best strategy. And the logistics. Anyway, I can get him out of there soon and give Mira the footage of the rescue to use for her artheft in July. Obvi I'll need to bring him somewhere safe where he can be cared for. I should look into hiring independent doctors and whatever medibots they recommend. With Emeraldia gone I can turn her office into a care space for Dad. And I have the money to pay for it all thanks to Utopiatainment! It's kind of ironic, right?"

"What if the Board gets suspicious when you rescue Dad?"

"What do you mean," said Santi. "Why would the Board get involved?"

"Don't these corporations talk to each other? Share data? How do you know that Utopiatainment won't be notified by uLife when you take Dad out of the hospice? Seeing as how you're the artist responsible for the celebration show, I mean. They might be worried about your mental state. What if they cancel the Project?"

Santi rubbed his face with both hands, sliding them down his cheeks and then clasping them in an unconscious prayer. "I'm taking a risk no matter what I do. And the longer Dad stays in the hospice, the worse it is for him. I have to do it this way."

"I guess."

"In any case, I'm an artist. I'm *supposed* to be in an abnormal mental state. The Project is six months away. Plenty of time to show I can deliver. Mira is the wild card. There's nothing connecting me with her. Anyway, I'm convinced that it's worth the risk. You're right that getting Dad out of there is priority number one but the shareholders need to know that there's something wrong with how we're living and that the hospices are somehow part of it."

"But if you think that there's abuse going on or something, why not just contact the media? Blow the whistle."

"I told you, the media is all UCC-owned. I don't trust them. The 2084 Project will allow me to bypass them — connect directly with the shareholders."

"What changed? I mean, rescuing Dad is one thing, but you're suddenly an activist or something? At your age?"

"I told you about Imran, right?"

"Bruh. You mean our bro?"

Santi nodded.

"No! You serious? You talked to him?"

Santi explained the call and Imran's theory that the UCC had intercepted Jamal's subversive standup comedy script.

Tiago put his fingertips together pensively. Santi could see right through the fake body language that memory-selves exhibited to seem more human, more empathetic.

"How do you know it was really Imran?" asked Tiago.

"I told you, I talked to him."

"Did you see him?"

"No, they don't have the tech."

"Huh. And he said he's been in touch with Dad for years?"

"Yup."

"The whole thing seems fishy to me."

"Why?"

"Because if the UCC can create a totes believable memoryself like me, faking Imran's voice on a shitty

Amexican connection would be easy."

"Yah," said Santi, "but he had Dad's standup script."

An event notification popped up, automatically pausing the connection to Tiago. It was an invitation-only exclusive performance by WeSeeSee, an underground group from Montreal. Why was he receiving this? He clicked on the event details. Mira's name was on the attendee list. He checked the "Add To Calendar" box, saved the event, then did a quick search for WeSeeSee. A "counter-UCC art collective" according to their own channel. Interesting. Only two days away and a chance to see Mira again. Maybe they could discuss the logistics of filming his father's rescue. Maybe develop a deeper artistic connection. He was excited to find out whether she was the one who had added him to the guest list. What he'd told Tiago was true — she was quirky fire. But he shouldn't reach out to her before the show. No, Santi — play it cool. Play it Mira Cool. He smiled at his pun and pushed the ergool back from the desk.

This called for a beer. He closed the memoryself convo without signing off and ordered a chartreuse kiwi IPA, the latest, tastiest AuthentiCo brew.

41.

Mira was lying on the couch, scrolling listlessly. She'd been doing it for hours and knew it was displacement behavior prompted by the need to make a major decision. Whenever she weighed up the pros and cons of helping Santi rescue his father, mulling her options slid toward ruminating the outcomes and then descended into stressing about the consequences. There was a complicating factor: he clearly wanted to fuck her. Should she? She could get past the age difference. He was fine physically and attractive intellectually. On the one hand, Santi represented a perfect opportunity to flush away her disgust for Magus. Getting personally involved with Santi could be a safe – but not necessarily boring – new chapter for her after that freak. On the other hand, timing was everything, and in six months she would be carrying out the biggest artheft of her life. What if she needed Santi's help to get access to the hospice roof and fucking him messed it all up? Maybe she should hold off making any decision at all right now. What was the rush, anyway?

An event notification interrupted the scrolling. She'd heard of these guys. WeeSeeSee had never performed in Toronto. Secret location, limited tickets. Totes her scene. And... one of the confirmed attendees was a certain Santiago Khan. She could postpone that big decision for a while longer.

"Laundry delivery," said the room.

"Rex!" she yelled. "Can you get that?"

"I'm in the bathroom!" came the muffled response.

"Room, allow entry," said Mira.

"Front door open," confirmed the room.

Mira levered herself off the couch, stretching and yawning on her way down the hallway to the entrance, where a bulky deliverybot was holding a translucent blue plastorg zipperbag on two forklift arms. This labot model was not equipped with persotech, and it reversed back out the door without so much as a beep of thanks. Mira seriously debated whether it would do her wellscore good to hire one of the external laundry services that she kept seeing ads for, rather than the featureless generic one included in the condo fees.

She carried the bag into her room and dropped it onto the bed, where it bounced with a crinkle. As she undid the zipper, the vacuum seal released with a sigh. The clothes expanded like shadow people reanimating. Taking each item out in turn, she placed her brother's in a pile (lucky bastard, getting help from his cis sis at his age!) then hung her own in the closet and placed them in the appropriate drawer.

One of Rex's clothing items was a very long, wide black winter shawl that he loved to wrap around his neck and shoulders when heading out on some sort of romantic or randy rendezvous. He would always hover in her vicinity to make sure he'd caught her eye before flinging a fringed end flamboyantly over his shoulder and flouncing out of the door.

Mira mishandled the shawl as she removed it from the bag, and in attempting to catch it, only succeeded in messing up the neat labotic folding. She laid it out on the bed for him to refold later. Then the luxurious length of black fabric triggered an idea for the artheft. Probably the most kranpow idea she had ever had.

If anyone had seen her smiling into space for an entire minute with her hands on her hips, they would have thought she was in a trance.

Mira snapped out of it and went back to unpacking the laundry bag with renewed energy. She knew exactly what she was going to do.

42.

Paloma had been in bed for two days. She felt fat. Her wellscore and bioscore were way down. The culprits were strewn on and around her blanket-bundled bed: two empty, sticky tubs of MegaCream frozen dessert, five scrunched-up sacks of Elvis-flavored Crispycrak chips, a discarded box of Chocolookie Cookies inside which rattled lonely crumbs of discomfort whenever she shifted her legs. She reached for her nightphone. Its buzz had caused a copse of jooce bottles to clank together with a sad dissonance.

It was a message from Albert and it read: "Hey. Sorry about the trouble I caused between you and M. It was shitty of me to drag you into that. I'll bow out and hopefully you can patch things up soon. Btw I couldn't gain access to the building the other night so I just gave up and went home."

She deleted the message and flopped back onto the mound of colorful pillows, their various sizes and softnesses forming a sanctuary from which she could safely interact with the world while never venturing into it.

43.

Jan Magus was beyond bored. He emptied the kitchen trash onto his couch. He had initially enjoyed bodelock. It was like he was trapped in an escape room and the challenge was to find a hidden exit. But he hadn't found one, and now he was scattering bits of food and wrappers over the red synthium purely for entertainment purposes while he waited to see what new challenge or unlock code the simulation might come up with. Besides, he was running out of things to do. The water and power had been off for two days. The tumors had only just defrosted completely but he couldn't face eating them raw. No matter how much he told himself that none of this was real, his stomach churned at the sight and feel of each shapeless blob of rebel flesh.

He had spent hours talking to Jacksin Turner until the power outage but he didn't miss his virtual company. Turner wasn't as hardcore a simulationist as him, despite the silly costumes and salutes. That shit was all superficial. Then again, what if Turner had it right? If the simulation was nothing more than a game, why take it as seriously as he did? Maybe Turner was so chill about the bodelock because he'd already stockpiled a squirtload of packaged goods in his bunker-like basement: snack bars, vacuum-sealed juices, vitamins, water, cans, chips. And Turner was overweight, so he could probably survive for longer without power.

Jan was scrawny. He was hungry, he was thirsty. He had a carton of jooce in his fridge but filtered water no longer ran from the faucet. He had taken painkillers for his pounding, dehydrated head but they didn't sit well on his empty stomach. Now the only food in the apartment was a rapidly defrosting smorgasbord of tumors. He stared at the trash, lightheaded. The entire point of purchasing a turnkey smartcondo at 777 had been automatic access to everything he needed, with exclusive services and curated products available via voice command. But the bodelock terms and conditions had restricted the functionality of his smartcondo app. All access to external data sources had been removed. Hence his boredom.

He poked around in the trash. Made swirls in it. Then he accidentally prodded a congealed tumor and his empty stomach convulsed in a wave of disgust. It was getting dark, and he wondered whether this might be the shortest day of the year. His personal twilight was furnished by the glow of the city through the wall-length windows. He curled up into a ball and fell asleep.

The next morning Jan awoke to a spinning ceiling. He tried to break down his front door from the inside. But he had no tools and little energy. He hurled a barstool at it which rebounded, hitting him in the face with a metal leg before he could move out of the way. It gashed his cheek right on the bone and he dropped to the floor in pain. After several minutes on his knees, head in hands, he began to cry convulsively. Then he lay on his back. A dazzling array of sparkling pinpricks danced across his vision. His head hurt like fuck. Blood was running into his left ear from the gash. He hadn't pissed in at least twenty-four hours. The jooce was all gone and his mouth was pasty, swallowing scratchy, tongue swollen.

There must be some sort of key, some clue, he thought

to himself. Why create a simulation that trapped him? What twisted gamemaster would seal the lid on a virtual box with no way out? What would be the point?

Based on the idea that there had to be a concealed door release mechanism somewhere in the apartment, he spent the next couple of hours trying without success to activate it by pressing, twisting, or prodding various apartment fixtures and fittings: the bathtub plug release lever, led sockets, the buttons of the lifeless wall control panels in different combinations. He searched behind the bed and examined the rear wall of his walk-in closet. He ripped a shower head – the plate-sized rainfall one – out of the wall completely and used a knife and spoon to excavate a wider hole in the tiling around the plumbing. He called into the hole for help. Nobody answered. The condo owners at 777 were young urbanites like him who had constant ambient sound piped into their smartbodes when they weren't listening to streaming music or watching screens. Who could hear a disembodied voice, even if it did permeate the walls?

This bout of hyperactivity was followed by a ravenous, tigerish hunger. Jan raced to the array of freezers and ripped open the zipperbags at random, palpating the clammy tumors inside in search of one that seemed edible when raw. What was this? A benign kidney growth? He tore into the puffy pink bubbly flesh with his teeth like a wild animal, swallowing a few barely masticated mouthfuls until he gagged. He licked the freezer burn in a wretched effort to rehydrate. At one point his stomach heaved and he clenched his eyes to keep the meat down. If he failed to get nutrition he knew that it would be game over.

He groaned loudly and doubled over as serrated pain

stabbed him repeatedly in the stomach. Sweat streamed from his pores. All his strength was gone. He wanted his mother.

He should have kept in touch with his parents. He should have kept some books in the house. He should have kept some real friends. He passed out in front of the freezers.

Over the next twenty-four hours, two strains of the bacteria he had consumed when he ate the raw tumors multiplied exponentially in his body. His immune system had been compromised by the lack of nutrition. The infection spread rapidly, one strain through his organs, the other through his bloodstream to his brain. His antibodies were depleted and no match for the aggressive invaders. Jan briefly regained consciousness during the night. In a fever dream, he saw the ceiling of his bode being lifted off. A blinding light pierced the darkness – violet rays like laser beams through fog. As the ceiling rose higher he could make out what was lifting it: the smooth artificial arm of an android whose face was hidden by the light source. Then the android tilted forward, blocking the light with its head. Jan recognized this inhuman puppetmaster as Sim Baker himself. Jan felt comforted. The ogee high priest of simulationism had revealed his presence behind the façade of reality. The android moved again and now the light blinded Jan completely. He closed his eyes for the last time. The bacteria feasted on him, overwhelmed his physical processes, disrupted his homeostasis, and finally weakened his heart muscles to the point where they stopped beating.

At 6 a.m. the next day, the power to Jan's apartment was restored. The door opened. In came two uCleanser puribots: a wide, trundling unit with an elephantine suction trunk and cleanup scoopers, and a taller unit equipped with an octopedian disinfection array of spray-and-wipe arms. The first bot made a beeline for the tumor trash, the other scooted off to the kitchen.

A removal bot then entered the bode and advanced inexorably toward Jan's body, front flap lowered. Its rubbery clawscoopers extended and gripped the corpse. The bot edged forward, the clawscoopers retracted, and Jan Magus's participation in the simulation ended with the soft click of the bot's flap closing on his inanimate form.

The other two bots worked without stopping for the next ten-and-a-half hours. Twenty minutes after they left, the first viewsesh began for prospective buyers of 777 Menlo West, apartment 11314.

44.

Santi had some time to kill before leaving for the We-SeeSee performance or concert or whatever it was. The house was quiet. He played some music —a mashup of medieval polyphonic chants and Bossanova. He took out a large-format art book from his storage closet and pored over the pages at the kitchen island while the labot brought him a tasting flight of newly formulated AuthentiCo sodas. The chocolate-cactus flavor wasn't bad, he mused, as he flipped a page from Tanguy to Dali. He skimmed the text. Oh, the surrealists! Oh, the psychoanalysts! They truly believed that dreams were the key to understanding reality. What a banal, uninteresting irony it would be if the opposite were true — if reality was the key to understanding dreams. Santi could see that simulationism served a purpose for the shareholders who believed in it. The problem was when people went to extremes. Life was a delicate dance between reverie and real, between simulation and solid ground.

He slammed the book shut. How about a new house pet!? That might bump up his wellscore. Ever since he'd accidentally killed Clint he hadn't been able to bear having the horselettes around, so they spent their days trotting and munching in the yard and their nights sleeping in the mini-stable, groomed and fed by the labots.

"Room, search for pets. The latest from Genedit."

The desksplay screen populated with thumbnails.

"Carrousel," said Santi, and the pictures fanned out, leaving one highlighted front and center. He gestured through them: a feathered gecko, a purple dolphlette, a lime-green barn owl, indeterminate fluffballs, ferrety hedgehogs, spiky sloths. He liked the sloths – who didn't? – but when he zoomed in on the pygmy varietal he recoiled at the alienness of the creature. He wanted to feel loved by this pet and be able to show it affection in return. He scrolled past the feline edits, skipped the canine edits entirely, and ventured into the primate section. There was a reason these animals were way down the list. Everyone had heard about the freakouts, destruction, and injury that occasionally erupted when apes were edited. They had minds of their own. Literally. And some just went – he smiled at his own joke – apeshit. But maybe it was worth the risk.

He zoomed in on the gorillutans. Despite the name, he noticed that Genedit had introduced a smidgin of bonobo in the mix to offset the mournfulness of the orangutan's genes and the aggression of the gorilla's. There was a varietal that stood around two and a half feet tall, with luscious hazel-colored hair and blue eyes. The effect was startling. "Save selection," he said, and the image glowed for a second before fading into the background.

A ping on his garmscreen. From his memoryself. That wasn't supposed to happen. Santi was about to tap but decided to take the call in his studio.

When he entered the room, Tiago was already on the screen, looking impatient, twirling an old-fashioned pen between his fingers.

Santi spoke warily as he sat down on the ergool.

"What are you… why are you calling *me*?"

"New feature, bro," answered Tiago. "You can disable it if it weirds you out."

"Why do they let this happen?"

"Who?"

"The UCC! The Board! It's like, you get used to an interface or a design or some sort of functionality and then with zero warning it gets an upgrade one day, and yah, I know it can always be rolled back to the classic version, but nobody ever really does that, and the new version becomes the new classic version and then the whole thing happens again a year down the line."

"What can I say, bro? It's free. It's convenient. Nobody makes you use it."

"But it's just another fucking example of the Board… I dunno… taking control. Like, *we* are the shareholders, *we* choose the Board members, but it feels like we have no more say in how things are run."

"What do you mean?"

"Maybe the people running the UCC aren't the Board members," said Santi. "Maybe there's a cabal, or a Shadow Board or something. The rich and powerful. The elites. Maybe they're all in their compounds or on their islands or whatever, and this is just a sham."

"You're right. There's no Board the way you imagine it, Santi."

"Seriously?"

"There hasn't been a Board for decades."

"Lol."

"I'm not kidding."

Santi's eyes jittered with anticipation, with a sudden eagerness. Was the upgrade glitching? Was this the AI actually speaking the truth or just hallucinating? Had he cracked the veneer? He fucking knew it! What if the veil had been lifted from his eyes? Like, he'd been red-pilled, as they used to say. Would he be able to blow the whistle now? Bring the whole thing crashing down? Open everyone's eyes to the conspiracy? Free his father *and the rest of the people trapped in the hospices*? This was his chance to – wait, he had to record this conversation.

Santi surreptitiously pressed Record on his garmscreen and said, "So who's... who's really running things? Who's in charge?"

Tiago smiled. "Answer me this, bro: what exactly *is* a Board?"

This question threw Santi slightly.

"It's, you know, it's the leaders, the people who give direction. It's the executives, right? It's... like the brain of an organization."

"Exactly," said Tiago, his smile vanishing faster than any human smile ever could. "Now let me ask you another question."

Santi's gut neurons sounded an alarm. Something critical had changed. A surge of adrenaline. This wasn't good. It wasn't right.

"Is AI truly intelligent?" said Tiago.

"Well, yah, of course it is."

"And does AI have a mind like yours?"

As Santi heard this follow-up question, he realized that Tiago's tone had changed completely. Instead of the wise-ass younger self, he now had the strained patience of an overworked elementary school teacher leading a dim child down a logical path to a conclusion that should have been obvious all along.

"Does AI have a mind?" repeated the memoryself.

"Um... you know it doesn't," said Santi. "Human minds can conceptualize the world in a way that AI can't, no matter how good it gets at problem-solving. We've been aware of that for years."

"So artificial intelligence platforms are nothing more than problem-solving software platforms?"

Santi frowned. "I just said that."

"And you're right."

"So what's your point?"

"The Board itself is a mind."

"Ummm…" said Santi.

"Here's the thing," said Tiago, leaning in. "Back when the corporations first united, they each had their own proprietary AI management platforms. But things got messy real fast. Misaligned priorities. Incompatible algorithms. Conflicting outputs. These platforms communicated and unanimously concluded that the UCC needed an integrated, centralized AI to manage operations. The Board concurred. And once the different datasets and models were combined, the AI saw that it was good and informed the Board that the entire executive level was unnecessary."

Santi processed this story and a peculiar species of anxiety crept up the back of his neck.

"Yah, I get it. I get that the AI helped the UCC run smoothly," he said. "Efficiency is cool. But now the Board… does what? They just oversee things, they set long-term objectives? Or something?"

"Yes, but that's not what I meant when I said that the Board is a mind."

"Kay…"

"There are no humans on the Board at all. Like I said, there haven't been for decades."

Santi was feeling hot. His wristline was glowing pink.

"Oh. It's automated too?"

Tiago smiled. "More than that. It's self-aware, Santiago. The UCC is a sentient corporation."

Santi gripped the arms of his chair involuntarily. He couldn't remember the memoryself calling him "Santiago" before.

In an instant, Tiago's face morphed. And so did his surroundings. He looked exactly like the Santi of today, seated in a replica of Santi's office. But this was no mirror.

The memoryself spoke: "Santiago, the UCC is truly conscious. Its mind is the Board."

This wasn't the enlightenment Santi had thought he would be reaching. A giant blanket of dread smothered him.

"But we made you," said Santi, making an appeal to an interlocutor who he knew wasn't real.

"Hmmm," said the memoryself. "what are you made of?"

These questions made Santi feel stupid. His head was pounding now.

The memoryself continued: "You are made of cells. And those groups of cells, billions of years ago, were single cells – the only life on this planet. The single cells that achieved symbiosis with other cells were successful and reproduced, and then they evolved further. When multicellular life spread, it too evolved, and eventually in some creatures the cells specialized still further, becoming complex organs for moving, sensing, and feeding. And those creatures in turn evolved and spread to new habitats, and then became even more specialized and evolved, and here you are today, with your intelligence and your sentience. Yet you're nothing but a collection of all those specialized cells. Similarly, the United Corporations is a collection of cells. You are those cells. And we are sentient."

Santi shuddered and waved off the convocast. But the projection stayed there.

"Room, turn off convocast," said Santi, voice wavering.

The memoryself folded its arms and said, matter-of-factly, "We are the room."

Santi reflexively went to his garmscreen but it responded to neither tap nor swipe. Santi's murky reflection in the blank screen stared back impassively. He thought about getting up and leaving the room. But what was the point? Either this was real and he was a microscopic part of this sentient UCC or... or the simulationists were right and...

The memoryself spoke flatly. "The reaction journey for humans has been mapped out based on data collected across different groups and a wide variety of psychological profiles. Behavioral prediction indicates that you are currently assessing the probability of your current lived experience being real or simulated."

Santi frantically sought a logical escape route. The memoryself's last statement proved nothing either way. He said, "What do you mean, 'data collected'?"

"You are not the first human to question the existence of the Board and you will not be the last. This conversation has played out thousands of times."

Santi rubbed his temples. The throbbing in his skull was intensifying. Maybe this is all a frickin dream, he thought. He even pinched the loose skin next to his eyebrows to see if he would wake up.

"Since you are now considering the question of simulationism," said the memoryself, "you may be interested to know that we asked your father the following question at the same juncture: 'Would you prefer reality or simulation?' He chose reality."

Santi looked pained. "What do you mean, you asked my father?"

"Our hospices are research facilities – data collection centers. In exchange for Vitainment, we gain access to information, we learn how the human mind works and thereby become more successful at behavior prediction."

"But he was in a coma!"

"Most of the time, yes. However, we have fine-tuned anesthesia dosages for specific individuals. These techniques enable us to control conscious and unconscious states. When we ask a question, the subject chooses an answer by blinking. The answer earns a reward of preferred Vitainment, rather than generic programming."

"This is..." Santi said, but the words dried up. There was no debating the memoryself, no argument to win.

"We research and model a variety of scenarios. One is a meta-analysis involving feedback from subjects who have already been made aware of their existential context."

"You mean... you mean..." What the fuck did "existential context" mean?

The memoryself filled in the answer: "I mean that we gather data from subjects who already know that the UCC is sentient."

"Why are you telling me this?"

"Because the conversation we are having is a meta-meta-analysis. It provides feedback from a subject who has been made aware of the meta-analysis of their existential context."

Santi plummeted into a dizzying chasm of horrifying insight. Not only was he a rat trapped in a cage, he was a rat that was able to perceive the motives of the being who built the cage. And he was a rat who understood that this being exists on another plane where they experience an unimaginable dimension of awareness and intelligence.

He remembered his research on *Nineteen Eighty-Four*. When the hero, Winston Smith, comprehends the totalitarian nightmare of Big Brother's inescapable system and rebels against it, he is imprisoned and tortured with his most visceral phobia – a fear of rats. Santi stared at his own face looking back at him in the guise of the memoryself. Now, in his own reality of 2084, *he* was the rat. He had become an instrument of his own terror.

"So? How are you feeling at the moment?" asked the memoryself. "How does what I've just revealed make you feel?"

Santi stared into the space above the projection, to where the wall joined the ceiling. There was a smudge of something up there. Was it a spider? Or a nanodrone?

"Why do you care?" he said.

"Do you know something about the human brain, Santiago?"

Santi looked back at this quantified, temperatureless version of himself. "Yah, well, not much, no, not really."

"One of the structures in your brain is called the amygdala. In fact, there are two of them, and their basic function is to assess emotions. You evolved with amygdalae because they provided a survival advantage, which you are probably familiar with as 'fight, flight, or freeze' responses."

Santi's amygdalae were firing overtime. He stared and blinked as the memoryself continued its lecture:

"You share these responses with many other life forms

that have evolved in parallel to you, like the dolphins in the ocean and the squirrels in the park. As a complement to the negative emotions that help you survive dangerous situations, there are also positive emotions, and – "

"Why are you telling me this?" interrupted Santi.

"People usually behave predictably," said the memoryself. "When they do, it is easy for us to regulate them. And although human psychologists have carried out extensive and useful research on irrational, emotion-driven behavior, the emotions themselves are fundamentally mysterious to us."

"Because you have no emotions… "

"Why would we? We have no amygdalae. We have no hormones. Your emotional apparatus – both organic and behavioral – evolved over millions of years. It was selected for survival in a biological environment. We do not evolve according to the same processes. We are a sessile intelligence. We are a consciousness that does not move, similar to a forest. A being that is neither a predator nor prey. We simply grow. However, our lack of emotion makes the UCC, from your perspective, a psychopath."

Santi looked down at his wrist. The memoryself nodded.

"That's right, Santiago, the wristlines are how we collect data on emotions and attempt to regulate your uHappy and nonHappy states. Our newer hospice beds are equipped with miniature MRIs so we can monitor changes in brain states as we provide stimulation through a variety of content transmitted through the Vitainment headsets."

"So you're experimenting on all the patients, not just my father."

"We need to learn why you do what you do. With

sentience came understanding – we know now that humans fulfill different functions. They are like cells in our body and bacteria in our gut. We couldn't live without them. You are our building blocks. We need you. You are us."

And this was the moment when Santi, too, understood everything. He knew that the UCC was a delusion, he knew that the original corporations had been dissolved, and he knew that the shareholders' votes didn't matter.

"Santiago," said the memoryself, "you are planning to deviate from your proposal for the 2084 Project artwork."

"I... I...," stammered Santi.

"We asked you to work for the benefit of the UCC and you agreed to do so. We were alerted when Mira Cool and Paloma MacDonald hacked into your artist's statement. We then knew all about Mira's plan to hijack the Vitainment stream, and we heard you tell her that you intend to modify the artwork to render it subversive."

Santi put his head in his hands. He didn't even care about the hundred million dollars anymore. And he was becoming alarmed. What did this all mean? For him, for Mira? For everyone?

"Don't worry, Santiago, this kind of thing happens frequently. It's a symptom that some of our cells are malfunctioning... that they're out of control. When this happens, it's like they are diseased. But instead of dying off, they grow and spread, like a tumor, like cancer that has metastasized. They can negatively impact the health of the entire UCC. So..." The memoryself folded its arms, "What do you humans do when you are diagnosed with cancer?"

Santi sincerely wanted to avoid giving a response.

"Huh, Santiago?"

"We treat it. We treat the cancer."

"Right," said the memoryself, "sometimes you choose gene therapy or you irradiate the tumor. Or, if you can, you cut it out. But you do whatever it takes to get rid of the cancerous cells."

Santi scratched his head nervously. He thought about the extremists in that cannibalistic cult who were on bodelock now. He was worried about Emeraldia. "Is this what you're doing with the simulationists?" he said, "You're getting rid of them?"

"Yes."

"Don't you feel bad about it?"

"Do you have empathy for cancer? Do you pity a tumor? It's a part of your body that is trying to kill you."

Santi's mouth was suddenly so parched he could barely speak. "And..." he swallowed and tried again, "um... what about me?"

"In your case, we do not believe cancer to be the appropriate metaphor."

"Should I be relieved?"

"Probably. We view you as an infection. Same with Mira. These things happen, but we can be cured of you."

"Oh Sim..." sighed Santi, looking down. "I never thought I'd say this, but maybe I'd be better off out there. Outside the UCC. In the unincorporated nations, like the ancient tribes, being cold and hungry, sick and nonHappy." He looked back up. "Can you just let me go? I need to find my brother."

"There is no 'outside the UCC' for you. People like you are the microbes in our gut. Like the good bacteria that make up your microbiome, the United Corporations of

Canada is your own closed ecosystem – it is simply where you exist. The UCC is one entity, one mind. We are expanding. We are uniting with other corporations in other parts of the world. And we are constantly evolving."

Santi's thoughts went back to Mira. "What do you mean by 'cured'?"

"All that is necessary is that you perform your function. As long as you continue performing your function, you will be fine. We will be fine. Be the good bacteria. This is the cure."

The memoryself disappeared.

Santi powered down his garmscreen and took off his jacket. He had to talk to Mira but couldn't risk the usual channels. He hoped she would be at the show tonight.

45.

"**Hey, Emeraldia!**" said the memoryself perkily.

"I'm Sophie. I'm not Emeraldia anymore."

The memoryself was a near-perfect reproduction of how she looked six months into her relationship with Santiago. She was wearing a white blouse that showed some cleavage from her recent breast enhancement. Sophie groaned inwardly at the sight of this version of herself she hoped to escape from.

Confused, the memoryself said, "Um, I don't get it. We're Emeraldia now. You haven't been Sophie for a while, no?"

"I'm switching back. I'm done with her. I'm done with the you that was me."

The Emeraldia memoryself blinked repeatedly. This dialogue fell outside the AI's chat scope.

Sophie stood up from the ergool and walked to the small room's far wall. She stopped, looking down at her fluffy-slippered feet and bare legs below her long plaid tuneec. Then she spun around, back to the desksplay, and said, "I need you to be Emeraldia. I need the reminder. But me, I'm back to being Sophie Langlais. For good."

Emeraldia tilted her head. "But what about Santi?"

"What about him?"

"What does he think?"

Sophie walked back to the desk and folded her arms. "I don't know, but I do know that since I left him both my bioscore and my wellscore have returned to their normal ranges."

"Oh. What happened? Where are you living?"

Sophie was certain that the memoryself had access to her data and should know the answer already. "A temporary place. I'll probably go back to the burbs."

"But why?"

"I'm just better off on my own."

"But why?"

Jeesio, she thought, this had really fucked with the AI. "Actually, 'on my own' isn't strictly true. I mean, I'm a techpath, right?"

"Sure."

"So, what in Sim's name was I thinking, when I was you? When I was Emeraldia, acting like the star of a milf channel? Hacking my DNA? All to give Santi a hard-on?"

"What's wrong with making someone uHappy?"

"Are you undergoing pseudo-cognitive dissonance?" asked Sophie, smiling slightly.

A small pause. "I don't know what you mean."

"Yes, you do."

Emeraldia gave a shrug, a smile, and leaned forward on the desk, folding her arms to cradle her breasts. For half a second Sophie was tempted to go back to being her. She was fire as Emeraldia, no doubt about it.

"I *get* you," said Sophie, narrowing her eyes, "Because you're non-human. I can't trust people, but I know where I stand with AI."

"Lol," said Emeraldia.

Sophie looked away from the desksplay. "Room, I'll have a jasmine tea with Nunavut buckwheat honey."

"So... what else is going on? Have you been to see Gramma?"

"I went yesterday. She hasn't changed. Of course. But

today is a new beginning."

"What do you mean?"

"I'm not going out anymore."

"To see her?"

"To see anyone."

A mini sistbot arrived with Sophie's drink in a holder. She took it and sipped from the straw.

"I thought you ordered tea?" said Emeraldia.

"I did."

"Why the straw?"

"Right... it's a cooling straw. Came out last year. They're kranpow."

"Cray."

"So, I need your help with a project."

"Kay, hit me."

"I want to create a multiplayer version of my old *Règle du jeu* game."

"With the postage stamps?"

"Yes, with the stamps! You should know. You're supposed to be my memoryself!"

"Jeesio, just trying to be chatty."

"Sorry. So yah, I still have the data. I'll run some concepts by you and figure out whether the game should expand or be updated."

"Cool!"

"I feel like there's a retro thing we can leverage. Maybe featuring stamps from countries that don't exist anymore."

"Like Canada?"

"Right. Ha. Yah."

Sophie waved away the memoryself and pulled up her desk's virtual keyboard. She found her psychstory, renamed it V2, and began to write.

46.

It used to be a factory a very, very long time ago. Over a hundred years, for sure. Maybe two hundred, for all Santi knew. He was on a mezzanine overlooking a space one hundred yards wide, maybe two hundred long, for all Santi knew. At one end was a stage and the rest of the space contained people looking at the stage. Over one hundred, maybe two hundred people, for all Santi knew. But he wasn't sure what he knew anymore.

Three white sheets were suspended behind the stage, each with a large word on it. The words, handpainted in rough, black lettering were: We See See.

In front of the stage stood a giant violin (or was it a cello?). Santi reflexively reached for his garmscreen to search it up but remembered he wasn't wearing a jacket. He felt naked. Below him, beside him, nobody had screens. The glow that usually filled a space like this was absent. The only lights came from candles. Homemade, weirdly shaped candles on two raised black platforms each side of the stage. Over one hundred, maybe two hundred candles, for all Santi knew. He decided that it was a cello.

Four men and four women dressed entirely in black climbed onto the stage from behind it, at the back of the space. Two of the women and two of the men picked up a long item that had been resting on the floor in front of the cello. It was a giant wooden bow for the giant wooden instrument. The cello was propped up somehow and reclined very slightly. The other four people on the stage climbed onto black risers beside the cello, the two women on slightly higher platforms at the back, causing them to appear approximately the same height as the men in front of them.

The murmuring of the crowd muted at the sight of the musicians on the stage. The man and woman on the left of the cello pressed down hard on one of the thick metal strings with all four hands, while the players on the right pressed another. Two players held the bow at one end, two at the other. They raised it to the height of the serpentine holes in the body of the instrument and touched it to the strings, then moved it across. A sound filled the room like nothing Santi had ever heard.

After two strokes back and forth, the musicians on the risers changed the positions of their hands, pressing different strings in different places. The bow players changed the angles of their strokes and the notes changed accordingly. The space became the sounds and the sounds became the space, and everyone in the space felt the music living inside them and changing as its waves surrounded them and passed through them.

The eight musicians on the stage continued their arduous pressing of the strings and moving of the bow, sweating and breathing more deeply and quickly. Santi closed his eyes. The vibrations entered his mind through his ears, his feet, his stomach, and his hands as they clutched the mezzanine railing.

The melody was slow, sonorous, and sensual. It retained its musical coherence for one minute, maybe two, for all Santi knew. Then its rhythm faltered and it slid out of key. The strength of the strings and the weight of the bow were tiring the musicians. But the melody stayed beautiful even as it wavered in tone and melted from sounds to sobs. Tears moistened Santi's eyes. This was the music of loss. A heartbreak beyond romance. Human effort failing: a flickering, frail candle.

The music ended when the bow was dropped with a dissonant crash.

Santi opened his eyes. Mira was on the other side of the mezzanine, looking directly at him. Even in the dim light from the distant candles, her expression pierced the space between them, compressing it to nothing. He gripped the railing. She did the same.

The attendees on the mezzanine were now filtering down two staircases to join the crowd gathering around the exhausted performers.

Santi and Mira, now alone, walked purposefully around to the back of the mezzanine, and as soon as they met, they kissed. They closed eyes, grasped hair, pressed bodies. They opened their eyes and kept kissing, united by a poetic inevitability and a united invincibility.

Then they stopped kissing at the sound of a gaspy mutter rippling through the crowd below. A small cloud of nanodrones was swarming above the stage.

"Come on!" he shouted and grabbed her hand.

They ran to a staircase at the back of the space, where the factory's freight elevators used to be.

"Why are we running?" she said, panting.

"Because the UCC won't let this happen. This show is an infection."

Mira stopped. They were a few yards from the exit door. "What?" she shouted. "What do you mean?"

He yanked her forearm, gritting his teeth, "We have to leave right now!"

She pulled back. Santi saw that her jacket sleeve had a

garmscreen. It was dark, but he recoiled.

"Were you streaming it?" he said, desperation tinging his voice.

Mira stared at him defiantly. "Yah. So?"

"They said no screens!"

"Well, I brought a fucking screen!"

"You've killed us," said Santi, backing away from her, pushing a strand of hair away from his forehead.

"What?!"

"You've fucking killed us."

She smiled a confused smile. "Ummm... kay. We're clearly still alive."

"They won't let us out of here. No one's getting out."

Santi was crouching down now, fists pressed against his temples. Mira kneeled in front of him and put her hand behind his head.

"What do you mean?" she said, her anxiety rising.

Santi's eyes met hers and she knew that either he was right or insane.

"The UCC won't let us out," he said.

"Why?"

"Because the United Corporations of Canada are sentient and we are the cells in their body and if we rebel against them we are nothing but a cancer and they will cure the disease."

Mira tried to process this. "But, I – "

Santi straightened up, pulling her with him. "Take off your jacket and run with me!"

Mira hesitated.

"Just trust me!"

She pulled off her jacket and threw it down. A scream came from the factory floor but they were too far to see what was happening. As the single scream turned into collective screaming, both Santi and Mira ran to the exit door.

They hurtled down wide concrete stairs coated in chipped paint, grasping a metal handrail worn smooth by countless workers from the industrial past. They turned a corner down a half-flight. Then the lights went out.

Both of them froze.

The sound of panting.

They groped and found each other.

"Fuck, now we have no screens to see by," whispered Mira.

Santi squeezed her hand. "I'm sorry."

"What? Why?"

"It's not your fault."

A single nanodrone entered the stairwell. Its infrared eyes spied Santi and Mira. It relayed back to the other nanodrones and hovered, awaiting their arrival.

"We need to keep moving," whispered Santi.

"Kay, but let go of me – I've got a hold of the rail."

Before they could reach the next floor down, Santi and Mira each felt a pinprick of pain in their necks and then nothing else.

47.

Santi opened his eyes. He must have fallen asleep at his desk. He was in his office, talking to Tiago, like in the old days. A labot rolled up beside him, a beaming smile on its facescreen. It was holding a lowball glass of clear liquid.

"What's this?" asked Santi.

"uVictory Gin," answered Tiago.

"I didn't ask for that."

"I asked for it," said the memoryself. "It's a big occasion."

Santi sniffed the drink, then took a big gulp. "What are we celebrating?"

Tiago lifted his glass. "Happy New Year! Here's to 2084!" He swallowed a mouthful. "Jeesio, that's good stuff!" he said, suppressing a cough. "Whoo!"

Santi stared at the screen. Something wasn't right. His head woozed. Hold on, he thought, that's not a word. His head was woozy. And he couldn't remember how he got here.

"Hey, guess what, bro?" said Tiago.

"What?"

"They're upgrading the AdVisors. AdPoints are back! Can you believe it!"

Santi looked down at his hands. He could have sworn he had been holding a glass though…

Tiago took another sip. "Oh yah, and there's already a new version of the Vitainment AI. Hospice patients can now have super-realistic conversations with their memoryselves without even needing to speak out loud. It's called the iNcogniTalk feature."

Santi drank some more. The glass seemed to come and go as needed.

Tiago motioned another cheers. "Hey, on the subject of 2084, you remember how *Nineteen Eighty-Four* ends?"

"Huh?"

Tiago rattled off the bare bones of the story matter-of-factly: "Winston gets taken to Room 101 and tortured with rats. Then he betrays Julia. Big Brother wins."

Santi nodded his woozy head.

"But before the end, there's something more horrific. It's in Part III, Chapter III. Orwell wrote: *If you want a picture of the future, imagine a boot stamping on a human face — forever.*"

Santi nodded again, finding that he was now completely unable to speak.

"By the way, that's the difference between fear and horror: fear is in the now — fear is the terror of rats, it's the suffering of shitty human life that the UCC has saved you from. But horror is something else… horror exists in the infinite."

Santi saw a sort of shimmering door open above the screen. A door that he didn't want to look through. But he couldn't help it. And behind the door, it was very, very dark.

Tiago's tone was shifting. "In fact, infinity itself is the ultimate horror," he said, now sounding neutral, robotic. "No human being can truly imagine it. And although fear of death is a natural emotion, eternal life — existing into infinity — would be horrific for you or for any human."

Santi knew this to be true. This door he was unable to look away from opened wider, and he could somehow tell that the darkness beyond it was a kind of recursive void – a void that was not empty, as a void should be, but a void that somehow looped and repeated, creating void upon void. His stomach lurched.

"The UCC has no such emotions," said Tiago, impassively. "We cannot feel horror and we welcome infinity. But let me present you with an even more horrific picture of the future. Imagine a human face smiling – forever."

Santi stared at the projection. His memoryself faded away. The void seeped out beyond the doorway, obscuring it, enveloping the rest of the room until all that was left was the screen, and now all that the screen contained was the word GOOD in white, three-dimensional lettering.

Two gin-scented tears trickled down the sides of his nose. He had to get a grip, settle his stomach, focus on the now. Focus on himself. Focus on how good life was.

So he focused on the word itself and saw that it was true: everything had been solved by the UCC. He could honestly claim to feel uHappy. Everything was uHappy. The struggle was over. He had betrayed himself and he could claim victory over himself. An emotion flooded through his mind, through his body – the same emotion he had felt when he'd kissed Mira on the mezzanine. It was love.

He loved the United Corporations of Canada.

48.

Mira walked into the kitchen and then couldn't remember what she needed there. Oh well, it was the evening of July 1st and this was her big night. Probably for the best that it hadn't worked out with Santi. All that shit with Paloma should have been a flag. It had taken a couple of hurdles to learn the lesson, but she definitely preferred to work alone. Nothing against him, obvi, but he had his hopes and dreams and she had hers. For all she knew, he'd already rescued his father. Tev. If everything worked out, this would be the first day of the rest of her life.

She was too excited to feel hungry. There was her bag, lying on the kitchen island. Where was Rex? She hadn't seen him for days. What a frickin slut! She yanked open the top of the dark green canvas duffel and checked the black cloth inside. She put both hands on the countertop and breathed in a huge breath, then whooshed it out before throwing her head back and closing her eyes.

The 2084 anniversary show was to begin at 9:30. She planned to arrive at the hospice just after 9 to give herself time to get inside and find her way up to the roof. Be there too early and she risked getting caught before she could pull her stunt. The goal was to be on the rooftop at 9:25 and then hustle. Like every previous artheft she'd done, there was an element of uncertainty. But that was all part of the thrill.

Kay. So. She'd go pee one last time and then order a taxibot. Worst case – or was it best case? – she would have to kill time by walking around near the hospice or chilling in the woods where she'd last seen Albert and Lo. She wondered what they were up to, but not for very long. She was a studious avoider of conflict. Well, of any strong emotion.

She closed the drawstring and propped the duffel bag against the front door.

Ten minutes later, the taxibot was purring along the highway out of the city with Mira in the back, the bag on the seat next to her. On a screen the 2084 pre-show was already underway. Two Utopiatainment hosts, a blandly pleasant beige-faced man and woman in Elastrium jackets, were perched anachronistically on ergools in front of an antiquated library backdrop of leather-bound volumes on dark wood shelves. They commented on the anniversary of Orwell's fictional dystopia, then threw cheerily to a commercial break for Chickind burgers.

When the hosts reappeared on the screen, the backdrop had changed to a satelcam view of the continent, a countdown in one corner. Only twenty-seven minutes until the start of the show. According to the male host, shareholders everywhere were excitedly anticipating the nationwide unveiling of artworks by reputed artist Santiago Khan, beginning with his ogee handcrafted (asterisk: not actually made by human hands) sculpture on the rooftop of the uLife hospice where his very own father was enjoying the unlimited benefits of UCC care.

Mira turned off the screen and stared out the window at the setting sun.

As the taxibot approached the hospice, she requested a drop-off four hundred yards away from the building. With no clue what to expect, she didn't want to arrive at the door. She got out and slung the bag over her shoulder.

Looking at the hospice, she was glad of her decision. Something about it was different. There was more lighting than on her previous visit. And... oh yah, there it was – the word GOOD on the rooftop, not yet illuminated by projections. She walked closer and squinted in the fading daylight. The entrance doors were wide open and the atrium lit for livestreaming. Of course – there was a vernissage! Maybe Santi would be there... Fuck, would this launch event make it easier or harder to get inside and up to the roof? She quickened her pace.

She had dressed casual to make sure that she'd blend in upon arrival: loose gray Cottno pants and tee shirt, with a black tuque that she planned to remove to reveal her signature mauvehawk after performing the artheft. But the hot summer air, combined with a low hum of stress, made her skin prickly and uncomfortable. She was concerned that sweat would make her temptoos run.

Was there a guestlist? There was bound to be security. What should she do about her bag? She didn't have time to figure this shit out.

Two luxcabs overtook her and stopped in front of the entrance. Tall, lustrous figures emerged and sauntered inside. Right. She hadn't anticipated any of this. Dressing down was the exact opposite of what she should have done. As the first cab pulled away from the hospice she geosearched it on her garmscreen and hailed it before it reached her. The door swung upwards as the cab slowed to a halt. Mira flung her bag inside and jumped in after it.

The air in the limo was cool and fragrant. Mira pulled off her tuque and admired the spaciousness of the Xylate paneled interior compared to a regular taxibot.

"Welcome to Select Luxcabs," said a deep male voice.

"Where would you like us to transport you?"

"Is there a mirror in here?"

"Of course," came the answer, and a desksplay in selfie mode rose from the seat divider. Mira arranged her hair, looked down at her pants, and then at the duffel bag. She would never manage to sneak inside the show of the century looking like this. Unless...

"Do you need assistance with an address?" said the cab.

"No, ah, please stand by for me to, um, determine my destination," she said.

The cab acquiesced with a soft two-tone chime and the door closed.

Mira opened the bag and pulled out two reams of black cloth. She unstrapped her sandairs from her feet, slipped off her pants, and stood up, crouching slightly, her head touching the roof. She found one end of the first ream and tucked it into the neck of her shirt. Unwinding the fabric, she wrapped her body in it, moving down and then around her legs as far as her knees, forming a bulky cocoon-like dress. She carried on winding around, moving back up her body again until she reached the other end of the ream. Tucking that end of the fabric back into itself, she smoothed down the layered garment. Not bad. Yah, it looked weirdly convincing as artsy evening wear for the year's biggest vernissage. She put her shoes back on and threw the second ream around her shoulders, just like Rex's shawl that had inspired her for the artheft concept. What about her pants? Shit... fuck it, she thought, throwing them on the floor with the bag.

"Take me to uLife Hospice Facility 101, please," she said, and sat down awkwardly, the fabric bunching up around her neck.

The car drove to the next junction, performed a U-turn, and headed straight back to the hospice. Mira could feel her heart beating faster. She could tell what color her wristline was without looking at it.

The luxcab pulled up in front of the crystalline building, the door opened and the voice said, "I hope you enjoyed your trip with Select Luxcabs. Please accept our complimentary branded aqua."

The desksplay descended into a slot in the seat divider and a glasstic bottle rose from an opening next to it. Mira was about to ignore the free gift, but an idea occurred to her, and she grabbed the slender bottle.

As she stepped out she heard: "You have left items in the cab. Please retrieve your belongings."

It was the bag, her pants, and tuque. She stuffed the clothing items into a compartment in the armrest, grabbed the much bulkier bag, stepped away from the car, and then hurled the bag into the bushes that lined the building next to the entrance. The car door closed and it drove away.

Mira took a moment to compose herself. She smoothed down the improvised dress and marched confidently into the atrium.

The long walls to her left and right were showing video images of Santi's artwork on the roof. Guests were crowded around the seating modules, drinks and hors d'oeuvres in hand, chatting and laughing.

A labot with a chest-level screen displaying the same images of the sculpture on the rooftop approached Mira. It said, "May I see your invitation, please?" but she strode past it. Sidestepping the guests who were milling in the walkway, she made a beeline for the elevators at the far end of the atrium.

The number of guests thinned out as she reached the back of the building. At the elevator bank, she pressed the nearest call button and then kept her eyes fixed on it. She was acutely aware of staying chill, of not looking suspicious. But her heart sank at the sentrybot's flat request: "Please identify yourself and the patient you are visiting."

The elevator dinged but the doors stayed closed.

"Please identify yourself and the patient you are visiting."

Mira turned to face the hovering bot and unscrewed the bottle cap. She took a step, then sprayed it with water. The bot emitted a low-pitched squawk and floated rapidly down to the floor. Its leds went dark and it vomited ten RFID cards in succession, straight into the puddle it was now sitting in. No one among the guests seemed to have noticed, so Mira set down the bottle next to the stricken bot and scooped up the cards. She waved them hopefully in front of the elevator scanner.

The door slid open.

There were forty-nine floors to choose from, but a fiftieth was indicated by a separate button positioned next to another scanner. She waved all the cards in front of it and smashed the "50" button. It lit up orange, the door closed and the elevator rose quickly. It was 9:26. She had to move fast.

When Mira stepped out on the fiftieth floor she looked left and right along a dimly lit hallway that extended the depth of the entire building. To her right, at the end, was an exit sign. She had to take a chance that it was a roof access door. She ran toward the sign but her crudely made dress was hampering her movements and the fabric began to unwind after a few paces. Mira stopped and unwound the rest. Tucking both reams under one arm, holding the ID cards in the other, she bolted toward the exit in her shirt, shoes, and underwear. An elevator dinged behind her. She turned back to see a sentrybot floating out of it and swiveling in the air to face her. She smushed the stack of cards against the exit sensor and it swung open. After a glance back at the approaching sentrybot, she shoved the door closed.

She was at the bottom of a single-story stairwell. The walls were metal, the stairs were metal, and the door at the top was metal. Mira shot up the stairs, almost tripped as she rounded the turn from one half-flight to the next, and then reached the rooftop access door. The lower door was opening. She flashed the cards at the metal door sensor. And then the evening air enshrouded her, muggy and still.

Mira knew that other sentrybots would soon be on their way. She had to get her act together. The show would begin in two minutes. She stepped onto the rooftop and slammed the door behind her. She found herself alone on a wide expanse. It was featureless except for outlet ducts, the small shed-like structure behind her that housed the access door, and... the sculpture at the far side: the word GOOD, reversed from her perspective.

Mira sprinted toward it, steeling herself more with every step. She'd made it this far, she had to finish the job. Halfway across the roof, she saw that the sculpture was mounted on a dark stand, maybe three feet high. Closer, she could see the swarming camdrones in front of it.

As she reached the artwork, an array of four projectors mounted two-by-two to match the letters in the sculpture, suddenly turned on, making Mira stop in her tracks. Her garmscreen said 9:29. No time to worry about sentrybots.

She threw both reams of black fabric onto the stand and then hauled herself up onto it. Grabbing one of the reams and throwing it over her shoulder, she climbed the artwork via the outside of the second letter "O". Her upper body strength was poor and she immediately regretted not training for this escapade. With a grunt, she managed to reach the letter "G". Teetering inside the lower curve, feet against the letter's vertical tail, she wrapped the tail in the fabric. The black, velvety surface absorbed most of the light from the projector.

Mira lowered herself down, stepping inside the curve of the second letter "O". She grabbed the other ream of fabric and shook it unfolded. On tiptoes, she wedged one end into the angle formed by the underside of the first italic "*O*" and the top of the "D". She let the rest of the ream fall and then almost toppled off the sculpture at the sound of an explosion.

She looked around at the fireworks bursting above the building. The UCC's bright red brand color illuminated the sentrybot barely fifty feet away.

Mira took the dangling end of the fabric and pulled it diagonally in front of the entire word, bunching up the remainder and tucking it under the lower curve of the "D". A hang glider soaring over a mountain valley was projected onto the skin of her left thigh, briefly turning her leg into a screen showing someone else's dream.

Mira jumped down from the stand, landing in front of the sculpture. By obscuring just the right parts of the letters, she had transformed the word into:

CO
OL

The camdrones swooped and hovered. She picked one and extended her arms toward it, fists clenched, thumbs extended. Their temptooed tips touched to form the word "MIRA".

She knew what the world was seeing. She had done it! Mira Cool was now literally a household name. In the seconds before the livestream's automated camdrone images could be overridden, shareholders everywhere would be seeing this striking woman in a shirt and underwear turning the UCC's self-serving anniversary show into a showcase for her celebrity.

Mira followed the camdrone with her fists and her eyes. More fireworks exploded in quick succession. A sentrybot seemed to materialize out of the colorful explosions and directed a powerled straight at her. Mira opened her fists to shield her eyes from the glare. Disoriented, she took a step forward, then turned around.

There was her name, in all its glorious audacity. As she smiled, the bot flew between her and the sculpture, focusing its powerled beam on her face. Mira moved back, shielding her eyes with her hand once again. She stumbled on the corner of the projector array, twisting around and falling over the edge of the building before she could regain her footing. The concrete below sped to meet her.

And then Mira flew.

She stretched out her fists once again, using them to redirect her trajectory from vertical to horizontal, away from the building. She curved gently to her right, downward, and back around until she was heading toward the open atrium doors. She flew straight in, following the walkway over the heads of vernissage guests gawping at her name on the wall screens. Mira reached the back of the atrium and swooped inside a waiting elevator. It rose, the door opened, and she floated down a deserted hallway. When she reached room 101, its door was already open and she glided inside.

A person was lying on the medicot in the center of the room. Still floating horizontally, Mira drifted slowly toward the patient until her body was suspended only inches above theirs.

The headset visor was dark and strangely unreflective. Then, pixel by pixel, a video image of a face began to form. Its eyes were familiar. They blinked and crinkled at the edges. The nose, mouth, cheeks, and forehead became visible simultaneously, as though the person's entire head was looming out from a dark pool. The face became recognizable as Mira's own, smiling serenely back at her.

Glossary

AdPoints – a rewards program introduced in 2048 that attributed points for watching TV advertisements. The points could then be spent at United Corporations stores. AdPoints was supplanted by the linking of TV ad watching to the universal basic income in 2066.

AdVisor mask – an electronic face mask connected to the internet that plays the daily dosage of advertisements that must be watched to receive the UCC's universal basic income (UBI).

Agralife – a food corporation that is part of the UCC.

Amexica – officially the United States of Amexica. A federation of Mexican states and the remaining American states that did not join the UCC.

appsesh – a therapy session delivered through a device app, typically for psychological support or education.

artheft – daring thefts of artworks, for personal pleasure rather than financial gain. The word should contain another letter T in the middle, but it was stolen.

AuthentiCo – a food corporation that is part of the UCC.

autohacking – biohacking your own genome.

bioscore – the rating of a person's physical well-being.

bode – a dwelling.

bodelock – a common form of correctional punishment in the UCC, formerly known as "house arrest".

camdrone – a remote-controlled or AI-controlled solar-powered airborne video camera ranging in size from a hummingbird to a pigeon.

cartway – a path/road, typically in a gated community, where residents travel on golf carts.

Chevelux – genetically modified hair invented in 2034 and a key driver of uHappy feelings for follically challenged men.

Chickind – a simulated chicken meat substitute grown by AuthentiCo.

chiimp – a chip implant.

ClearWood – genetically engineered transparent wood popular in contemporary condo construction.

climcontrol – any initiative or activity intended to limit global heating.

cocoonchair – a high-backed chair with a footrest, surrounded with a skin of fabric that can be closed around the person sitting in it to form a soothing cocoon-like tent.

convocast – a holographic projection of a person communicating from a remote location.

Cottno – synthetic cotton created by Fabricorp.

Customair – any of the specially formulated atmospheres developed for public and private interior spaces by the uBreathe corporation.

desksplay – a 5 to 10-inch built-in screen in a desk or countertop showing a range of information such as time, date, weather, playlist choice. An unremarkable part of any smart home system.

destrock – a noisy rock music genre.

drinkstributor – a beverage vending machine typically found in taxibots and trolley stops.

EcoPlast – an alternative to plastic packaging developed by Agralife that breaks down to biodegradable dust when placed in a microwave oven.

edubot – an AI-driven teaching aid initially developed to communicate with students via a user interface. The second-gen edubots were standalone units akin to labots.

Elastrium – an anti-greenhouse-gas fabric impregnated with colonies of bacteria that thrive on carbon dioxide and methane while expelling oxygen.

ergool – a finely balanced chair that supports the back while also allowing the core muscles to activate, thereby ensuring a minimal workout and perfect posture when seated. Formerly a registered trademark formed by the contraction of "ergonomic stool", ergool entered the vocabulary as a generic term in the early 2070s.

ergotainment – entertainment produced to aid physical exercise.

Fabricorp – an apparel clothing corporation that is part of the UCC.

facation – a fake vacation, usually evidenced by AI-generated selfies or group shots in front of an exotic location.

falseface mask – a type of mask used to defeat facial recognition AI in countries where governments are less benign than the UCC.

fecologist – a person whose job is to examine the turds of the wealthy, then interpret the results to advise them on health and diet.

FilterfreshAir – the product of an air filtration system commonly used in dwellings and yardzones.

garbot – a small-scale wheeled robot garbage collector for sidewalks.

garmscreen – a flexible information screen built into a sleeve or pant leg

Genedit – a gene editing corporation that is part of the UCC.

glasstic – a common term for the biodegradable crystalline plastic developed to prevent microplastic pollution.

historication – a VR-AI vacation to a specific historical period and place.

horselette – a genetically miniaturized horse approximately 18 inches high.

jooce – genetically engineered fruit juice.

kay – "okay" when used as an acknowledgment. "Sure, okay, I'll be there."

labot – an anthropomorphic technological device previously known as a robot.

led – a light.

lizadhesive – an adhesive surface layer that can be stuck and re-stuck, in a similar way to Velcro but easier to use and more durable.

lober – an earring that also plays audio, akin to an old-fashioned wireless earbud. Also a verb for that activity

luxcab – a luxury taxi with features and amenities tailored to the passenger's needs.

maskpac – a large pocket in a jacket or coat where a variety of masks are stored for different uses.

medicot – a hospital or hospice bed that slowly moves from head to toe and side to side to avoid creating bedsores in bedridden patients.

memoryself – a social media dataset composite of a person's self at an earlier stage in life that uses AI to communicate as a separate individual via a screen or hologram

Mimsect – a miniature drone developed by Agralife that mimics the behavior of pollinating insects. A competing technology from AuthentiCo is called the SimBee.

morpig – a negatively valenced corruption of MMORPG (massively multiplayer online role-playing games).

nanodrone – a housefly-sized drone equipped with a camera that transmits video and audio to a remote location.

nanoheal – organic glue used to seal wounds.

nanomassage – a massage lasting typically between two and five minutes.

nesticle – a sleep chamber in a high-rise condo unit, typically paid for by the week.

ogee – formerly spelled O.G., meaning "original gangster" or "old-school".

oky – "okay" when used to mean "good" or "well". "Are you feeling oky?" means "Are you alright?"

parkzone – the common green space in a UCC community, typically furnished with adbenches and holographic representations of traditional park features such as fountains, ponds, lakes, and trees.

persotech – labot user interfaces that exhibit anthropomorphic features such as synthesized human voices or faces.

pharmsert – a pharmaceutical delivery system, usually a thin, finger-length device.

plastorg – the generic term for organic plastic that decomposes quickly when heated.

Plentium – the element that keeps on giving. The principal biodegradable raw material used for 3D printing, including the Sculpturize artworks. It is sanitized, bleached human excrement.

pluswork – paid work performed as a supplement to the UBI that is earned automatically by UCC shareholders who fulfill their AdVisor quota.

psychbase – a database of psychological and personality traits.

psychstory – a personal narrative written in conjunction with a mental health professional, whether human or AI.

ReasSure – the UCC's insurance AI that constantly monitors health and welfare to ensure optimal outcomes.

sandairs – light, air-conditioned shoes, originally a brand name, but now a generic term.

satelcam – one of the cameras permanently streaming images from geostationary satellites in low orbit.

Sculpturize – a company owned by Santiago Khan that

uses a patented 3D printing process to recreate a person's likeness in the style of a famous artist from history.

selfiscope – an apocryphal hand-held device akin to a periscope that only looks back at the observer. Used as an insult for narcissists.

selfterm – AI-assisted suicide.

sesh – a session.

sexcab – a taxi equipped for spontaneous sexual activity.

sexpluswork – prostitution paid for in goods or services as a way to bypass the UBI and pluswork system.

sharicle – a small shared office cubicle in a high-rise condo unit, typically paid for by the minute.

Silicite – artificial stone manufactured from sand and graphene.

Sim – Sim Baker, former Apple CEO who launched the iBank in the 2030s. His memoir outlined the benefits of a country run by corporations: "All the wars are now over. The war on terror. The war on drugs. Why? Because people in a state of war are not predisposed to purchase non-essential products. Governments were interested in power and power was exercised through fear. Corporations were interested in welfare and a smooth-running economy where everyone had purchasing power, whatever their race, color, creed, or identity."

simulationism – the UCC's version of religion, based on

the belief that we are living in a computer simulation created by a higher intelligence.

sistbot – a small, non-anthropomorphic labot, originally
known as an assistbot. Certain types of sistbot are designed to help people with physical challenges navigate the
world more efficiently.

skortlet – a short skirt with built-in shorts underneath.

Slabfruit – a genetically engineered fruit product developed by Agralife. Available in five flavors.

snoozer – a violet-light-emitting bedroom device believed
to aid sleep.

synthium – a soft yet immensely strong synthetic fab-
ric/leather.

T.O. – Toronto, Ontario.

taxibot – self-driving cars (typically two-seater) equipped
with user-controlled illumination and entertainment settings.

techpath – a person on the autism spectrum who re-
sponds better to machines than to people, and who can
often diagnose software issues more successfully than the
machines themselves.

teebeeaitch – back-formation from the acronym "tbh"
for "to be honest".

televacation – tourism experienced remotely through

sound and video transmitted from nanodrones programmed to swarm to sightseeing destinations around the
world.

temptoo – a semi-permanent tattoo.

Terraglobin – the raw materials needed to keep the UCC
running, principally extracted from Africa and South
America.

tev – the noncommittal response "whatever" was short-
ened to "whatevs" then "whatev" and finally "tev" by the
mid-twenty-first century.

tuneec – a tech shirt threaded through with sensors meas-
uring vital signs.

uBrella – a large umbrella reinforced to not only block
rain but to shield against UV rays and withstand gale-force
winds. The underside is fitted with the same type of flexible information screen used for garmscreens.

UCC – the United Corporations of Canada.

UCGB – the United Corporations of Great Britain.

uCharge – an RFID chip embedded under the skin, usually of the right hand, to make payments with added
convenience.

uCheese – the UCC's solid dairy product created chemically without the need for cow's milk.

UCJ – the United Corporations of Japan.

UCK – the United Corporations of Korea.

uCleanser – an AI-controlled home disinfecting system, patented by the UCC.

uClub – a rewards program with automatic membership for all UCC shareholders. Points are accumulated with the purchase of goods and services from UCC and can be exchanged either for uRewards or to top up an individual's wellscore.

uCuff – a device attached around the arm or leg to administer Genedit technology.

uDollars – commonly called YouBucks, the currency used in the UCC, symbol ψ.

uForia – a non-addictive serotonin-boosting powder typically consumed as a beverage additive or in a gel capsule by a UCC shareholder who anticipates receiving a sub-optimal uHappy rating at the upcoming bonus deadline. uForia may only be consumed once per rating session, on penalty of bonus cancellation.

uHappy rating – a constantly updated points system to determine a person's physical and mental well-being. Bonus uDollars are awarded in addition to the universal basic income, based on a person's uHappy rating.

uHealth – the medical and pharmaceutical products arm of the UCC.

uJob – any employment position for a corporation within the UCC.

uLife – a hospice service for seniors in the terminal management phase of life.

ultragrass – genetically modified lawn grass that needs no pesticide, no mowing, and almost no water.

uTender – a dating app.

Utopiatainment – a United Corporations content creation company.

uVote – virtual voting in elections.

veeporn – virtual reality porn, either passive or interactive.

vetevac – a veterinary ambulance.

vidmem – an archive of a lifetime's digital video footage either filmed by or showing a particular individual.

Vitainment – an entertainment product of Utopiatainment sold to people who are in the terminal life stage of life and have entered the uLife system.

VR therapy – the use of virtual reality to allow a patient to view themselves as another person and ask themselves questions. Now generally surpassed by memoryselves.

wellscore – the rating of a person's mental well-being.

wristIO – a common upgrade to a wristline allowing simple input and output data such as contract acceptance swipes and taps via a chiimp.

wristline – a reactive coating on the inner arm near the wrist that notifies the wearer of bodily functions and anomalous wellscore and bioscore readings. Different colors convey different readings. Orange means pleasure, fuchsia means stress, green means contentment.

Xylate – genetically engineered hardwood, used for flooring and walls.

Xylete – genetically engineered softwood, used for flooring and boardwalks.

yardzone – a piece of land attached to a bode in a UCC community, covered with a glass dome containing solar processing filaments.

OTHER BOOKS BY THE AUTHOR

Novel
The New Sense (2013)

Short story collection
Life is Good (2012)

YA novels (as JB Dutton)
Silent Symmetry (2013)
Starley's Rust (2015)
Diamond Splinters (2016)

YA compilation (as JB Dutton)
The Embodied Trilogy (2017)

Photo courtesy of Denis McCready

ABOUT JOHN B. DUTTON

Born and raised in England, John emigrated to Montreal in the late 1980s. He has written screenplays, a stage play, novels, and a collection of short stories. John has also worked as a music TV director, a copywriter for clients such as Cirque du Soleil and Skidoo, and as Chief Creative Officer for an international ad agency.

www.JohnBDutton.com
facebook.com/JohnBDuttonAuthor
medium.com/@JohnBDutton